The Incomers
Moira McPartlin

Published by Fledgling Press 2012
www.fledglingpress.co.uk
Printed and bound by:
Martins The Printers, Berwick-upon-Tweed, TD15 1RS
ISBN: 9781905916450

Cover design by Thomas Crielly

Dedication

For Norah Elizabeth McPartlin.
Thanks Mum.

…see me through the eyes of history
propaganda of the past
see me as you've been told
see me as you've heard
now, see for yourself
see me as **you** see me
see me as **I** see myself
see me as I am

(extract of *see me* taken from *ancient voices
speak urban poetry: son of moyo chirandu* -poems
by tawona sithole)

Chapter One

Ellie closes her eyes and squeezes the baby tight against her churning stomach. The plane is descending, a voice tells her this, but where is the ground? She sees only dirty clouds. The cabin shakes and rumbles like the ground at home when the mine blasts new rock. Her ears hurt and her head fills with mud. They are going to crash; this she knows for sure and she clutches the beaded *juju* round her neck and prays to her God for forgiveness. Her poor baby, to die so young. The stewardess asks the gentleman in the seat next to Ellie to extinguish his cigarette and fasten his seat belt.

The sudden sunlight hitting the small portal makes Ellie blink. She picks out the shadow of the plane in the dark grey water on the earth below. The plane dips to the right until the wing tip almost skims the surface of the waves and Ellie sees the reflection of the fuselage rush up to meet her. Why does stewardess walk up and down, calm? They are going to crash into the water. A voice speaks all around again and instructs everyone to look out of the right hand windows. The passengers turn their eyes towards Ellie and stare now, where they avoided her gaze before.

'The Forth Bridges,' the voice announces. 'The famous red railway bridge is over sixty years old but look at the lovely new road bridge, opened only two years ago by Her Majesty Queen Elizabeth II.'

Ellie can tell this is a great excitement and hugs Nat and smiles. They are not going to crash.

When Ellie steps out of the airplane door she gasps as

her breath leaps back to hide in her mouth. As she touches her feet onto the hard concrete the hairs on her arms jump out of their pores, she feels a tingle creep then shake her body; her teeth rattle in her mouth39. Her toes go numb and her legs cannot move. The baby begins to cry and she forces her legs awake to trot to the airport building.

There is no problem with her passport; this was dealt with in London.

James grabs her and Nat and hugs them tight as soon as she walks into the arrivals hall. Her husband has lost weight, Ellie thinks as she pats his back to confirm she is now here with him. As their lips close around their world she tastes again the cool mint of her husband and remembers that first time she tasted his toothpaste, in the hot cab of the white Landrover he drove in her homeland. He had leaned towards her and jabbed his ribs with the gear stick and she had giggled; he only smiled confidently, took her face in his cool hands and pulled her towards him. Ellie had been scared one of the nuns would see them but if they did, they never mentioned it.

James loads her two bags onto a trolley and takes the baby into his arms. Ellie marvels again how such a white man can beget such a black baby.

The dirty clouds have parted revealing a piercing blue sky to welcome Ellie to Scotland, and yet she hesitates to go back outside. James hands her back the child, shrugs his jacket off and throws it over her shoulders.

'Oh Ellie, I'm sorry, I brought a coat and blanket for you but they're in the car; it's not far, if we hurry it will warm you up.'
He tries to grab her hand but Ellie pushes him away.

''S ok, 's fine.' She takes a deep breath and pulls the baby's shawl tighter around his body. He begins to cry again as if he too knows what is coming. Ellie grabs the bottom of her skirts and stamps her feet before allowing herself to be ushered toward a green Landrover.

The baby stops crying as soon as Ellie wraps them both in the blanket and gives him her breast. Her feet now throb as they begin to warm under the hot blast from the heater. She is surprised to see the shiny new bridge so soon after leaving the airport.

'The Forth Bridges,' she says.

'Yes, how did you know?'

'A voice on the plane told me.'

James laughs. 'A voice? That was the captain.'

'I know it is the captain. Do you think I am some ignoramus?'

He points to the other side of the bridge. 'The Kingdom of Fife.'

'So I come from one Kingdom to another. Where are the King and Queen of this Kingdom?'

'Gone, hundreds of years ago.'

'Then we shall be the new King and Queen of Fife,' she holds up the now sleeping baby, 'and Nat can be Prince.'

James pushes his hand under her blanket and grabs a chunk of her thigh.

'I can't wait to get you back to our palace.'

Ellie bows her head and smiles, but her voice remains closed.

Their silence stretches. James coughs.

'How was your flight? You must be tired. You must be hungry.'

He stretches round to reach the back seat. The vehicle swerves and Ellie gasps as she sees a bush come towards her. James pulls the steering wheel round and drops a packet on her lap, all in one move.

'I asked Cook to make you a sandwich; I thought you might be hungry.'

Ellie finds enough breath from her fright to say, 'Thank you, 's ok, I am fine.' Her mother had packed some food for her journey and she could not eat even that. She knows she will eat when she is ready.

Everything is green and grey where folds of fields ripple towards hilly horizons. The road is smooth, a black scissor-cut slicing through the green. At one point on this road the Landrover stops and lets another car from the right pass, but it is not a crossroads. There is a concrete circle topped with a mound of earth in the middle of the road, but the road goes round the mound. James laughs.

'You want to see your face – it's called a roundabout.'

'A round-a-bout.' Ellie says to herself and wonders if she will ever be able to learn to drive on these roads with such obstructions. And so many different cars to avoid.

About a mile later James pulls the Landrover hard over into a single track road guarded by a brick house with a roof like the hat of a witch.

'That's one of the Lodges, the beginning of the estate grounds.' James smiles towards her. 'We'll soon be home.'

Even though it is cold, James drives with his sleeves rolled up and Ellie finds her fingers twitch with the urge to stroke the golden hair on his arms, but she stops herself. It has been three months since she last saw him and she

4

finds she is shy. She hugs her son instead. He feels warm against her stomach and Ellie realises she is still cold despite wearing the thick wool coat James brought her.

'I need to pop into the big hoose before I take you to your new home. The Fairbairns aren't at home this season and the cook needs more money for provisions.'

Ellie wonders if this big hoose is bigger than the Fairbairns' house in her country.

'This must be an extensive farm.' The baby stirs with her voice.

At home her own family has some land to farm, but it is out in the open where everyone can see how far it stretches to the horizon and they can see the herd of goats and the crops failing when the rains do not come.

'Here,' James says, 'all the fields around are owned by the estate but farmed by tenants who pay their dues to the big hoose. The estate grounds are for hosting parties and shooting birds and deer, for fun as well as to eat. When the shooting season is over, the family will move to their other concerns in other countries.'

'My country.'

Ellie realised when she met James that these people make their living off others' labour and by agreeing to marry their Factor, Ellie had signed into that deal. She will have to learn to live with that.

The black road bumps over a ramp to a crunchy grey gravel track. A tall symmetrical line of shiny green bushes shelters a square house standing proud of its three storeys; its door is framed by pillars. Many, many windows, even windows on the roof, reflect the late afternoon sun. To the side of the main house, a squat block which looks like an afterthought, gives the house the shape of a lopsided

5

L. Ellie wonders how many people it takes to clean such a house and where do these people go when the family moves to shoot larger wild beasts than deer. James stops the Landrover at the bottom of a sweeping staircase of stone steps.

'You stay here, I won't be a minute.'

Windows at the base of the house blank Ellie. The engine noise dies now that the ignition has been turned off and leaves a silence that fills with bird song. A brown bird flutters to the ground and hops and jabs, hops and jabs at the lawn until it is rewarded with a plump worm. Ellie has never seen such a drab fellow before.

Nat wakes and wrestles with the blanket, wriggling to be laid down on the floor.

'Shsh, shsh.' Ellie pushes the blanket back and offers her swollen breast again and he grabs at her with his chubby fist and greedy mouth. Her tummy tugs as he latches on and she lays her head back to wait for the scrape of tiny teeth. Nat, still in his first year, is too old for breast feeding; James advised her in his last letter. She knows her husband is jealous; he wants her breast for himself. Even though she wishes to please James, it is too soon to wean her baby. What did men know of children?

James bounds down the steps two at a time, clearing the last three in one jump to land square at the vehicle door.

'Right, let's get you two home.' He climbs into the seat and stares at her.

'What are you doing? Someone might see.' He pulls the blanket up over the baby's head to cover her breast.

Ellie can feel her scalp itch with anger. 'What is this, are you ashamed of your wife and baby?'

James rakes his hand through his thick curls. 'No, it's not that, it's just that women around here don't feed their babies outside.'

Ellie tugs the blanket off the baby. She can feel her face hot while her feet still throb with cold. 'Well, I am not from around here, Mr Mason, and I will feed my baby where and when I want.'

She tucks the blanket around the baby's rump and strokes his head then rests her own on the back of the seat and closes her eyes. Now she thinks she wants to hurry to her new home and close the door on what others might think.

The house James takes her to is a short drive down a lane to another witch's hat, with tiny windows staring out to an overgrown garden. Dense forest crowds the sides of the house. When Ellie steps down onto the gravel the breath is whipped from her lungs by what she now knows is the sharp cold air of Scottish winter.

James leads her past a green door hidden by tangled rose bushes and ushers her around the corner towards the forest. They squeeze through a rusty wrought iron gate that James fastens behind him.

'Do the Fairbairns cut down the trees here for their mine as they do in my country?'

James laughs. 'No, these trees are part of the estate. This forest is tiny compared to the forests in your country. There is no money to be made from these trees.' He points to a stone wall with a back gate that leads to a track. Beyond this Ellie can see another forest.

'That is the biggest forest around here,' James says. 'No more than a wood really. It belongs to the Scottish

Co-operative Society, and they will keep it safe from loggers.'

The back garden is perfect for her. A small patch of tangled bush could be pulled and the ground cultivated. A rickety shed needs fixing but it has a good roof. She frowns at the trees shading the northern end of the garden then remembers where she is. This is good, she thinks.

James leans into her. 'Don't worry; we'll soon have those weeds cleared.'

Weeds? Where she is from there are few weeds, only food growing in the wrong place.

James leads her through the back door into a kitchen and Ellie closes it behind her. She feels safe in here, even though the house is colder than outside. James dashes round flicking light switches and fiddling with a green stove in the corner.

'The house has been lying empty for a while but the cook said someone had been up to air the place.' He kicks the green stove and rattles its front door open. 'They've put this on but it's died down. It just needs a kick up the backside.' He moves to Ellie and Nat and crushes them in a cuddle. 'Once the stove is roaring we should never let it die.'

The Pairty Line

'Did ye hear who's moved intae the estate?'

'Aye, a big bloody black wumman.'

'Huv ye seen 'er then?'

'Naw, ah jist heard, eh.'

'Jist what ye'd expect fae they toffs, like. They spend a' thir time in the jungle then bring thir coons, back here tae oor village.'

'Is she workin' fur the toffs then?'

'Naw, she's mairrit tae the factor, eh.'

'Really, that braw bit boy wi' the blond hair? Ah wis hoping Oor Denise wid get a look in wi' him.'

'Your Denise disnae stand a chance, they toffs aye stick thegither. Onywey, they say the blackie hus a bairn tae him.'

'Really? So whit colour's the bairn, like?'

'Black as coal.'

'Goad, who'd huv thocht.'

Click - 'Did ye hear that?'

'Aye, is it them again?'

'Git aff this pairty line, ye nosey basturd.'

Click. 'That telt them.'

Chapter Two

'Ellie, stop futtering with that stove and come over here.' James grabs two fistfuls of her backside and whirls her before smacking his mouth over hers. Even after two weeks she still cannot believe how warm his lips are in this cold house. His hands rummage over her body before he stuffs them up her jumper.

'Yow!' She twists free of him; his hands are not so warm.

'Here, I have a present for you.' He picks out a glossy book from his briefcase and by the way her strong man is holding it she knows it is heavy.

'Mrs Watson, the cook, gave it to me. It's for you. She thought you might like to learn about some of our plants.' He thumps the book on the table. 'I told her you were a country girl just like her.'

Ellie reaches over and touches the glossy cover of the book. 'Which country are we talking about here?'

The first week after her arrival, Ellie scoured and cleaned the house and always had a kettle boiling to welcome a guest, and although she had no kola nut to make the welcome complete she had the packet of biscuits, half covered with chocolate, which James assured her would be adequate. But now two weeks have passed and she has yet to meet anyone from the big hoose or the village. They know she is here and yet no one comes. James says they are just giving her time to settle in. In her home the women of the village would bring gifts to a new bride to ease the lonely sickness of leaving her fatherland. This is not so here. What is this place she follows her husband to?

Ellie drags the book towards her and reads the title: *"The Encyclopaedia of British Plants – Edible and Poisonous"*. She does not understand. Does this Mrs Watson believe Ellie to be some kind of witch doctor to be appeased with delivered gifts or to be trained in local folklore?

'Why could she not bring this gift to me herself?'

'She is a busy woman. Come on, Ellie, it won't hurt you to have a look inside and maybe try and be a little bit pleased. You know Mrs Watson has been out to the Suwokono estate loads of times, she is very knowledgeable about your country's cooking. She just wants to help you fit in here.' James stands back and looks at her with that funny stern mask he wears sometimes when he reads letters from his mother.

'Why do you have to be so suspicious all the time? Have you never heard of hospitality?'

'Gifts like this normally come at a price.'

Suspicious? Ellie is suspicious of the lack of direct hospitality here, but chooses to press her tongue on the top of her mouth to trap these words. She traces her finger over the glossy cover which is torn on one corner. If she licks her finger and rubs the torn section it heals for a moment but reopens when the pressure is released. She will tape that later, she thinks. She has never owned such a book. The books in the mission were used many, many times over; ripped and torn and damaged by the variations of the climate. She opens the cover and sees that someone has written on the first page 'Wilhelmina Flemming. Christmas 1965.'

11

'This book is only months old, why would she give it to me? It is too good to give to me.'

'I'm not sure, I think Wilhelmina might be the sister who died last month. Maybe Cook's having a clear out.' He scrapes the chair back and stands over her.

Ellie peels back some pages and lets them flutter through her fingers, breathing in the intoxicating smell of the new print; the pages stop and remain open at *Elderflower*.

'Fragrant white cluster flowers, grows in plenty in hedgerows. Flowers can be used for herbal tea, cordials, wine and champagne,' she reads aloud.

'You could make me some wine to drink in the evenings. I bet it would taste better than that disgusting palm stuff you used to inflict on me.'

'I think you did not protest too much about my brother's palm wine at the time,' she says, ready to remind him of the time he disgraced himself and had to be put to bed in her family's compound. But a look at his beaming face jams her tongue behind her teeth. He seems so innocent that she wonders how many children she looks after in this house. As he reddens with his bubbling enthusiasm, he dips his head and the golden mop of hair falls to hide his face. Ellie feels a pang that she might not live up to his expectations of her. When she smiles and pats his hand she sees him visibly relax.

'Sure, I will make your wine. I will make you the best champagne in this Kingdom and we will sit in the garden and sip, and eat wild strawberries and we will watch the villagers struggle to the pub, past these stinky fish and chip shops you have told me about.' She rubs her thumb over the torn cover.

'You might regret giving me this book.'

James pushes in his chair. 'I have to go,' he kisses her on the forehead.

Before he leaves the room he pauses by the open door of the small bedroom and peers in at Nat, snoozing his afternoon away. Ellie smiles as she watches this young man she calls her husband back out of the room and ease the door closed without a sound.

Ellie circuits the house with a duster, trying to keep busy, but every other minute she returns to the table and stares at the book. She puts the kettle on the boiling ring and rattles the caddy to see how long the tea will last before she is forced to go to the village shop. She opens the lid and sniffs the powdered rubbish that is not real tea to her. She misses her tea: she misses the bitter bite on her tongue and the burnt aftertaste left when the cup has drained back to the cracked clay. This dust she has here has the flavour of mud.

She flicks the pages of the book, just to look at the pictures while she waits for the kettle to whistle, then sits to read a new page. When the growing season arrives she can make her own tea. There are many possibilities out there in the garden and the surrounding forest she has yet to explore. The afternoon gloom creeps across the floor to where she sits, forcing her to turn on the tall twisted wooden lamp that waits in the corner like a palm, giving instant light, illuminating what is now her life.

In Ellie's home village — in a remote district a few miles from the great river — light comes from daylight or oil lamps. The first day her father took her to the mission school in the big town was the first time Ellie saw electric lights. She remembers her tears and being mystified by many things in the town, but that small white switch which held the power to light up a whole room for intermittent periods of time was the most mystifying of all.

The Pairty Line

'Ye'll never guess, eh? Effie MacCulloch hus seen the coon.'

'Where?'

'Doon at the burn collecting water.'

'Git away wi ye. Whit wid she be daein' that fur? Huv they no got running water up at the estate?'

'Aye, but they say she cannae drink oor water, it makes her sick so she hus tae collect it fae the burn.'

'Niver? Whit dis she look like?'

'Mawkit, she walks aboot in bare feet and her hair is hingin' wi' grease.'

'Lazy bitch.'

'That's no aw. She cannae clean her hoose eyther, that's fur sure.'

'How dae ye mean like?'

'They say it's a pig sty. Auld Mrs McGeever hud that hoose afore and it wis spotless. Noo apparently there's rats running aboot and gress growing oot the chimney pot.'

'Dirty bitch.'

'Aye well, if ah git rats in ma hoose ah'll be goan up there tae tell her.'

'Good fur you.'

Chapter Three

'You can't go out looking like that.'

James stands in the doorway wearing the smile of a cub. Ellie reviews her best skirt and bodice, still warm from the iron and with her restless fingers twists the scarf she had intended to wrap round her hair; she snaps it tight in front of her eyes.

'And what is wrong with this, Mr Factor-man?' She flicks the tie across the room towards James as if to lash him but knows she will miss well short of the mark.

'You're going to Hollyburn Post Office, not a garden party at your President's Palace.'

Ellie turns from him; she does not wish to talk about the President's Palace; she does not want to be reminded of home.

James disappears out of the room and returns with a pair of his loose khaki trousers.

'Put these on. They might be a bit tight around that magnificent rump of yours but they'll do until you get some decent skirts and dresses.'

Ellie fails to prevent the gasp that pops her lips open. She remembers packing all her fine clothes. Her mother, the finest seamstress in the village had taught her daughter well. Even at the age of fifty that wily old mama could still transform the cloth delivered for the designs of rich clients. The clients never guessed how mama somehow always over-estimated the amount of cloth needed. The result was that Ellie could combine or dye the off-cuts and create modern clothes of many textures, patterns and colours. As Ellie examines the trousers for size she mutters to herself that no man is going to change her style.

James looks at his watch. 'You better not leave the trip to the shops any later, you don't want to scare the children spilling out of school at dinner time, do you?'

Ellie lifts her bowed head and stares at her husband. 'Why are you so mean to me today? These children will need to encounter this black woman sometime.' She snuffs the tear that is trapped in her closed throat. 'Or do you intend to keep me locked up in this witch's hat forever?'

'I'm only joking.'

James pouts a hurt face but she does not care. Ever since they came to this house his list of rules has increased.

'Come on,' he says, 'I'll get Nat and give you a lift up in the Landrover.'

Ellie holds up her hand. 'No, you look after Nat; I want to do this alone.' She sees a look of relief shadow his brows, then he says,

'But you'll be ages, I have work to do.'

'I will take your bicycle.'

'What?' His laugh stings her. 'You can't even ride it.'

Ellie masks what she thinks is the look of a stern king cobra. She will need to lay down some rules of her own soon, she thinks.

'There is no need to laugh at me, Mr James Mason, I have been practicing on the road round the house while the baby takes his nap, I will be fine,' she says as she traps her mass of tight curls in her scarf. Then she dumps the khaki trousers on the table, pulls on her short wool coat and gathers her skirt into one hand. As she hooks a string shopping bag over her head and shoulder she says,

'If I am to be accepted in this place, they can get used to my fine clothes as well as my black face.'

Her release is complete as she pushes off with the bicycle and feels the cool air chaffing her chubby knees where her skirt hitches over her thighs.

Bicycling round the house had been easy and flat, but as soon as Ellie peddles through the estate's main gates she feels her breath shorten. The road to the village is uphill and soon her legs tire. Perspiration soaks her armpits and trickles down her back to the cleft at her buttocks. At one point she wobbles so much she is forced to stop, just where a red and white sign shouts 30 to her. She begins to push the bicycle.

A house sits on the bank above the road. Ellie sees a little girl of about ten years old appear round its side, struggling with a washing basket full of clothes. The girl stops dead and gapes. Ellie raises her hand and shouts, 'Hello!'

The girl's eyes and mouth open wider, as if she had not expected words from Ellie's mouth. Then she clamps her mouth closed, smiles and lifts her hand, dropping the basket.

Ellie is about to move off when a tall skinny woman appears out the door and glares at her, then hustles the girl inside, banging the door hard, so hard Ellie can feel it slam in her face. The discarded heap of washing, with the yellow basket on top, looks like a mud turtle crawling back to his river bed.

One smile will do for today, Ellie thinks. As Sister Bernadette would say, 'You should always eat an elephant with a teaspoon.'

As the road evens off she hitches up her skirt again, remounts and pedals hard to stop another wobble. Houses, two storeys tall, line each side of the road. Ellie sees a couple of women walking towards her; both are pulled bent by shopping bags. They chatter noisily to each other despite having cigarettes glued to their lips.

Ellie has never seen women smoking outside before; she wants to stop and look but knows she should not. The women stop talking, stop walking. One dumps her bags on the ground and switches them round to different hands, never taking her eyes from Ellie. It is as if she is trying to stare her out. Ellie lowers her gaze and cycles on, pedalling faster until she at last spots the newspaper billboard James told her to look out for.

The shop door opens into an airy interior with a wide counter at the back, leaving a long open expanse for Ellie to cross. On the right hand side of the shop is a cubicle made from panels of wood and glass, with a high counter to one side of it, below a notice board. The shop smells old and rotting and the dry air almost makes Ellie gag. Standing at the shop counter is a customer, a woman wearing plastic on her head. As Ellie approaches she can detect a smell like oily fish from the woman, or maybe it is something more intimate.

This store is not like the markets Ellie is used to where every conceivable type of merchandise is crammed, higgledy piggledy, along each side of the road and in every inch of space in makeshift sheds. In good years the vast varieties of vegetables and fruit of different colours and sizes clamber for room on the tables and bins set outside the stores. Here, the fruit and vegetables are stacked in a dark corner on wire shelves, and the choice offered is potatoes, carrots, onion and turnip, or swede, as they call it here.

One skinny leek hangs limp and pathetic over the side like a sea-sick sailor. No cooking herbs, no plantain, no decent fruit. Only apples and oranges and bananas and huge green apples which Ellie discovers, reading a hand-written cardboard sign, are called 'cookers'. Some of the oranges look misshapen and rough. Ellie picks one up and examines it. A woman in a green apron works a silver machine that slashes through a lump of meat like a machete to grass. She carves off slivers onto a piece of wax paper. Her voice cuts into Ellie's thoughts, never faltering the slicing stride, her muscles bulging against rolled-back shirt sleeves.

'You don't want to buy those oranges, hen, unless you know how to make marmalade, that is.'

The fishy woman turns and looks at Ellie with suspicious eyes. The plastic on her head is one of those silly rain-mate things advertised in *The Sunday Post*. Ellie thinks it is ridiculous these are sold in a country where the rain drives straight at your face in horizontal sheets; a rain so cold and severe that a little piece of plastic is useless. Today it is not even threatening rain; the rain-mate must have another function Ellie is ignorant of.

The slicing woman shouts to an open door lined on one side with cardboard boxes.

'Can you come back here and serve this …' Her face flushes and she looks back to her task.

A tubby man who looks about the age of forty, but Ellie thinks would probably look younger if he lost some fat, pushes past the boxes. He is losing his hair but seems to be growing it long on one side to comb over his crown.

He strokes it now as he looks around the room before his gaze settles on Ellie for a second, then moves away again. She waits; he almost looks at her as he shouts in a slow voice as if she is stupid,

'What – can - ah – get – you - hen?'

In her careful mission school accent, Ellie reads out her list to her audience of three and steps over to the meat counter while the man begins to place each item on the counter.

'What is this?' she says, pointing to a pinkish-grey dappled square that looks like dog shit.

'That's haslet. It's lovely,' the fish woman says.

The lady in the green apron hands a loose sliver to Ellie. 'Here, try it, hen.'

She tastes a dry salted concoction that makes her nose wrinkle and her tongue stick to her mouth; it tastes like shit.

Green-apron laughs, 'No, ah'm no keen on it either.'

The fish woman, clutching her purse to her breast, moves over to Ellie and looks her in the eye.

'Dae ye normally eat lions and stuff then, ye ken,' she says nodding towards the door, 'ye ken, where you come fae?'

Ellie looks at the woman and says in a slow clear voice, 'Only when there are no humans to eat,' and is relieved when she hears a snigger come from the sliced meat counter.

A bell tinkles as the shop door opens and a small woman with short cropped grey hair enters. She is wearing trousers, which Ellie thinks is unusual for women in this country. Maybe she too much wears the trousers of her husband.

'There – is – a – PARCEL – for – you – Mrs Winski,' Funny-hair man says, drawing a box in the air. He addresses the woman in the same shouting voice he uses toward Ellie and she thinks if this is his natural voice, it must drive Green-apron crazy.

Mrs Winski smiles and nods but says nothing. She moves to the vegetable rack and begins to prod potatoes and carrots with the same disgust Ellie has for them, then she begins to rifle through a rack of seed packets that Ellie had failed to notice. Ellie does not know how to cultivate here but she knows where to find out. Her teacher, Sister Bernadette, told Ellie's class stories from her home in Scotland; told them each town and village has a building filled with books. A building you can walk into and find a book and take it home to read for a whole month.

'Is there a library in this village?' Ellie asks Funny-hair.

'A library? No' here, hen, no. You'll have to go intae the toon fur that.' His voice drops to a normal pitch now he discovers she can understand him.

'The Toon.' Ellie repeats, 'What is this Toon? How far?'

'Aucheneden,' Fish-lady says. 'Ye can get the bus there,' she points to the shop door, 'every twenty minutes fae the bus stop across the road.' She holds out her purse and jingles money. 'You need money, coins. To pay the conductress.'

Ellie holds up her own beaded purse. 'Yes, thank you.'

The rest of the transactions are conducted in silence. Fish-lady with the plastic rain-mate pays for her haslet but lingers by the counter. Green-apron moves to the glass and wood cubicle which she opens out to allow her to push a parcel the size of a boot box through.

'You'll be alright for your sausages and cabbage now, Mrs Winski,' she says.

Mrs Winski smiles and nods her head.

Ellie thinks she has cleared a high hurdle and leaves the shop with her purchases but as she closes the door she hears Fish-lady say,

'Who let the nig-nog in?'

'Don't ask me, Lily,' Green-apron replies.

Ellie crashes blindly into the arms of a tall man standing outside the shop by her bicycle. She pushes herself off his coal-scented coat and looks up into a pair of sad, tired eyes. The black wiry hair that peeks out below his flat hat is speckled with grey.

'Pardon, pardon,' he says in a thick accent.

'No, no, please, you must excuse me.'

He bows to Ellie, clicks his highly polished shoe heels and touches his flat hat. As Ellie bows back, she hears the door open and watches him rush forward to relieve Mrs Winski of her burden.

Mrs Winski turns to Ellie and smiles.

'Good day to you, miss,' she says. Then turns to her husband, hooks her arm through his and gives it a little pat.

The Pairty Line

'A bike? Whit, she rode it tae the shops, like?'

'That's whit ah said.'

'Well, ah wished ah'd seen that. Did ye speak tae her?'

'Well, ah niver actually seen her ma self, but ah hud it oan guid authority that she rode a bike tae the shops.'

'Whit wis she wearing?'

'Some big clash o' colours. Nettie Marshall said it wis like huvin' yir eyeballs assaultit wi a packet o' Smarties, eh?'

'Ah wished ah'd been there.'

'Ye widnae if ye hud smelt her.'

'Whit dae ye mean, like?'

'Stinkin'. Foreign cookin' smells and stuff – ye ken like the Chinkies and thon greasy Eyties.'

'NO!'

'Aye, mingin'.'

'That pair young fella. Imagine huvin' tae live wi' that?'

'Aye, well, he made his ain bed, eh?'

'Aye, ah suppose.'

Chapter Four

'You won't need to go into the town.   Dod, the gardener up at the big hoose will give you all you'll need to plant a garden,' James tells her as they lie in bed on Saturday morning.   Nat curls nested between them, warm and settled with no intention of waking up.

The library visit had appealed to Ellie and the notion of venturing to the toon appealed even more but now, here is her husband, her keeper, advising her it is not necessary. Ellie holds her disappointment close to her breast, like a talisman.   She will wait to see what this Dod has to offer her, then she will decide for herself.

A little brown bird with a bright red puffed-up chest perches on the windowsill and looks in at Ellie.

'Hello, little friend, you seem hungry — or maybe just greedy, is it?'

Nat sits on the floor playing; putting cotton reels into an empty tin tea caddy. Ellie picks him and his toys up, places him in the washing basket and drags it under the table.   Her baby is starting to roll and will soon be crawling on his belly like a caterpillar, she thinks.

'There, you will be safe from snakes and falling spiders under there,' she chuckles. 'Now do not move.'

Ellie dips her hand into the oat bin and, with one hand balanced under the other to catch spills, she tiptoes to the back door, eases the handle down with her elbow and steps out into the cool morning.   She pulls in a deep breath and enjoys the chill as it cleanses her lungs.   The bird hops off the sill and onto the coal bunker from where it watches her scatter grain along the line of the window ledge.

A shadow crosses her and in the window she sees the reflection of a man, head bent against the day. She turns to see Mr Winski disappear from her vision, behind the shed, and along the track that skirts the side of the house. Her first instinct is to call out a greeting, but the noise of a bump from the room behind sends her rushing back in to the house to find Nat sitting by the sink cupboard, a tin of Vim powder scattered all around him. His hands pat the dust, he grins up at her to show how clever he is. He moves a hand to his mouth.

'Stop!' Ellie screams.

The baby's eyes blink and his plump face screws up; he bubbles and shakes his head, muttering despair in his own language.

Ellie grabs him and pins his hands to his side. She sets the tap running and stuffs his hand under it, hooking her arm round his tubby belly to control his struggling. Even though he is small he screams and wriggles so much she thinks she might drop him.

The basin in the sink is filling but his hand is still covered with the powder so she dumps him in the water, clothes and all, only just managing to stop herself laughing at his shocked face. She squeezes a globule of Fairy Liquid and with the tips of her fingers she rubs the tiny hand clean.

A huge sob escapes Nat as he tries to nestle into Ellie's breast. When she is satisfied he is safe, she lifts him up and hugs him so tight she realises she might hurt him.

'Mama's sorry,' she says as she nibbles his ear and coos. 'You are so yummy I could eat you.'

Now she is soaked too. The floor will have to wait. There are too many cupboards in this house; there are too many things to harm him. She had forgotten the tin was under there, but she shouldn't have left Nat alone, even for a minute. Tonight she will throw them in the bin. In her home village her mother used only natural cleansers. From now on she will save the wood ash from the living room stove and she will make her own soap, not the strong perfumed muck that stings and dries her skin.

When they are both dry and changed and Nat's sobs have reduced to whimpering sighs, Ellie decides she is finished with this kitchen for today. She wraps the baby in his sling, tucking his feet in to keep them warm and pulls him round to her back. She can feel his sweet baby breath on her neck and knows that with all the fuss he will be sleeping soon.

Before she leaves the house Ellie pulls the plant book from the shelf and turns to the section for spring, she knows this month is the beginning of the growing season here. She absorbs the pictures and reads the unusual names aloud; *alexanders, bisort, borage.* When she comes to one she knows; *bulrush,* she thinks of her church classes and slams the book shut. The mission is behind her now. This is her new life. She is the wife of the factor of the estate, no longer the poor mission girl.

She considers tearing the glossy coloured page of illustrations to take with her, but that would be sinful. Even though she was only a girl her father taught her to respect books, always. Books were scarce and sacred. Learning was important to him, for that she should be grateful. She throws a couple of shovelfuls of coal in the stove and puts the soup on to simmer for James' lunch.

27

The back door she leaves unlocked and creeps past the red breast swelling his belly on her oats.

The garden has a rotten wooden gate which opens onto the track. In one direction, after a few yards, the track widens into a country road that leads to the village. In the other, it works its way between the estate perimeter and the Co-operative Woods. Ellie looks for signs of Mr Winski, but there are none. James must fix the gate before Nat is old enough to play in the garden – this he always says, but the job is not done. Men must be reminded of jobs that do not sit on their noses. Not far from her gate, on the opposite side of the track, is an ancient metal farm gate with tall posts, each embossed with flowers. Ellie runs her finger over the ridges and wonders what the flowers signified to the craftsman who made this gate which now hangs off its hinges; the bottom half consumed by the ground through years of disuse. It is open just wide enough for Ellie to squeeze through with her baby.

As she ducks her head to clear a thicket of overgrown briar, she can smell the damp moss and clean water of another world. She hears a faint trickle but sees no stream, or burn, as they call them here. James has given her a pair of Wellington boots. Not green like his. Somehow he managed to find, in the big hoose, a child's red pair that fit Ellie. He was so excited when he came in, his felt hat pulled over his brow, hiding his eyes. She could see the smile tugging at the corners of his mouth; he had something behind his back. She grabbed for it and he backed off into the stove and swore when his hand touched the side. He threw the wellies onto the middle of the floor as he ran for the sink and the cold tap.

The soles squelch into the faint path and Ellie tries to

ignore the rub of the boots, tight on her stout calves. She should nick the tops to give her more room but does not want to upset her husband who now nurses a scorched hand for these wellies.

Ellie follows a broken stone wall which leads further into the woods and finds a ramshackle hut about five feet square, cowering behind a fallen tree trunk. It has no door and Ellie can see inside to the remnants of someone's life. Coal sacks are ripped open and coarsely sewn back together to form bedding, heaped on one corner of a torn, single mattress. A rusty tin kettle is cobweb covered, and leaves have gathered where they have blown in over the autumn. The slight breeze that sighs outside is funnelled through cracks in the walls, giving them voice. Like a migrating bird, the occupant has flown for the winter.

Ellie steps into a glade and counts the varieties of plants she believes she can use. New shoots brave enough to raise a head before the cold season has breathed its last breath. Flattened orange grass is rotting, oozing its goodness into the soil for its next generation. Ellie pats round her back to feel the warm hump that hugs her so close. She pulls a few young shoots and puts them in her pocket, remembering the spot from where she took them. She would identify them tonight and mark up a list of all their uses.

As she stretches forward and plucks out a white fragrant flower, she notices a stone semi-submerged in the earth. She squats down and begins to tug vegetation off the stone but is careful not to tear out its roots. She finds what looks like a gravestone. She kneels back, bottom on heels and looks around; there are more stones to the left, lying in a line. She shuffles her knees across to the other

29

side of the glade and pulls back thorny branches to find free-standing stones.

This is a graveyard, but where is the church? She knows Christian burials must be on blessed ground. Is that what this is or some Scottish ritual she does not yet know of? One stone is in better condition than the others. She can make out the form of embossed letters under the moss and rubs her hand across it. The moss is soft and damp and comes off the stone easily. Some of the etching is chipped and not so easy to read. It is a name, Sister Agnes; there is a date but she cannot make it out. This is a nun's grave, she is sure.

A rustle from the woods towards the village alerts Ellie to the fact she is not alone. She lifts a stick and stands up, watching the space where she first heard the sound, but when it comes again it is further to her left.

'Mr Winski?' she says in a voice not loud enough to wake the baby.

She raises the stick and grabs her skirt ready for flight when a brown and white dog carrying its own stick in its mouth, crashes through a bush and bounds in Ellie's direction. There are many dogs in her village at home, many fierce dogs that she has stood her ground with. This dog will know she is not afraid. Its stubby two-inch tail works its back end into a *shekere* shake. When it sees Ellie it stops and looks at her, then it looks back to the wood, then at Ellie, then back to the wood again before racing to her feet, dropping the stick on the ground and looking up with lolling tongue.

With one finger and thumb Ellie picks up the slime covered present and throws it into the bushes.

'Wow!' A voice sounds, before a dark head appears

from the thick brush.

It is a priest dressed in black raincoat and black wellies.

He laughs, 'You almost got me there, young lady.'

Ellie suppresses the urge to turn and run. The priest seems to have been expecting her to be there. He steps forward and holds out his hand.

'Father Grattan,' he says in a crumbling voice. 'You must be Mrs Mason, James's wife; I've been meaning to visit but thought I would give you time to settle in.'

'Ellie, my name is Ellie. How do you know I am Mrs Mason?' Ellie asks.

The priest laughs again. 'Oh yes, very good, I imagine you will need that sense of humour if you want to fit in to Hollyburn.'

He brushes his coat sleeve and takes a packet of cigarettes out of his pocket. He offers the packet to Ellie, but she waves him away, then he pops a cigarette in his mouth straight from the packet. When he lights the end Ellie is surprised at her feeling of pollution in this clear air.

His cheeks hollow as he drags deeply, holding the smoke in his mouth before blowing it out of one corner. It is as if he wants to keep it inside him for ever, Ellie thinks.

'I hear you've already been to the shops.'

Ellie nods.

'And on a bike? Good for you.'

Ellie becomes aware that the dog is back and nudging her leg with its head, staring at the stick. She looks down and the Father chuckles. He has an easy laugh for a priest. The priests Ellie knows from home are serious pious men; hard men, removed from the people; white men who train black boys to be superior and teach them to steal and use

31

fear against their own people. She feels Father Grattan could be a friend but then he spoils it by saying

'I haven't seen James at church since he came back.'

Ellie's body straightens. 'I did not know James went to church.'

The priest drags in more smoke; he racks a cough and wipes his mouth with a white handkerchief.

'It would be good to see you both there sometime,' he says, then picks up the stick and throws it, sending the little dog bouncing into the forest.

'Well, Ellie, it was nice meeting you.' He walks behind her back. 'And the little fellow too.'

Under her coat Ellie feels goose pimples explode up her arm and grasp her neck. She does not understand this feeling. Despite its failings the Church had been good to her, filled her full of education but in the process somehow left her empty. The Church had been telling her people for decades that they know best, but like an animal who chews its paw off to escape a trap, sometimes instinct tells you what is best.

The Pairty Line

'Did ye ken that the new pit manager wis a Catholic? Ah'll tell ye, they Tims ur takin' owre.'

'Now dinnae stert, ye ken my man's a Catholic.'

'Oh aye, sorry, ah forgot. But he jist seems so normal, eh? – Kin ye hear that?'

'Whit?'

'That effin' pairty line. – Git aff the line, nosey. – Sometimes ah wonder if thon pairty line is a Catholic, they ayeweys seem to hing aboot when am oan aboot thum.'

'Well, ye shouldnae go oan aboot thum should ye? It's no nice.'

'No, ah suppose no.'

'Onyweys, the Catholics irnae as bad as thon Orange Men, nor the Masons fur that matter. It's thaim an' thir Ludges ah cannae be daein' wi'.'

'And whit's that suppose tae mean? Ma Da's a Mason.'

'Well, ye've heard whit it's like doon the pit, it's aw men thegither until it comes tae votin' fur a shop steward, then they aw break ranks and vote fur thir ain.'

'Noo dinnae you be spoutin' yer politics shite tae me.'

'Ah'm no, aw ah'm sayin' is ma man wis best man fur the job and the Masons and Orangemen ganged up and votit against him – jist cause he's a Catholic.'

'Ah think yer jist bein' owre sensitive.'

'Mebbes aye, mebbes naw, but that's whit happened, eh? The Catholics pay thir dues the same as a'b'dy else, ye ken?'

'Ah niver says they didnae.'

'Aye well, let's leave it at that then.'

Chapter Five

'I did not know you went to church.'

James raises his head from his newspaper and stares at Ellie.

'What do you mean?'

'I met a priest in the forest and he asked why you had not been to church. I did not know you went to church.'

'Ellie, for God's sake what are you talking about? We were married in the Catholic Church, your nuns insisted on it, remember?'

'Why did you marry me, James?' Ellie's mouth is dry as she speaks the words and places a red leather prayer book on the table.

'Is it because of this?'

James stares at the book but doesn't touch it or pick it up.

'Where did you get this?'

'I found this when I was putting away your washing. There is an interesting card inside.' The breath is held inside her body. She has said too much and must not now breathe until her husband has spoken. She knows she should not be talking to her husband in this way. If he were one of her own she would be beaten for such insolence.

They had met on the road close to her village. Ellie remembers the look of her world, bold and brash like its people. That day her mother lifted her head from over the bubbling cooking pot, balanced on its three legs in the fire pit outside her hut, and as she watched her daughter approach her mouth grinned but her eyes wept.

'Daughter, it is the way of things,' she said, handing Ellie a bowl of steaming pepper soup. 'You have made a life for yourself. Your brother's family need a home. To make room for you here would be too difficult.'

Ellie had known before her visit this would be the outcome but she had not anticipated that her mother's acceptance of old customs would tear the fibres of her heart. Her time as a pupil at the mission school and her training to be a nurse at the clinic had shown Ellie her home with new eyes. Before she left she had thought nothing of walking miles through the bush, collecting firewood. Each day, without complaint, she would rise from her bed at dawn to help her mother pound rice for the men's breakfast, before going with the other women to the vegetable field to tend her crops. In the town she had grown used to water from a tap, not from a well. Her new life was of comfort, and yet she did not want to walk away from her home.

She ate with her mother in silence as she watched village children in the next compound play with their makeshift toys: four tin lids wired together with coat hangers, a wooden box on top to fashion a vehicle similar to the trucks which trundled past the village on the President's new road, to the President's new gold mine. This road, the Jewel of Independence, had displaced Ellie's brother's family and now denied her the home she had been taken from ten years earlier. Her brother's plight had made Ellie's decision easier.

A chicken sat in a wheelbarrow and cackled at its luck, saved from the pot for one more day. When Ellie rose, her mother pressed a bag of prepared manioc into her hand

35

and pushed her to leave. In return Ellie handed over the few grubby notes she had earned that month in the clinic. The children in the yard laughed and chattered, oblivious to their hard life. As Ellie turned they tugged at her skirt, hoping for a treat from the town. Although she pretended not to have anything, they persisted until she handed over the small amount of sweets she had brought for them; it was not much but it was all they asked for. For them, maybe, it was not so hard: it was the life they knew.

Ellie heard the rumble of the bus, checked her watch and realised it was on time – impossible. She picked up her skirt and dashed past the remaining shacks. Her city sandals flapped and threw up the thirsty red earth,

A puff of black smoke belched from the bus that sagged at the back axle. Ellie widened her stride as she saw it lurch over a rut in the roadside and bump back onto the hardcore. Many pairs of eyes stared at her from the back seats and Ellie heard a chorus of 'Stop!' One red brake light blinked and the bus slowed enough to allow Ellie to catch up. The tight grip on her lungs eased as she heaved herself onto the step. She clung to a handhold by the door as her face pressed close to a woman with an obvious sugar cane habit. A gummy grin welcomed her. The bus hopped forward once and then rumbled along at a speed slower than walking.

The smell of fresh oranges could not hide the earthy odour of bodies nor the smell from two goats tied to the roof. Ellie was so used to washing every day in a deodorized haze, she had forgotten her native essence, but on this crowded transport she remembered she was the daughter of this land no matter what the mission had taught her.

The bus was filled mainly with women returning from the market with their unsold goods. They would return in five days with more goods to sell. The hypnotic sway of the bright beads and crucifix hanging from the driving mirrors lulled Ellie into her own thoughts.

She had nowhere to go but back to the clinic to continue with her nurse's training. There was enough work for her and her colleagues; there was enough work in this disease-ridden country for armies of nurses. She should not be so sad to be denied her home. After she left the mission school she had wanted nothing but to return home. In all her years there she never stopped missing her mother and the wide open sky. She thought she wanted nothing more than a simple life of cooking and preparing food; of collecting water and hoeing and planting and living. It was a hard life for a woman but in the town she had witnessed a life no better. She had planned to go home after her schooling until the nuns had persuaded her to try a month at the medical clinic up river. They scolded her and scratched her conscience, reminding her that even if she persisted in her refusal to take her orders she could still pay the church for her education and serve God by helping to save these poor Africans.

Ellie held her head up high with pride the first day she wore her uniform, the fact it had been worn by other nurses before her did not matter. The cleaning and scrubbing were easy chores but the actual task of nursing was proving too great for Ellie. Each time she witnessed the flow of another person's blood she felt weak and her mouth filled with saliva. Many times during small operations she would faint onto the floor of the clinic and the doctor and nurses would push her to the side with their feet to avoid infecting their scrubbed hands. This was not the only reason Ellie longed to return to her fatherland; she missed the crops, the work in the women's field; she missed the feel of the red earth on her hands and the thrill of watching plants grow and mature until they were ready for the pot. She missed the gentle people of her village. The town was dirty and its people greedy and mean.

The blast of a horn brought Ellie back to the swaying bus. Shouts reverberated from the back seats and crescendoed to the front. The driver swore as he crunched the gears while stamping on the brake. The bus slowed and the front tipped off the road to the herald of another horn blast. A mass of bodies were thrown to the side and screams replaced the shouts. Ellie bashed her forehead against the door and only glimpsed a construction truck, piled high with rubble, speed off ahead of them before a trickle of blood ran into her eye. The driver lifted Ellie back from the door and pulled it open to allow her and the rest of his human cargo to spill out onto the roadside.

The bus lay skewed, its front wheel in a ditch beside the raised road. Many passengers squatted down to examine the damage, some stood. Most of the women loaded their goods on their heads and walked off as they used to do before the bus was in operation. The driver lit a cigarette, scratched his crotch then scratched his head. Ellie sat down on top of her bag in the shade of the broken bus to wait for salvation.

Machetes glinted in the afternoon sun as two younger men from the bus hacked at a young tree by the side of the bush. Ellie watched them as the sweat ran down their shoulder blades and disappeared under their vests. Three other men helped them carry the felled trunk to wedge below the axle. The women were shooed from their shady spot into the blazing sun, and under the driver's instructions the men worked together rolling a large rock under the trunk to create a lever.

As the remaining women clucked, 'Ah, ah, our strong men, so strong, so brave', Ellie looked to the horizon where she saw a pink cloud. She narrowed her eyes to make out the form. There was not another bus due this way for many days. Was this another construction truck coming to push them further into the ground? Other women noticed; they sat forward to gape. Some rose and began to walk towards the road. Water was passed round by those who had more than others.

A quivering image emerged from the dust. Like a hog escaping from bush fire, a white Landrover hurtled towards the stranded villagers. The men at the bus ignored this intrusion, intent on their task. The Landrover drew up behind the bus and stopped. Ellie peered towards the dust coated windscreen and felt her mouth dry, even although she had just tasted a second sip of water from her toothless friend. A white man was driving, but it was a black man who jumped out of the passenger side and shouted in English, 'What happens here, my friends?'

A bus load of black faces stared at him.

Ellie stepped forward and translated for the bus driver. The driver wiped his brow with the bottom of his tee shirt.

'Tell them we can manage,' he said to Ellie, but before Ellie had a chance to speak the white man stepped out of the Landrover and walked towards them.

'We have a winch, we can pull you out.'

The deep voice sang. His voice had the same ring as Sister Bernadette, and Ellie realised this man was Scottish.

39

He was taller than his passenger and so white, like a ghost. Ellie thought his white hair looked so soft that she wanted to touch it to see if it was like silk. This man before her had waves in his hair like the shifting sands. His white shirt was open and she could see blonde hair curling towards his throat. Ellie swallowed and found she could not talk. He looked like the picture of Archangel Gabriel she had in her epistle.

Both intruders looked at her.

'She speaks English,' the passenger said.

The angel smiled at her and held out his hand for her to shake.

'Hi, I'm James. James Mason.'

Ellie stared at the hand and then at his face which she saw was deepening with colour. His eyes were the colour of the big river.

'I know, I know, stupid name,' he said. 'My mum is a huge fan of the flicks.'

He pushed his hand towards her again, and she knew she must take it. She placed her hand in his and was surprised at how cool it was. His grasp was firm over her limp one. She was tempted to return the pressure but held herself back and could not help staring at their two hands entwined; black on white, white on black. Fingers and palms joined in this first meeting over the dry dusty earth of her fatherland.

Ellie had never believed in love at first sight, but when she met James she believed this was a man who would never beat a woman. They were married within six months; James had agreed to obey her tribal tradition of bearing gifts to her family compound and the nuns had insisted on a Nuptial Mass in the mission church. And although she knew James was a Catholic, he had appeared ambivalent to both rituals, insisting he only wanted them to be together, no matter what it took.

When she found the prayer book, in the house of the witch's hat, at the bottom of his drawer, with his name and an address in Perth written in childish writing on the first page, she realised she knew nothing of him or his motives for marrying her. At first she stared at the contents unable to believe what she was reading. She put it back in the drawer determined to forget it and never mention it, but like a stick in a river her mind became stuck in a current of thought she could not escape.

Ellie feels she paces many miles on her kitchen floor before she returns to the drawer and takes the prayer book back into her shaking hands. James stares at the book.

'I haven't used this for years, not since I left school, in fact.'

'The priest seems to think he has not seen your face in his church for a while, but not that long.'

'He's just an old woman, I wouldn't listen to what he says,' James says, pushing the prayer book away from him.

'Why did you keep it if you have not used it?'

Ellie's palms feel damp. Her husband still does not look at her face. He finds the grain running through the table top more interesting, she thinks.

'My mother gave it to me for my confirmation. It's not for throwing out, Ellie, you should realise that.'

This is true. Ellie herself still wears always the *juju* her mother gave her for protection before the birth of Nat. A *juju* filled with tribal magic, a magic she turned her back on when she went to the mission.

Ellie picks the book up by its cover, turns it upside down and gives it a shake. Pages of coloured markers fluttered to the table. Pictures of saints, of Our Lady's Ascension, Saints' relics and many depicting the various guises of Jesus. Ellie bends and between her finger nails she picks up a tattered black and white scrap as if it is tainted with a poison she wants to avoid.

She holds it up between her husband and herself and begins to read.

'Society of the Holy Childhood, The Missionary Apostolate of Catholic Faith.' She stops and looks at him; he has a puzzled look on his face but under that puzzle she sees something else, something she has not seen before in him. Wariness.

'And what is the purpose of this noble organisation? "To save the lives of children forsaken by their pagan parents or to redeem them from slavery and to give them the grace of baptism and a Christian education."' She stops again, but James continues to stare at the table.

She can see a vein throb in his temple and her heart begins to beat hard. Like a child stepping into the river to swim, she knows the crocodile is there but cannot step back once cool water soothes her aching feet.

Ellie clears her throat of the small lump of bile that rests there. 'Condition one: "To say a Hail Mary" and other stuff — easy. Two is better: "To make a small contribution for the work of the Black Babies Society."' She spits the words out at him. '"On average one "Black Baby" is rescued for every two shillings and six pence received.   Member's name: James Mason."' Ellie drops the card and places her hand flat on the table before easing herself into her chair; without the table she feels she will sink to the floor. When she had found the card she had raged to herself and paced but now she needs to sit.

'You have done well for the Society: you have saved one "Black Baby" and begat another.'

James narrows his eyes; she can see the back of his jaw working as if he is chewing hide. Ellie stands again and places the kettle on the stove. She feels she has maybe gone too far, she does not want to see steam escape from his ears like in the cartoons. The deep breath she takes as she turns back to him explodes in the silence. He picks up the card and reads it, then places it back in the prayer book at a particular page and carries the book out of the room, closing the kitchen door behind him. The silence drums in Ellie's ears so hard she wills her husband to shout, to throw something. He is so quiet, there is no steam, there is no sound, as if he holds his breath throughout the whole exchange. Then the door to their bedroom slams so hard the pot rattles on the stove and Nat screams from his nap.

Ellie looks at the closed door and wonders what she has started.

The Pairty Line

'Ur ye goan tae the bingo the night?'

'Aye, an' ah better win cos ah'm skint.'

'How come yer skint, it's only Friday? Did yer man no gi' ye yir hoosekeepin' last nicht?'

'Him, the useless basturd. He's back shift this week, left tae catch the pit bus at wan o'clock, but couldnae git further than the club. He only gied me half the hoosekeepin' when he stoatit hame at closin'. Couldnae leave hiself short, could he?'

'Goad knows why ye pit up wi' that.'

'It isnae his fault really. He says the new pit manager's a right wee Hitler, ayeways changing the shifts roond. Ma man hates the back shift.'

'He's a pair wee sowl, that man o' yours.'

'Dinnae gie me yir snash. It is a shame.'

'Aye aw right.'

'And, he's pit a new rule in place.'

'Who?'

'Gallagher, the manager – if ye miss a shift yir barred fae gettin' overtime.'

'Really, that's awfy.'

'Ah ken, so not only ur we doon a day's wages, he'll git nae Sunday shift. Ah'll be even mair skint next week, eh?'

'Better git yersel tae the bingo everyday next week then.'

'Ah ken, otherwise ah'll huv tae bump my rent payment aff fur anither fortnight. The arrears ur fair mountin' up.'

44

Chapter Six

James refuses to speak to her. Even though the bed is cold he confines himself to sleep on the edge, as if fearing to touch her even when he sleeps. She wakes each morning to find him gone. An empty bowl with vicious dried-on cornflakes and a cup half full of cold tea his only message to her. He must eat lunch at the big hoose because he misses his midday meal at home, and in the evening he slouches in at six thirty, cold from the early evening dark, his eyes tired but determined. Ellie lays his meal out for him and watches him eat in silence before he rises, leaving his picked-at plate on the table for her to clear away. He then disappears to run a bath and go to bed to read estate journals. Once she tries to speak to him, to tell him of Nat's new tooth, but the words clot in her mouth.

Ellie thinks this silence will last forever, then on Saturday he comes home stating he has instructions to take the Fairbairn boys to mass on Sunday and Ellie should come with him. It is an order from James, not a request. The sight of his hardening jaw clips her protesting tongue before she sentences herself to another week of silence.

As he leaves the house to chop logs for the wood burner he throws Ellie his parting argument.

'This is part of my duties; this is where the priest knows me from.'

The Fairbairn boys from the big hoose are home for the half term; their parents, as usual, absent. The boys, being about twelve and fourteen could be considered old enough to look after themselves, but instructions must be obeyed. With no one to look after Nat, Ellie is forced to take him too.

Ellie and James pick the boys up at the big hoose a quarter of an hour before the service is due to begin. The younger boy lumbers into the car and slumps in the back as if he were sleepwalking. The elder stinks of alcohol, curls up in the corner and falls asleep as soon as he clambers in to the back seat. Neither boy speaks to Ellie or James, nor does she expect them to, and even when Nat holds out his hand to them, the smaller boy looks straight ahead with sleep in his eyes.

Ellie has only ever passed by the high hedge that skirts the back of the church when out on her foraging trips, but each time she passes she feels guilty. The nuns would be shocked to discover she had turned her back on them. The church stands sentry on the edge of the village: a grey monstrosity that looks with narrowed, accusing windows toward Ellie. She wraps her coat closer around her as the Landrover parks at the side door.

James takes a long brass key from his pocket and opens the heavy varnished side door of the church; the village parishioners enter the church through the commoners' front door. The church is vast, bigger even than her country's cathedral. This church has many, many seats and a ceiling so high Ellie is sure angels reside there. The side altar looks onto the main altar which glows under the majesty of a golden tabernacle surrounded by burning candles. The smell of stale incense claws at her throat. A life-size statue of Our Lady obscures the left half of the main church from Ellie's view but she knows, from the scuffling and coughing, that people occupy these pews.

On the right side of the church she watches a flock of parishioners, young and old, make their way up the aisle and genuflect before filing into wooden benches. There is only room for about ten worshipers in the side altar so Ellie moves in behind the boys and closer to the door.

The church is colder than anything Ellie has felt since she arrived in this country. Colder than the house, colder even than the frosty mornings when she first stooped at her front door to pick up the milk bottles, their silver tops pecked ragged by the greedy birds who stole the frozen cream that settled there. Her nose begins to run. Nat too, begins to snuffle and she opens her coat and bundles him inside. He has been snuffling more these days, and she worries he will catch some horrible disease from these sullen pale-faced Fairbairn children. He has had no other contact with children since they arrived in this country.

In Ellie's homeland the children are quiet in church, respectful and devout. Here, in this church, children cry and rattle their toys along the wooden seats. Someone has a cough they cannot contain and at one point it sounds as though something ruptures in their chest. Ellie pulls her coat further round Nat. Two girls in the front row snigger and talk in loud quick voices she cannot understand. When Ellie cranes forward to see more, she notices they look directly at her. She meets their eyes and they both bow their heads but the sniggering does not cease. Ellie's gaze moves round the rest of the congregation and finds they all look at her; some with open curiosity.

A tinny bell rings and five altar boys in white robes file through a door opposite the side altar, followed by Father Grattan. He looks different in his green robes. Ellie thinks he suits the colour and wonders, not for the first time, why priests choose to wear mostly black when there are so many wonderful colours in their wardrobe.

The altar-boys walk into the aisle, genuflect and climb the altar steps. When the priest sees Ellie and James he smiles towards them and Ellie's mouth dries. She looks back to the congregation and spots the little curly-headed girl from the house by the road sign. She is half way down the church in the middle of a row. The congregation turn their attention to the priest, but the curly-headed girl is intent on Ellie. When Ellie nods her head and smiles towards her, a grin crosses the girl's face and makes Ellie's heart calm. A tall, dark-haired man beside the girl puts his hand on her shoulder and the girl lowers her head. Ellie cannot be sure from the distance between them but she imagines that hand sends a message the girl knows well. On the other side of the girl, with her head bent and eyes closed, stands the skinny woman.

Ellie's gaze moves along the line to a tall teenage boy with floppy dark hair and spots, who looks embarrassed to be there. Next to him is a girl with long straight greasy blonde hair. She is examining her nails and fiddling with her hair until a chubby lady in a blue coat and black mantilla catches her hand and places a hymn book in it.

Ellie is glad of Nat's heat to warm her throughout the service and is relieved when James ushers them out into the winter sunshine and back to the car. As they drive past the front steps Ellie sees the little girl wave to them and the father take her hand in his and pull her towards the open side gate. Ellie can see he is not pleased.

'Who is that family?' she asks.

'How should I know?' James replies. 'You should know by now the estate hardly ever mixes with the village.'

It appears the mood does not shift easily from her husband's shoulders.

When they arrive back at the witch's hat house, Ellie puts the baby on the floor to play while she cooks James bacon and eggs the way they like food fried here, in lard. James stares at his plate but does not eat.

Ellie sits opposite him and takes a deep breath.

'Husband, I am sorry. I should not have spoken to you in that way.' She bows her head. 'I was wrong.'

Still he is silent.

'I will do anything to make things right, but I cannot take back my words.' Her apology is lumpy on her tongue; this is not the way it sounded when she rehearsed it in church.

He looks at her. 'You asked me why I married you. Why did you marry me? Was it for a passport out of that hellhole country of yours?' His voice is calm but she can feel the venom on his tongue.

'Is this what you think? I thought we loved each other.' She is aware of Nat's eyes on her, this boy of theirs is not so stupid and like antelope in the bush, can detect when danger is near.

James stands and pushes his chair back. 'So did I.'

Ellie jumps up and reaches for his arm but does not touch him. 'Can you remember the first time you came to my land?'

'Yes.'

'It was strange, no? You knew no one and you were surrounded by black faces. But you were boss man so all was OK.' She can see the tension in his face relax a little. 'It is the same for me here, all around are white faces, only I am not boss man, I am a black woman.' Ellie

49

sits down and holds her hands together as if in prayer. 'How strange do you think that feels?' She watches him open the kitchen door. 'I ask you to give me some time, husband, time to learn new ways and time to rid myself of old suspicions,' Ellie says to the closing door. Her words reach his ears, this she knows, but do they reach his heart?

The Pairty Line

'Did ye hear aboot Geordie Macintyre?'

'Aye, awful sad i'nt it.'

'Mind you, ah saw him last week and he wis as yella as a banana.'

'Cirosus o' the livir wis it no?'

'Ah heard it wis the cancer.'

'Awful. Mind you, ah reckon he'll no' be missed, she hud a hell o' a life wi' um.'

'Noo, ye shouldnae be speaking ill o' the dead.'

'No, ah suppose. But speakin o' bananas, that black wumman wis at the chapel on Sunday.'

'Get away wi' ye.'

'Did yer man no' say?'

'Aye, very funny, ye ken fine well he niver goes.'

'Well she dis. Who wid huv thocht it, eh? Ur they no' suppose tae worship witch doctors and false gods. Ah saw it on the telly, loads o' thon blackies runnin' aboot wi' nae claes oan, breasts hingin' aw weys. Mind you she couldnae dae that here, eh?'

'Goad no. Whit wis she wearin though?'

'A coat made oot o' tiger skin, ah heard.'

'She must huv brought that wi' her, like.'

'Aye, ah suppose so, it's no the sort o' thing ye cun buy up the toon onywey.'

'Goad's truth, no.'

Chapter Seven

Ellie sits at her kitchen table, looks at the feeble banana cradled in her hand and wonders if she will ever taste anything decent again. Her belly aches for roasted yam. Her mouth waters for the taste of peanut and bean stew. She licks her lips to try to remember the taste of pepper soup or plantain, seasoned and fried in sweet oil. Jollof rice, she is sure she can make here with these limited ingredients. The kettle on the stove whistles and she groans at the thought of another cup of tea like lizard spit. She hangs the bananas back on the hook she insisted they have, and that James laughs at.

'There are no spiders in these bananas to bite you,' he had told her when she first asked him to hang the hook in the kitchen.

'Better to continue with old ways than to have a bite on your bum,' she had said in return.

The fruit bowl full of drab apples and oranges taunts her so she drags the plant book towards her and tries to ignore these inadequate selections. She flicks the pages and thinks about the person who gave her the book; she met the cook only once, back home.

James had requested Ellie's presence to attend a Presidential reception. He had been working on some deal for the Fairbairns' mine commissions or something grand like that. It was well known in the British community that the factor from the Suwokono estate had married a girl from the mission clinic the month before and the

52

Fairbairns thought it would be good form to have the black bride attend. Ellie's wishes were of no concern.

Before she dressed she had already been to the toilet twice to be sick. The second time she went with an empty stomach and the gut-wrenching feeling she had as every muscle in her abdomen heaved, had sent her reeling to the bathroom floor. She was still lying there when James came in to hurry her along.

'I cannot go.'

'Don't be silly, of course you can go.'

'You do not understand. I hate this man.'

James laughed. 'Doesn't everyone?' He lifted her to her feet and set her on the toilet seat.

'Come on, you have to do this for me, just this once.'

'I do not feel well.'

'You'll be fine. I'll be there to look after you.'

Ellie had somehow managed to smooth her face into a beguiling smile and swallow the bile that was rising again at the sight of the President.

Her head bowed as she shook his hand and he looked past her at more important persons further down the line. She stumbled to a seat in the corner of the room and thought if she could just stay there for the evening no one would bother her. Waiters in white shirts with ragged collars wheeled round the room, offering drinks and canapés to those standing, and although she knew they saw her, no one offered her a drink.

Their looks said, 'Who does she think she is? A village girl, dressed to impress, thinks she is better than us; let her thirst for the milk of a lizard before she will be served by a man.'

Ellie's eyes searched for James, but he was engaged in

deep conversation with the President's brother and one of the government ministers. He had no need for her and she wondered why he had been so insistent she attend.

The small head of a woman with tight grey hair appeared round a door. Ellie watched her black beetle eyes appraise the room, nodding and moving her lips as if reporting back to some hidden assailant on her shoulder. The eyes settled on Ellie and a frown creased her brow. A bare white arm with shirt sleeves rolled above the elbow shot out from behind the door and grabbed the sleeve of a passing waiter. Much hand waving and pointing followed before the waiter dragged his feet towards Ellie.

'You have to eat something.'

'I do not want anything, thank you.'

'Ms Watson says eat.' He dropped an empty plate on her lap and shoved a tray of food in front of her face. 'Ms Watson says no one leaves her table hungry.'

There was no table beside Ellie and she did not want to put the plate on the floor. She looked around for James but he was bowed in talk with the President and a man in military uniform. He was admiring the President's crucifix and many medals; he should not encourage him, Ellie thought.

Ellie picked up a small piece of food. 'Thank you,' she said to the waiter's retreating back.

She surveyed the food on her plate; the smells snaked to her nose and wriggled through to her brain. Before she ate she looked towards the door and the two eyes willing her to eat. The rough biscuit was made from grain and topped with some kind of paste; Ellie nibbled the end off it. The foreign flavours burst on her palate and she struggled to swallow the mouthful, but it soon crumbled in her mouth and the smoky flavour of the meat warmed her belly and satisfied her mind. She realised with regret that she enjoyed this food. Against her will she lifted her head and smiled at the curly-headed woman who returned her smile with a sharp nod before retreating behind the door.

Ellie later discovered that the cook from the big hoose in Scotland had been sent for to prepare traditional Scottish fare for the President and what she had eaten was a small oatcake smeared with smoked venison pâté.

Ellie closes the book. She will go and thank Mrs Watson for her present and for insisting that she eat something at the reception that day back home. She will introduce her to Nat, everyone loves the baby.

Ellie wraps him up in his blanket because he is snuffling and even though spring is maturing there is still chill air outside the cosy kitchen. There is a knocking sound. Ellie wonders if there is something wrong with the stove, but it happens again and she realises it comes from the door. It would be good to speak to someone, even if it is the priest come to call. Her voice is reserved for Nat and the birds. James still remains sullen after her misunderstanding about the 'Children's Society.'

The door hammers again but this time as if the person is fleeing from an evil spirit. Ellie forgets how long she stands in the middle of the floor with the baby in her arms. She does not want to miss her visitor, so she sits Nat in the playpen and rushes to greet her guest. She only wishes she had kolanut to greet them properly.

Ellie is confronted by a woman of about fifty but it is hard to tell, everyone here looks the same to her. Is her visitor Green-apron from the shop?

'Did I leave something?'

'Pardon.'

'In the shop?'

'What are you talking about, woman?'

The words spit out of her mouth and Ellie can feel her face heat. She now notices that this woman has pursed lips and a furry upper lip that looks as if she is balancing a caterpillar there. Ellie watches for it to fall off. No matter how hard she tries she cannot stop looking.

'My name is Nurse Lynn.'

Ellie holds out her hand to shake, but the nurse glares at it as if she has been offered a handful of monkey shit and pushes past Ellie into the house.

'Dr Wishart asked me to call in and check up on Baby.'

She ruffles through a little brown bag and pulls out a dung-coloured folder.

'It is reported here that you have been resident in Hollyburn for over a month and yet have not registered with the doctor.' She scowls at Ellie. 'Is that true?'

'True. Would you like a cup of tea? I am sorry I have no kolanut to offer you.' Ellie can feel her heart thumping. Did she do something wrong, why had James not told her about this?

'You should have been to see him before now.'

'Who?'

'Dr Wishart, of course.' The tone of the woman's voice tells Ellie that she imagines her black face means she is an imbecile.

Ellie looks at her hands.

Caterpillar-lip holds up the folder. 'No excuses. I don't care who you are, Baby's health comes first.'

Ellie sits down on her kitchen chair and pulls Nat up on her knee. Then she notices the table with the book and the picked plants spread out around; young nettles she plans to make tea with. Ellie is tempted to try that now to see what the reaction will be. She wants to tell this intruder that she had begun her nursing training but instead lets the nurse loose on her and her family.

Nurse Lynn thinks she knows best, that is clear from her superior sounding questions, but when Ellie looks at her left hand she notices there is no wedding ring. Ellie fingers her own ring. Even the nuns have wedding rings.

'When was he weaned?'

Ellie shakes her head.

'Not weaned? Ridiculous, never heard of such a thing at his age.'

'There is enough milk here for many years to come,' Ellie says.

'What? Ridiculous, we must begin to wean Baby.'

Ellie looks at the woman and considers arguing then holds both palms up to the ceiling. She is the mother and will do as she pleases without interference once she has closed the door behind this woman's back.

'He does eat some solids.' Ellie strokes his head. 'Do you not, my prince?' She can tell from the screwed up caterpillar that this does not impress.

'What solids?'

'Porridge.'

'Good. Potty training?'

'Excuse?'

The woman puffs her chest and stretches her neck rigid like a woman carrying a heavy load on her head.

'Have you started potty training yet?' She spits out

each syllable with the venom of a cobra. 'You know, getting him out of nappies.'

'No, ma'am.' Ellie clamps her hand over her mouth; she should not have said that, she should have known better. She will not bow to this woman who does not wear a ring.

'He has not yet finished his first year in this world, he does not walk yet.' Ellie finds her voice is small, insignificant and wills her strength to return.

The caterpillar twitches a hint of a smile.

'Better to start early; boys are lazy, you know, slower than girls. Give him to me a moment.'

Ellie watches the woman's hands as she unravels Nat from his blanket and coat.

Nat's little lip pouts as the nurse pulls his trousers and nappy down and he looks at Ellie as if to say, why is she doing this to me? He bawls when she begins to tug the jumper with the too-tight neck over his head.

'No, no, I will attend to this,' Ellie says, jumping up and grabbing the baby from the nurse. She eases the jumper over his ears and then over his head. She should have packed it away before, but James' mother knitted it for Nat and James was so pleased at this first sign of acceptance that he insists Nat wear it at every opportunity.

When Ellie puts Nat on the floor he reaches his hands out to her and flexes his fingers open then back to fists, grabbing the air.

'Up, up,' he says.

The caterpillar lady frowns. 'Does he say any more?'

'Not in English,' Ellie says. This is not the truth, but she is sick of these questions and she feels her strength drip back into her blood.

58

Nat begins to whimper and snuffle.

'For goodness' sake, woman, pick the child up and stop his blubbering,' Caterpillar says as she bumbles out of her officious blue coat and snaps her bag open.

Ellie picks him up, hugs him close and whispers, 'Be brave, little warrior,' in his ear.

'Come on, come on, I don't have all day to waste here.'

'I did not ask you to visit.' Ellie plonks the baby on the edge of the table and sits down again, balancing him with one hand under his arm.

When the nurse picks him up, he begins to scream. One teardrop suspends in each eye, like a spider on a bush, before rolling tracks down his cheeks.

'Now, what is all this nonsense about?' the nurse admonishes.

Ellie coos to her baby and feels her heart ache at his tears. He looks like a plump aubergine with chubby arms and legs sticking out from a white vest. She can feel her own tears rising from love and anger but she will not let this woman see.

The nurse rams a sharp thermometer under his arm and orders Ellie to hold his arm in place. She then looks in his ears with a silver cylinder with a funnel on the end. Despite herself Ellie bites back a laugh. When she first saw these at the clinic she thought they looked like the cake icing contraption she found in the mission's kitchen drawer.

'Stick out your tongue, boy.'

Ellie's head snaps back as if she has been slapped.

'His name is Nat.'

Nat stares at the nurse with defiance, eyelashes dewed with lost tears. His mouth clamps shut, tighter than a nutshell.

'Come, little one, open wide,' Ellie says.

He turns to look at her with the sorrowful look of his father. She will not let her little boy suffer this way.

Ellie reaches into a drawer and pulls out some coconut candy. Nat's fist begins to grab.

'No, only if you open up for Nursey,' Ellie says.

'What is this you are proposing to give the child?'

Ellie holds it up. 'It is a candy from home – it is wonderful that my people have worked out how to send items through the post,' she says, wrestling her anger, 'Just like Mrs Winski.'

'I don't think you should be giving this child this native food, you should let him settle down to our diet.'

Ellie's anger percolates to boiling; she knows she should calm down, but she cannot.

'Your diet? Meat pies and chips that taste of monkey shit. I will feed this child what I wish. Are you going to look in his mouth or not?' Nat has been sitting with his mouth open showing off his newly formed teeth during the exchange.

The nurse tuts and slaps a wooden stick on his tongue. Then she runs her hands up and down his body, lifting his vest and examining his skin. Her fingers pause on the dark mark Nat has carried on his back from birth.

'What is this bruise?'

'It is a mark of the birth.'

'Are you sure, it looks like a bruise?'

'I do not beat my child.'

The nurse rubs her finger across the palm of Nat's hand.

'What is this rash?'

Ellie had rubbed cream into his hands to soothe the

Vim rash, but it refused to heal.

'A little dry skin is all.'

'Ask the doctor for something when you register.'

Ellie ignores this and pulls the baby back to her, carries him through to the bedroom and wraps him in a blanket to put him down to sleep. He whimpers for a little then sticks his thumb in his mouth, all the while staring up at Ellie with those sorrowful eyes.

'You should discourage thumb sucking.' The nurse is behind Ellie, searching his room with her eyes. Ellie puts her hand up to push the woman out, but the nurse steps back from the threat of her touch and turns to the kitchen.

When Ellie comes out of the room, Caterpillar is bending over the new play pen fingering the clothes pegs and bag that Nat loves to play with.

'How many hours does he spend in there?'

'Not many, only when I have to go out to the garden.' Ellie stands tall and realises she is taller than the woman. 'I do not neglect my son.'

'No one is suggesting that.'

Ellie hands over the blue coat. 'You may leave us now. Please do not come back. I will visit the doctor if that is what is required.'

As she shuts the door, a couple of tears escape before Ellie pushes the rest away. She picks up the discarded sweet, closes her eyes on this world and sucks on the taste of her homeland.

The Pairty Line

'Did ye hear the ambulance through the night?'

'Aye, whit wis it, - the pit?'

'Aye, a rockfall, eh? It wis that nice young chap that hus jist moved here fae the west. Ye ken, the newly mairrit couple that flittit intae the Mooney's auld hoose?'

'Aw no. No' that nice chap. How is he?'

'Broon breid.'

'NO!'

'They say that Inglish pit manager is goan bananas. Course, he'll jist be worried aboot his ain job.'

'Aye but these things happen aw the time.'

'No' in his pit, he reckons.'

'Aye well he'll sin fund oot about that man-killer he's landed wi', won't he?'

'Aye. Ah suppose.'

'Did the young fella's wife no jist huv a wee bairn?'

'Aye, it'll no be lang afore that Nurse Lynn is roond there flingin' her weight aboot, trying tae interfere.'

'Sumbudy should dae sumthing aboot her, eh?'

'Ah ken, she's jist a twistit auld spinster that'll cause sum serious harm wan o' these days.'

Chapter Eight

Ellie is still hissing like a snake when she lifts Nat from his nap and swaddles him into his clothes and sling. The long tarmac lane James drove her along that first hopeful day is the quickest way to the big hoose, but Ellie wants to explore the woods on the way and give herself more time to calm down. She is in no mood for visiting but she has paced the lino until the floorboards creak, she has to get out of this house.

Armed with her basket and wearing her red wellies, Ellie leaves through her back door. She hears a footfall and sees the back of Mr Winski disappearing into the woods further up the track. She is sure it is he; the thick heavy black jackets are common wear in Hollyburn but his cap is different from the cloth flats worn by the men she has encountered so far. She steps out through the garden gate and looks to the direction he went, in what she guesses is also the direction of the big hoose. There must surely be a gate further along the track that will lead her back into the estate grounds.

New growth of stingy nettles curl through a thicket of bramble thorns and Ellie calculates tea and soup and wine. James had quipped, before his mood, that a mug of nettle soup would put colour in her cheeks. Very funny.

The light dims as she walks deeper into the wood and she realises that the night will soon draw over the sky. Something called British Summer Time will happen at the end of this month when the clocks are moved forward an hour to fix the daylight saving given to the farmers in winter. Why this need to change time? In her land everyone rises when it is light and retires when it grows dark; the palm oil used for lighting is precious, so why waste it?

She can smell damp earth, reminding her of the bush at home during the rainy season, when the ground springs from its knees and embraces the sky with lush green shoots and a promise more than it lives up to.

She has read in the book now sitting permanently on her kitchen table, that many varieties of fungi grow on the forest floor and she plans to study them and examine the tree trunks for signs of growth. Her heart warms as she imagines her husband's face when she presents him with something other than potatoes and carrots or turnip to eat.

The baby is snuffling into her back now and she thinks he will be ill by nightfall. It was wrong of her to take him outside on this damp afternoon. She should return home and visit Mrs Watson another day.

An animal cry shudders from the woods just ahead of where she stands.

'What is that?' she says to herself.

'At?' Nat says.

'Shh.' Ellie had forgotten her parrot son.

Like an antelope caught by a wild dog, the cry is helpless. This is followed by a low moan. Ellie feels her heart tighten.

She creeps forward to see if it is an animal in a trap. She knows there are few predators in these woods. Once off the path the trees thicken and her feet sink in moss and composting leaves. She stops and ducks behind a tree when she sees the figure of a man. The hand she places round her back and rests on the rump of Nat, she prays will hush his parrot chatter.

Mr Winski sits on a fallen tree. His head hangs low between his legs with his arms covering his head as if protecting it from falling objects. He rocks forwards and backwards, moaning. When he stops rocking he lifts his head and hammers both his fists into the trunk beside him. Ellie can see blood oozing from his knuckles. She wants to go to him and stop this. The tortured cry screams from his mouth and he resumes his rocking and moaning. An intruder should not witness this amount of pain if they cannot help. One foot behind the other, she backs away.

Nat sneezes, a baby sneeze but Mr Winski's head snaps up and he turns his blotched, tear-stained eyes towards her. Before Ellie runs from this man she sees in his eyes the deep humiliation of defeat.

The Pairty Line

'They say the Pole wis tae blame.'

'Whit fur?'

'The accident at the pit.'

'Are you still harpin' oan aboot that? Onyweys, ah heard the young lad wis still drunk fae the nicht before. He should niver huv been allowed underground. The manager'll swing fur this wan. But - whit aboot the latest – ah heard that the meenister's a nancy boy.'

'Dinnae haver, who telt ye that?'

'Ma man brought it back fae the club.'

'Aye well, he wid love that.'

'Whit dae ye mean?'

'Nithin'. So tell me, how dae the brains o' the village work it oot?'

'Well, he, the meenister, like, he's stertit up this youth club. Aw the young yins go tae his hoose on a Sunday nicht an' ur supposed tae speak aboot Christ an' stuff.'

'Well whit's wrang wi that?'

'It jist disnae seem richt, that's aw.'

'Ah tell ye, it's hellish. Onybody that tries tae dae guid in this village is shot doon in flames.'

'Ah'm jist saying, like.'

'Well dinnae, ah'll no hear anither word aboot it. It's jist idle gossip eh?'

Chapter Nine

The garden at the back of the big hoose is surrounded by a
stone wall as tall and as wide as a shea tree. A small iron
gate closes under an arched doorway and seems to be the
only way in. Ellie peers through the gate and gasps at the
green that is abundant in there.

A man in a flat cap and wearing a black jacket with
leather across the shoulders is bent over a twiggy bush
snapping pieces off with hooked scissors. She is tempted
to speak, but she clips her tongue back behind her teeth.
The gold dog that lies by the shed lifts its head, thumps its
tail twice and lies down again.

James tried to dig her vegetable patch but his Estate
Factor hands are soft, and as he dug blisters appeared on
the soft ridges where the fingers sprouted from his palms.
So Ellie had taken the spade against his loud but tapered
protests and dug a trench fifteen feet long and ten feet
wide, turning the hard black clay earth over two feet deep.
As she dug she could feel the sweat run down her back
and on her brow and between her legs, and she felt warm
for the first time since she left her red dirt land.

James had bought her some packets of seeds from the
shop called Wool Worths, explaining that the stock in the
village store was so old it was a wonder it hadn't taken
root on the display stand. He promised to take her to this
Wool Worths one day, and Ellie was sure she would not let
him forget that promise.

His mood is still cool, but like a stone in the constant
stream of the river, his resolve to remain silent to her is

smoothing in the trickle of their everyday routine.

A noise in a tree brings her back to the garden: the sound of two planks being drilled and rattled together alerts her to the presence of a woodpecker. She scans the trees but cannot find him.

'Listen,' she says to Nat.

'At?' he whispers as he pops his head out of the shawl and looks round.

'Shsh.'

'Shsh,' he mimics, breathing angels wings on her neck.

They stand like statues and listen to the sound grow louder. Out the corner of her eye Ellie sees a flash of red, the only bright colour she has seen in the estate apart from her own skirts and scarves.

'Shsh,' she breathes in.

She can feel Nat hold his breath and the reward comes to them from heaven. The red flash attaches itself to a tree. The bird sparks them a wicked grin before its long black beak drills into the bark with a rapid-fire ratatattat; it stops, looks round at them with a satisfied smile and dashes off into the forest.

Nat lets the breath go with a big huff and a cough. 'At,' he whispers.

'A bird.'

'At.'

'A very pretty birdie. In the forests of your motherland there are many pretty birds. My mother, your grandmother, tells of a time when the forests sang so loudly with bird song the earth rumbled with joy.'

Ellie did not add that now the earth rumbles to the sound of construction trucks and mine detonation or that the birds had fled, their song replaced by industrial saws cutting timber to be carried underground.

The high wall of the garden obscures the house and when it does finally come into view, Ellie is startled that she has forgotten how large it is. The square windows on all floors are shuttered, like the eyelids of the dead. Or are they just indifferent?

The birdsong which has followed her here remains in the forest as she steps onto gravel. A dog barks in the distance, perhaps from the village, certainly too far away to be the gold dog. Then there is silence, at least she thinks of it as silence until her ears tune into the sound of music, a murmur of a radio drifting from the direction of a low building attached to the side of the house. Ellie picks her way, tiptoeing on the gravel; then she stops.

I am an imbecile, she thinks; I am not a thief, I have come to visit. I have come to pay my respects, to pass the time of day and thank the cook for her gift. She places her feet firmly on the gravel and clump, clump, clumps her wellies hard, scattering stone chips in her wake

As she rounds the corner of the house she sees the woman she remembers from the President's reception tipping rubbish from a plastic bucket into a larger tin bin. When the woman turns and sees Ellie her mouth makes an 'O' shape.

Her hair is so tightly curled it is almost as curly as Ellie's, but Ellie suspects this lady's hair is the result of a practice called a Permanent Wave.

The woman puts the plastic bucket down on the ground, wipes her hands on her apron and holds out her hand for Ellie to shake. Ellie thinks this is strange after the Nurse's reaction to her offer, but she takes it anyway.

'Ah'm Maggie Watson,' she says, 'and you are Mrs

Mason.' She stands back and looks at Ellie with honest eyes. 'Ah'm cook, housekeeper and general dogsbody around here.' Her voice is soft but strong in the local dialect, like the woman in the shop.

'Hello, Mrs Watson, my name is Ellie.' Ellie turns round to show her back. 'And this is Nat. Say hello to Mrs Watson, Nat.'

'Hiya, wee man,' Mrs Watson says.

' 'ya,' Nat responds.

'Och, isn't he lovely?'

'Yes, he is.' Ellie clears her throat. 'Thank you for the book.'

The older lady purses her wrinkled lips and bats Ellie's words away.

'Och, it's nothing.'

'It is very generous. Too new to give away to me.'

'It wis ma sister Minnie's. Ah gave it tae her for Christmas, just before she passed over. Ah don't know why, ah knew she hadn't long tae go. Ah thought it might spark some new life intae her.'

'I am sorry for your loss.'

'Not at all, girl. We all have tae go sometime. As long as you can get a use of the book, there'll be no waste; ah hate waste, so ah do. Ah know how your people love tae live off the land, not that ah mean that in a bad way, you understand, it's just, you know, oh dear, ah just meant ...'

Ellie laughs and realises that she has not heard her own laugh for a long time, it feels good.

'Ah had meant tae come tae visit down at the lodge, but felt ah should let you settle in first.' Mrs Watson continues. 'The folk round here aren't intae each others houses all the time. Mind you, they still like to ken your

70

business.'

Ellie feels her blood warm with the guilt of her attack on the inhospitality of the villagers.

''S'ok,' she says, but does not know what to say next. Should she mention the President's residence? It is obvious that Mrs Watson does not recognise her and she does not want to embarrass the woman who has been kind to her by reminding her of the earlier meeting.

'My husband tells me you like my country's food.'

'Aye, it's great tae use different stuff tae cook with. Mind you, ah suppose ah'm luckier than most, the walled garden can throw out some exotic stuff. And it wasn't that long ago when the food rationing stopped here, you know. Ah remember it wis years before we saw bananas again after the war.' She stops and turns red. 'Sorry ah didn't mean …'

Ellie laughs, 'It is alright, I quite like bananas, but I prefer mangoes and papaya.'

'Aye, well, the Fairbairns have a grand contact in India who sends over spices and stuff, and of course when they go back to Africa they send back all manner of stuff fae the bazaars. Just you let me know when you get homesick, hen, and ah'll see if ah can find you some of your home spices.'

Mrs Watson taps her nose and says, 'Don't you be letting on tae the village mind or they'll be calling us a witches' coven. That auld bugger in the garden thinks the spinach is the only exotic thing he should be growing.' She crosses her arms and looks pleased with herself then she jumps and uncrosses them again.

'Sorry, hen, much as ah'd love tae stand here gabbing with you, ah must get on. Next time pop round about two-ish, that's my quiet time. Toodle 'oo.' She lifts her plastic bucket and returns into the back door, shouting, 'Toodle 'oo, Nat,' over her shoulder.

Ellie watches the door close and wishes she could follow, wishes she could sit down and talk more with Mrs Watson about the spices of India and the markets of home where the exotics are sent from. Ellie lifts her head and walks away from the house. She has made a friend who is too busy to talk to her. She will need to find some excuse to come back and talk to Mrs Watson again. And perhaps next time she will have the opportunity to speak to the man in the garden about his plants.

The Pairty Line

'Ah got lovely pieces o' cod roe and finnin haddie fae Davie the day.'

'Lucky you, he niver hus ony finnin haddie left by the time he gets roond tae ma street.'

'Aye well, ye ken how that is, eh?'

'No, how like?'

'He gies it aw tae that Nora Wilson. And that's no aw he gies her by the sound o' things.'

'Whit dae ye mean?'

'Dinnae be sae naive. He delivers her fish tae the door. She'll no' staun' oot in the street like the rest o' us huv tae. Sometimes he's in there mair than five meenits. Ye ken whit that means?'

'No! No wi' Davie, he stinks o' fish.'

'Aye well, she niver hus ony problems gettin' her finnin haddie that's fur sure, eh?'

'Bit whit aboot her man?'

'He's constant back shift and unlike some, he niver misses a shift.'

'Dinnae stert.'

'Ah'm only sayin.'

'Aye well, ma man's on the wagon noo. We're hoping tae go on holiday this year.'

'That'll be a first.'

'Did ye no hear me, dinnae stert.'

'Aye, richt enough, ye hae enough sorrows without me gien ye ony mair. At least your man kin go tae work kenning ye widnae cheat on him, eh?'

'Aye, if you say so.'

Chapter Ten

The Wednesday after Ellie's visit to the big hoose, James leaves the house without eating his breakfast.

'Can you go up to the village and buy fish from the fish van?' he says as he pulls on his coat and hands her extra housekeeping money. 'It stops in front of the Post Office about half past four,' are his parting words.

They always have fish on a Friday, which James brings home with him. The fish van that honks its horn round the streets in the village also delivers to the big hoose. James arranges his order with Mrs Watson without ever consulting Ellie. In the days after her arrival at the witch's hat house James presents her with packets of assorted butchered meat on the Saturday and the Wednesday, and on the Friday she receives limp grey fish along with a bag of orange grains.

'What is this?'

'It's coating for the fish,' James says as he dumps the parcels on the table and leaves her to her woman's work.

That first time Ellie fries the fish in butter and sprinkles the orange grain over the top. She presents it to James with mashed potatoes and diced turnip.

'What the hell is this?'

'Your tea.' But it did not take many glances at her husband's horrified face to tell her she has it all wrong.

James scrapes the food into the bin.

'Wait there,' he says and slams out of the house.

As she hears the Landrover rev up and skid away she places her hands to her forehead to try to calm her throbbing head. She picks up her fork and breaks off a piece of the fish. The fish disintegrates into tiny flakes. It is hot on her tongue and the cold dried orange tastes like evening desert sand. A knot twists in her stomach and churns the empty juices until they bring water to her mouth. Her dinner also finds itself in the bin and she spits in the sink to rid her mouth of the bile there.

Ellie sets her mind to blank as she washes the plates and the frying pan and stores them in the back of the cupboard. She opens a jar of Heinz baby food and begins to spoon the cold gloop into Nat's mouth. He bubbles it out and begins to cry. The jar is full but as she looks at it she realises that it too is shit, and sends it to join the rest of their meal in the bin. What is wrong with her? A woman who cannot feed her family; she would be outcast if she were in her fatherland.

She grabs the tin of oats from the counter and begins to work it together with the top of the morning's milk which she has saved in a stone jar and hid in the pantry for her baby. This she simmers on the range until it is thick and smooth. Then soothing him with her breast, she lets the meal cool a little and is soon ladling spoonfuls into the eager mouth of the chubby boy. Ellie places a little on her lips and takes pleasure in the hunger it quells in her belly. She deserves to go hungry; she is such a lazy wife. Nat slurps and smacks his lips with delight. At least he does not complain about her food.

She hears the Landrover return when she is clearing away his plate. A glorious smell of hot vinegar drifts in from outside, and James carries a bundle wrapped in newspaper and lays it on the table. Ellie is scared to look up and see anger on his face, but he lifts her chin and kisses her nose.

'Come on, woman, there is only one way to learn how to make the best fish and chips and that is to taste the Master's: one Lorenzo's breaded fish supper and one normal fish supper.' He opens the newspaper parcel to reveal two separate newspaper packs.

'Quick, get some plates; we don't want it to get cold.'

He places one packet on a plate and shoves it towards Ellie. Her belly rumbles like distant thunder. She picks at the paper; it is warm and covers her fingers in gritty news print. She peels it back further and gasps at the golden sticks and the bright orange fish that lies limp on top.

James lifts one chip and holds it in front of her. 'These are chips; you cut the potato up into fingers and deep-fry them.'

Ellie copies her husband and lifts up a chip between finger and thumb and bites the end off. It is cool on the outside and hot in the middle. Vinegar vapours tickle her nose. She then flakes a piece of fish as she sees her husband do, and pops a piece in her mouth. It is smooth with a crunchy edge. This food she finds to her liking.

James jumps up and begins to rummage around in the pot cupboard. He almost disappears before he comes out dragging a large pan that is streaked around all sides with heavy dark lines. Ellie feels her face warm. This cupboard she intended to clean the day before, but the sky was bright and she chose to walk in the forest with Nat. Now her husband truly knows what a lazy wife she is. But he is still smiling as he takes the lid off the pan and tugs out a yellow-coloured wire basket and sniffs inside. He holds up his prize with a grin.

'This is a chip pan. I knew there would be one. It's a

76

bit grotty, I admit, but that is what it is. It is filled with lard. You know, cooking fat.'

'Animal fat?' Ellie asks.

He washes his hands and comes to the table and opens his packet.

'Yes, and you heat it high, but not so high it goes on fire.'

'Will I be able to cook this food?'

'It will be fine as long as you don't let it heat too long.' He shovels some of the food in his mouth, then picks up a single chip and blows on it before handing it to Nat. Nat shakes his head; his belly is full of oats.

'Tell you what, Ellie, you scrub that pan and I will buy lard from the butcher van when he comes to the big hoose, and tomorrow evening you and I will cook up some chips.'

He looks over at the open cupboard door. 'You might want to clean out some of those cupboards. It's filthy under there. The people who had this house before us must have been living in a pig sty.'

The tongue in Ellie's mouth moves to protest in her defence. She had tried to work hard in her first week, but still has much to do.

They make their chips the next day, but Ellie remains unhappy about the way fat needs to be so hot and she hates the way her belly bloats when she has eaten. The packets of meat are easier; she knows how to cook chicken and the larger pieces of meat she treats like goat and hog. But there is only so much she can do with the vegetables; every meal tastes the same.

Now he wants fish on a Wednesday too.

With the baby strapped snug to her back against the

late afternoon chill, Ellie struggles at the hill. When she reaches the house by the road sign she stops and pushes the bike, hoping to see the girl again, hoping for that smile, but it is only the skinny woman she sees. With no hope of a smile, Ellie watches the woman scrubbing at the brick wall bordering the house and wonders what she gains. Then she sees the words, daubed with red paint. 'English Bas go home' seems to scream hatred from the bricks, and Ellie thinks that this is perhaps not nice for the skinny woman who is making no headway at removing the words. Underneath the red paint, in smaller white letters, Ellie reads: 'fuck the pope'.

'You will need to paint that out,' Ellie says, almost to herself.

The woman turns and points her sharp face in Ellie's direction. Her eyes widen then narrow in defence. Her chin lifts up and with the look of a lion towards a hyena, she turns back to her work. Ellie shrugs and walks on and wonders how such a woman can give birth to a butterfly daughter.

The sky is dreary and a persistent dark cloud shadows Ellie as if she is the only one in the village to be rained on. She sees little boys in green and white shirts playing soccer in a school playground; it is a single storey hut which looks more like a workshop than a school, she thinks. Goalposts lie in a corner of the park waiting for someone to erect them, but the boys do not care; they have jumpers piled up. Ellie climbs back onto her bike and starts to cross the bridge spanning the burn which gives its name to the village. 'FTP' is painted red on the bridge too.

There are more boys, this time in blue jumpers, playing outside a bigger double storey building. Their goal posts

78

are standing tall and gleaming. Brilliant white.

Two girls walk down the street pushing a miniature baby carriage, one hand each on the handle bar. The sun is shining on their heads. When they see Ellie they turn and trundle into a side street.

Up ahead of her, Ellie spots the curly head of a little girl. It could be the butterfly but she cannot be sure. The girl is skipping along, one sock at her ankle, the other pulled to her knee. A grey skirt hangs down below her brown suede coat but Ellie can see, even at a distance, that this child is dressed differently from the other children here. She has proper shoes the colour of her coat; she is not clumping about in those horrible black Wellington boots the rest of them wear.

The little curly mop flutters into the shop and Ellie is sure it is her.

A white van, with a smiling fish painted on the side panel, is parked at the corner of the street and five women queue on the pavement beside it, clucking and smoking whilst clutching their huge purses to their chests like Bibles. What do they carry in these monstrosities? Ellie watches a man in a white coat lift slabs of yellow fish and throw them on the weighing machine. He laughs and chats and the woman he is serving digs him in the ribs with her elbow and hoots like a barn owl. They seem established. Ellie decides she will not stand outside to wait her turn, she will use her time to go into the shop to buy rice; she always needs rice.

She holds her breath as she opens the door and hears the tinkle of the bell above her head. The girl is standing with her head down. She is tugging at the front of her hair as if she wants it to grow quicker. The green-apron lady is filling shelves with blue tins and the funny-hair-man comes from the back shop and hands the girl a box.

'Here you go, hen, Ruskoline.' His voice is low and not shouting like before.

'Can I have the penny tray, please?' The girl asks in a crisp clear voice, an accent like Sister Philomena who came from somewhere near Robin Hood's Sherwood Forest. Ellie remembers being told the story of the green man who robs from the rich and gives to the poor, something that surely will never happen in her own country.

The tray is a palate of colours. Thin, red strips like string, rainbow-sprinkled discs, paper-covered squares of orange and black. The black ones have the face of a black boy grinning. The man looks up at Ellie as he holds open a white paper bag for the child to drop in her selection from the tray: two black boy sweets, some red string and a pastel-coloured disc. He takes the money the child hands him in exchange for her bag of sweets and scuttles to the till with one eye still on Ellie. As he hands over change he says,

'Oh wait, ye've got something on yer forehead.' He moves his hand forward as if to touch her but the girl springs back.

'No,' she shouts, 'you can't!' She clutches the box and the bag of sweets and looks round the shop. Her eyes are moist when she turns to Ellie.

'I'm sorry,' she says, to no one in particular, before running out.

She only faces her for a second, but in that time Ellie sees the dark smudge on the girl's forehead, like the symbolic chalk her people ceremoniously put on their face and toes during festival.

'Well what wis a' that aboot?' Funny-hair says.

'Are ye blind or just stupit?' Green-apron asks him from the shelves, still, it seems, with no intention of serving Ellie. 'They've been in and oot aw day wi' their heathen marks.'

'Who?'

'The Papes. It's Ash Wednesday, remember. Father Grattan dabs them aw wi' ash oot his grate and it's suppose tae send them tae heaven.' She thumbs at the door. 'That new family, the Pit Manager and his tribe - another bunch o' Papes.'

Funny-hair shrugs and turns towards Ellie.

'What can ah get you, hen?'

It takes the man too long to find the rice in his back room and when Ellie leaves the shop the fish van has gone. She can hear his horn blast from further into the village but the rows of houses, in criss-cross streets joined with paths and walkways, stand in her way like a bush where a machete cannot clear a path. Ellie knows she will not penetrate that part of the jungle.

'Oh no, what will we do now, Nat?' But no parrot answer comes back. She picks up her bike that has fallen over outside the shop and starts to freewheel down the road.

James stares at the plate of food she places in front of him.

'And what's this?'

'Macaroni and cheese.' She holds up a small *Macaroni Cook Book*. 'A little girl gave it to me, the macaroni too. It has lots and lots of recipes in it.' She flicks through the pages.

'Macaroni Supreme, Cameroni Macaroni, Chic'aroni

Delight and one I think I will try on Friday, Macaroni Surprise.' She slams the book shut and places it on top of her other book, she will soon have her own library. 'S'great stuff, even Nat can eat it.'

'And what happened to the fish?'

Ellie stares at her plate.

'No fish, just macaroni today.'

When she starts down the hill Ellie sees the girl trail ahead of her. The skip has been replaced with a slow drag of feet. Her head is down and her shoulders slump; well shod feet scuff the ground like a boy returning from a fruitless hunting trip. Ellie peddles past her and stops by the kerbside.

'Hello, little butterfly.'

The girl looks up; her eyes are wet, her face streaked with dirt and her forehead mark has rubbed off leaving a red rash from a scrubbing.

'I hate it here,' the girl sobs, with more drama than is needed, Ellie thinks. A huge sigh exaggerates from the girl before she continues, 'Everyone at school hates me. The people at the church hate us. They say we are English snobs, but we're not. I was born in Scotland; it's not my fault they moved when I was wee. My mum cries all the time, Dad is angry when he comes home from work, and I hate Ash Wednesday. I hate my mum for making me go to the shops.

'Why did she have to make me go? She never goes out with the ash on. When Father Grattan put that big blob on me this morning I knew I would look stupid, even Eric Creighton laughed at me and he had more, and Carol is allowed to rub hers off because her mum doesn't care, but it's a sin to rub it off. Now my mum will kill me because I've rubbed it off.'

She stops at last and takes a big gulp of air and Ellie hopes she doesn't start again at the same speed because she wants to understand what this girl has just told her. She remembers Ash Wednesday in the mission, but there everyone had a mark and wore it with pride. Ellie did not realise today was that day and her husband did not tell her that his fasting was the reason for his request for fish. Like evenings in the mangrove the air within her marriage still swarms with many pests to be swatted away or killed.

'I hate going to the shops too, you know, but 's not that bad here,' Ellie says.

The girl shrugs and heaves another dramatic sigh.

'I love the forest,' Ellie says. 'The birds are friendly there. A little red breast comes to say hello each morning.' Ellie laughs and the girl snaps her head up and two bright intelligent eyes glisten with unshed tears, but a little smile tweaks at down-turned mouth and two dimples stud pale cheeks.

Ellie can feel she is winning over the little girl. 'But sometimes you meet some interesting people on the way to the shops, hey?'

The little smile broadens.

Ellie points to her bike basket with the solitary bag of rice.

'And now I miss the fish van and my man will be angry, like this.' She makes a fierce face. The girl laughs.

'You tell me, girl, what I give my man to eat when he is not allowed to eat meat on Ash Wednesday.

'We sometimes have macaroni and cheese.'

'What is this macaroni?'

'You don't know what macaroni is?' The girl giggles. 'It's the yummiest thing in the whole world. Mum's is the best, but the stuff we get for school dinners is horrible and gunky.

'And where will I get this macaroni, it grows on trees?'

'Oh no, silly, from the shops.' She stops and looks at Ellie and Ellie can feel her laugh rumble as the little girl looks towards the village then to Ellie and they both laugh at the same time. Then, like a veil being pulled down, the girl's face turns upside down and she is sad again.

'Mum's going to kill me.'

'Why?'

She points to her forehead.

'Ashes.'

Ellie bends down to a puddle at the side of the pavement and picks up a marble of mud. She rolls it around between her finger and her thumb.

'My people still use the earth's gifts to mark our status. In my village we use chalk but 's just the same.'

She steps to the girl and with her finger dabs a mark on her forehead. The little girl closes her eyes and says,

'Remember, man, that thou art dust, and unto dust thou shalt return.'

'Amen,' Ellie says and looks round to check no one is watching then looks up at the sky when a rumble begins in her belly again and she allow herself a laugh at her foolishness.

'See we are still here, not struck down dead.' She holds out her hand. 'My name is Ellie.'

The butterfly looks at it before taking it and shaking it up and down several times.

'I'm Mary.'

When she stops she turns Ellie's hand over and traces her finger along her life line.

'What a lovely colour your hand is, the colour of the pansies at our last house.'

Ellie feels a tear form in her eye as if this is the nicest thing anyone has ever said to her, which is nonsense. James says many nice things to her; she just cannot recall them now.

'Look.' Mary holds her hand up. 'Look at mine, all bony and white and pink.' Then her eyes widen. 'I know. I could get you some macaroni.' She pulls Ellie's hand. 'Come on, I'll ask Mum'

Ellie thinks of the skinny woman scrubbing and pulls her hand free.

'No, 's ok.'

A line of cars begin to pass Ellie as she picks up her bike and wheels it beside the girl. The occupants of the first stare out at Ellie and her new friend and she wonders how they must look, this black woman and the little white girl. Mary stands beside her and watches them file past. In the back of one car a girl with blonde hair and a face like a dried mango presses her nose against the window and stares. Ellie recognises her. She is the sniggering one from the front of the church. The girl lifts her hand and Mary waves back.

'That's Carol, she's my best friend.'

But by the grim look on Mary's face Ellie is not so sure.

'They will be going to church. I don't need to go, I went at school this morning, Carol will go as many times as she can because she wants more stars than me.'

Ellie has no idea what Mary is talking about. Mary

scampers across the road.

'Wait here.'

After a couple of moments the girl comes rushing down the driveway clutching a blue and yellow box.

'Mum's gone to church, but she won't mind, she has two packets and it's not stealing if you give it back, is it?' She then hands over the book. 'And I thought you might like this too. It's mine, I sent away for it last year but I'm a rubbish cook and Mum is always too busy to help me. I just get in her road.' Mary looks severe as she pushes it into Ellie's hand.

'Take it, it's a present.'

Ellie accepts her gift with a bow.

'Thank you, Mary, you may have saved my marriage,' she says as she opens the book at the first page.

'Can you read it all right?'

Ellie feels her face warm and her heart sinks but she can see the child knows no better. No doubt she is also in the Society of the Holy Childhood.

'Yes, I can read, Mary. I will bring a new box of macaroni back to your mother tomorrow.'

Only when Ellie cycles back through the estate gate does she realise she had not introduced Nat to Mary. No one, it seems, notices the sleeping baby strapped to her back.

The Pairty Line

'Jub, jub lips.'

'Whit?'

'That's how ah heard that bitch Bunty in the shop describing the black lassie tae the Postie.'

'Well, whit's wrang wi' that? You cry'd her a coon.'

'Aye well, ah've decidit that's no' very nice. The lassie husnae din me ony herm. And huv ye seen her wee pick-a-ninny baby? He's jist like a wee black doll. Shiny skin and tight curly hair. He's a wee smasher, so he is.'

'You're goan soft in yir auld age.'

'Aye well, mebbes ah huv, ah'm no gettin' ony younger that's fur sure.'

'How's yer piles?'

'Dinnae ask – the doctor wants me tae get them done, but ah'm no keen on hospitals.'

'Why no' like?'

'Ah went fur an oot patients and aw the dochtirs ur Pakis.'

'No' aw eh thum, shairly no?'

'Aye, aw. Nice chaps mind, and braw tae look at as well, but ah couldnae unnerstaun a word they said.'

'Goad, ye didnae want sumbudy like that rummaging aboot yer piles, eh?'

'Ah ken. They say they dinnae yaise bog roll. They yaise thir haun's tae wipe thir bums.'

'No! That cannae be right.'

'Ah'm telling ye they yaise thir hauns.'

'Goad's truth whit next, eh?'

Chapter Eleven

She almost asks James to go to the shop for the replacement macaroni. Ellie wakes in the night with a dripping nose and her throat burning like a pepper pod. When she swings her legs out of bed and puts her feet on the cold linoleum floor, she sets off a round of sneezing violent enough to rattle the foundations of the house while her husband sleeps on. Ellie knows this cold is an excuse not to go to the shop, and she knows cold or no cold she will force herself to go.

The chattering in the small room tells her the baby has woken with the birds. While Ellie prepares the breakfast for her men she rehearses what she will say to the skinny woman. Will she offer her hand in greeting? The box of macaroni might appear as an offering. Should she take another gift to the woman? Has Mary told her mother? Ellie will impress on the woman that her daughter is indeed kind to strangers in their land. All mothers love to hear praise of their children. The introduction to Nat should perhaps come first; everyone loves a baby. What if she sees the skinny woman on the way to the shops? Can she offer a greeting without explaining she will call back?

There is no sign of the skinny woman at the road sign but Ellie can see that the wall has a fresh coat or two of white paint.

She hears the racket before she comes to the small school. Children cavort in the yard. She looks at her watch, 10.30, must be morning recess. The children look so pink and fresh and alien to her. Ellie shivers. Clustered together in a pack they seem somehow threatening, but that is silly; they are children playing a children's game. Two little girls play with small balls, bouncing two in succession against the walls singing 'one, two, three ol-ee-ray, four, five, six ol-ee-ray, seven, eight, nine ol-ee-ray, ten ol-ee-ray, postman.' This rhyme means nothing to Ellie, but she realises that she may not have picked it up as it should have been. The people in this village speak a fast, undistinguishable kind of English when they are not being watched.

One girl, with long curls like tubing, tied up with a red ribbon, manages to keep her balls in constant play while another drops one ball after only two bounces and runs to retrieve it from amongst a group of girls skipping. Ellie searches the mass of bobbing heads for that one curly head she now knows. A tall boy with straw hair and dried snot caked to his nose stops wrestling a smaller boy in a grubby grey shirt and gapes across the expanse of the playing field to where Ellie stands. A grin spreads over his face and he begins to swing his arms and bow his legs in parody of a chimpanzee.

'Hoo, hoo, hoo,' he says as he waddles towards her. The grey shirt and others follow him, copying his walk: an army of comic chimpanzees. They are mocking her, she knows, but she cannot move. Even though she can feel her nose dripping and she wants to take the hankie out of her pocket and wipe it, the only movement Ellie makes is to place her hand on her baby who nestles behind her back. The comic army advancing towards her root her toes into the pavement. She sniffs up the drip as best she can and hopes these children do not think she is crying.

Like a farmer with a bull, she knows she can show no fear. She spots the curly head standing with a tall, fat blonde girl who looks as though she should be working out in the fields, rather than playing in a children's playground. It is the waving girl from the car. The blonde girl is holding Mary's arm and jumping in front of her, preventing Mary from moving forward. Every time Mary tries to pass, the girl blocks her way. Mary points and when the girl turns, Mary skips round her and runs helter skelter past the boys to where Ellie stands. The little girl's face is white, but her cheeks are flushed. She stares with bug eyes at Ellie but does not speak to her when she reaches the fence. She turns her back on the fence and says in a small voice,

'Stop this.'

The boys halt their approach but the big snot-nosed boy steps forward and says,

'What's this, you protecting a coon now?'

'Don't say that, Eric Creighton. It's not nice.'

Such bravery, Ellie thinks, as she blows into her hankie; a mouse against an elephant.

'Who's gonnae stop me, you? You're just a toffy-nosed English bitch.'

Ellie stuffs the hankie into her pocket and steps nearer the fence ready to defend that comment, but has no need.

'I'll stop you, Eric Creighton.' A growl comes from behind the crowd.

All the children, including Mary, drop their heads and cower back to create a path for the owner of the voice to walk through.

She wears a mask so hideous that Ellie puts her hand to her mouth to stop her gasp escaping. The woman's head is a mass of red hair the colour of the western sky, her face is cracked with sand and her cheeks and lips smeared with red ochre. How could anyone find this mask attractive?

'Get back to the playground, children, and stop all this nonsense.'

There is a shuffling of feet, but the children continue to hover around the woman.

'Now!' She roars. They scatter like birds from the trees after gunshot.

Ellie notices the blonde girl take Mary's hand and lead her away. Mary looks round and smiles to Ellie but the girl tugs her forward and begins to run, dragging her with her.

The mask turns on Ellie. 'I would appreciate it if you would not disrupt the children's playtime by standing at the fence.'

'How do I disrupt? I merely cycle to the shop.'

The mask woman snorts. 'Your presence is disruptive enough.'

Ellie puffs her chest like an adder. 'And I thought this was a free country, I will go where and when I please. Please take your attitude and teach your children to respect other races and other culture. Is that not what you should teach them from the Bible? *"One law shall be to him that is homeborn, and unto the stranger that sojourneth among you."* Exodus chapter 12, verse 49.'

'How dare you preach the Bible to me?'

Ellie pushes her bike away, she has heard enough. 'I dare because I understand it more than you. Good day, Miss.'

She leaves her mark open-mouthed and speechless. When a rumble begins in her chest, Ellie enjoys the flow of the laughter coursing its way through her body. Behind her ear she can hear the small gurgles of a little boy who enjoys the sound of his mother's laughter.

'You are lucky you did not cast your eyes on that hideous mask, Nat. Do you think she will be a Miss? No man would want to wake up to that face in the morning.'

Ellie chuckles to her baby before expelling a triumphant sneeze.

Green-apron is the only one serving in the shop. Ellie watches her eyebrow raise a fraction when asked for macaroni, but no comment is made. Ellie snuffles while the lady pulls the box from the shelf and lays it on the counter.

'Got a bad cold, haven't you?'

'Yes, it starts just this morning.'

'Expect you won't be used to this colder weather, that'll be it. Need to wrap up warm, stay indoors'

Ellie sighs, 'I think colds come from germs, not weather.'

Green-apron looks hard at Ellie. 'Aye, well, that maybe so where you come from, hen, but here colds come from the rain and the damp.' She reaches under the counter and places a white box in front of Ellie. 'That's what you need - Beecham's Powders, that'll sort you out.'

'No thank you, I have my own remedy.'

The woman laughs a tiny sweet laugh Ellie feels she keeps in a box for customers.

'Aye, ah thought you might. Well, suit yourself.'

The door is closed firm against Ellie's knock but she knows the skinny one is inside; the net curtain covering one of the front windows does not hide the shadow

92

moving behind. Ellie leaves the box of macaroni on the door step and calls through the letterbox,

'I am returning what your daughter lends to me. Thank you, missus, you have a very kind little girl.'

She just hopes that she has not thrown Mary into a deep pool of trouble.

'Is this the place a mother will have her son growing into a man? A place where children mock and adults treat her no better,' Ellie coos to her son as she unties the binding. Nat smiles to her, understanding the tone of her words and not their true meaning. She knows by the glow in his cheeks that he enjoys these short bike rides to the shops. The air is good for him even if it is filled with unkind thoughts and coal smoke. She will take him again. These people will not turn them away forever, this she feels is truth.

The day disappears in washing and cooking and playing with Nat. Soon the afternoon fades and the kitchen window becomes a mirror to reflect Ellie's life. The stove dominates the room, lids rattle as pots simmer. The table is set for tea and a small jam jar holding a posy of foliage sits between the place mats, the baby yawns and slouches in his highchair.

'An early night for you. I need to talk to Papa,' Ellie tells him as she rubs his cheek with her thumb before lifting him and sitting him on the rag rug. She turns both taps and fills the stone sink with warm water. He screams, as always, when she pulls off his top but settles in the sink with a splash and a giggle. Black skin shines against the dull off-white enamel.

Ellie washes his skin for the last time with the soap

she made from wood ash, the soap her husband says is ridiculous and that she must stop making. She will hurry; the clock tells her James will be home soon.

The door opens just as she pulls a warmed vest over her son's head. This time he does not scream.

Cobble-sized slabs of pastel pink, green and blue soap are thrown on the table, almost knocking over the posy jar. The fragrant smell surprises Ellie. The pit soap her husband had warned he would bring her is not black with a strong carbolic smell as she'd imagined. The perfume is sweet.

'Will this sting eyes?' She asks her husband who now looks to her for thanks.

'There is only one way to find out. But if it does we will have to find something else. Forget the idea of making soap from wood ash. You'll be locked up, woman.'

His tone is hard but she can see that he has humour in his mouth. He picks up a curl of her hair and twists it round his finger.

'We can try it out tonight. You can let me wash your back.'

This suggestion would normally bring a laugh to her belly but she can only force a smile. A bubble of sadness stops her like a cork stuck fast in a bottle. James pulls a chair out and sits next to them.

'What's up?'

Ellie hands her half-naked baby to his father and rests her eyes against the palms of her hands. Tears push against the cork in her chest but hold fast. Ellie feels a pressure in her belly is making her head ache.

'The children make fun of me and Nat – monkey noises.' She hears her voice quiver; there is a crack in her

94

throat and the cork releases.

'The teacher,' she sobs, 'she is as bad.'

'Tell me what happened, from the beginning,' James says while rubbing Nat's back with the heel of his hand. He then tickles him until he giggles.

'Is Mummy being silly, Nat, heh? Let's hear mummy's silly story.'

''S'not funny.'

James frowns at her but keeps his voice soft when he says, 'I know but there is no point getting Nat upset. He was with you, did they shout at him?'

'No, 's ok, he was asleep - I think.'

James pulls the top of Nat's pyjamas over his head and leaves his bottom free for Ellie to put on his nappy.

He hands Nat his keys and waits until the boy is engrossed with them before turning his attention to Ellie again.

'So, tell me.'

Ellie blows her nose and begins. James is correct; she should not upset her son. She starts at the beginning with the painting on the wall. She tells of the boys. When she mentions Mary she watches him frown. When she tells him of the teacher and how she had quoted the scripture, he laughs.

'Good for you, I bet she loved that!'

''S not funny.'

'What would you like me to do, Ellie?'

This she does not expect: some form of action offered from her husband. In her fatherland this could lead to serious trouble, but she is not in her country. She looks at him with her son on his knee. In Nat she can see his father and the same truculent expression. What does she want him to do? She sticks her tongue to the top of her mouth to stop the words 'take me home' escaping.

She raises herself up from the seat and lifts a nappy from the laundry pile. Nat should be covered before he puddles on his father or the floor.

'I want you to understand what it is like for me here,' she says to the towelling material in her hand. 'Yes, that is what I want from you. Just understand.'

'Ellie, you knew before you came here it would be hard. It is never easy. You have to try to fit in.' He waves his hand down her body. 'I mean, look at you; look at the way you dress. When are you going to start wearing western clothes?'

Ellie smoothes her hands down her skirt and unhooks the apron that hangs on the kitchen door. She ties it round her waist.

'Just try to understand, James,' she says as she takes the baby from him, prises the keys out of Nat's tight fist and leaves the room before James can say more.

Ellie knows there is something to help her cold in the forest; she just does not know what yet.

She sniffs all through dinner.

'For God's sake, Ellie, take something for that cold.'

James pushes the chair back with a teeth-rattling scrape on the linoleum and stomps through to the living room. Ellie hears the theme tune to *Coronation Street* and hears the metallic grind of the actors' voices, and she wonders again why people spend so much time absorbed in the dull lives of others.

She smears the fine covering of coal dust from the book with the flat of her hand and wipes it off against her pinny. She passes her clean hand over the shiny cover and presses down the sellotape covering the tear. Did Wilhelmina ever look through this book with a glimmer of hope to cure her ills? Mrs Watson had inferred the cancer ate her sister from the inside.

Ellie had seen such a thing in her village before she went off to school. Five members of one family had been eaten alive with the cancer. Some of the older people had said it was the family's mother who put a curse on them, put a curse on her own family because they would not look after her in her old age. Now she is alone and branded a sorcerer; she is lucky she is not killed herself.

Ellie shakes her head at such nonsense. Superstitious havers, James would say.

The book is well laid out, organised by the seasons of the year. She turns to the spring pages again which are filled with pictures of leaves and a few flowers.

Raspberry leaf seems to be the thing for her sore throat, and sage, of course. She knows sage; there is something similar in her country. She finds nothing in this book for her runny nose, which is OK, the mucus should leave her body and her nose can drip it out.

Next morning Ellie wakes with the dull ache and sore throat still raging in her head. The house is chilled. Still only March and James tells her last night it will be a few months before she will feel warm sunshine, but he warns her not to expect too much.

James sleeps on his back with his arms stretched over his head. The blonde hairs under his armpits are fine like wisps of down, she notices small goose pimples on his arms, and she eases the blankets up and covers him to his neck.

The kitchen holds the warmth of last night's stove. Ellie rakes it with care and places a small bundle of kindling on the quiet embers to give the fire "a kick up the backside." Soon it flares. She stands with the fire door open just for a few minutes and indulges in the roasting heat before she piles the coal on top and closes the door.

She measures porridge oats in the pan and mixes them with water from the tap then throws in a handful of salt as she stirs it with a wooden spoon – clockwise, always clockwise as James has taught her to do.

It is still dark outside but Ellie can see rods of rain fall from the sky and splash against the window. She has a notion to go gather her herbs now. She examines the picture in the book, still lying open at the page, and thinks these raspberry plants are not far from the house, they are tangled in the hedge that lines the path from the house into the forest. The sage covers the nuns' graves, too far to go in this weather. She stirs the pot to boiling. The raspberry leaves are almost at her door. The porridge pot spits at Ellie as she moves it onto the simmer plate to make room for the filled kettle on the hot plate.

James's heavy jacket hangs by the back door. Ellie grabs it off the hook and pulls it over her shoulders. She smells his sweet smell and thinks she should crawl back to bed, to curl up warm under those soft downy armpits, but she can feel another sneeze wriggle up her nose and the burning in her throat, and she decides she wants to try this potion. As she slips her feet into her wellies and steps out into the dark wet morning, a small space in Ellie's head clears. She lifts her face and accepts the rain, sticks out her tongue and catches the cool drops. She closes her eyelids and washes the sleep from the corners of her eyes, snorts like a horse and cools her poor rasped nose.

A flashlight has a home on the shelf by the back door; Ellie reaches back in and grabs this before leaving the house. The garden gate is open. James always leaves it open, and Ellie struggles to push down her anger. He knows how hard she works in her garden and yet he invites the forest animals in to feast off her labours. The flashlight shows her the way through the glistening crisscross of spider's webs woven so carefully during the night only to be torn down in daylight. The spectacular show of beauty halts Ellie's progress.

To spoil the gossamer work is a sin, but she knows she must. She feels the delicate filaments kiss her face as she pads towards the forest, afraid of disturbing the tranquil peace. The heavy rain steps up a couple of paces to a torrent and she realises she should not linger as she picks a handful of leaves, careful not to bruise them. The comfy light of her kitchen entices her home to check in her book, she must not make a mistake. The kettle's whistle welcomes her back and she gasps at the steamy heat as she steps through the door.

The leaves lie in her hand wet and fragile, their points reaching out for the life that is oozing from the veins. Although she feels guilty, she knows she has only taken a few and the bush will not suffer; it will still be able to bear flowers for the bees and fruit for Ellie and the birds. They will have a fine harvest, she thinks. That will be something to look forward to, fruit other than apples and oranges. Ellie stirs the porridge, which has stuck to the bottom of the pot, and she fears James will notice. She pours some into a bowl and balances a saucer on top then places it in the bottom oven to keep warm for her man.

The leaf held against the picture on the book confirms she is right. A tiny black spider scurries from under a stalk and runs around the table trying to find the way home. Ellie coaxes it into her hand and releases it out the back door. She runs the cold tap over the leaves and places them in a mug which she fills with boiling water and watches as the leaves float to the surface. She is sad to see another tiny spider which she spoons out, too late to save. The brew should infuse for five minutes.

'Come on, lazy,' she says as she pulls back the covers from James. Then she sneezes into a paper hankie swiped just in time from the bedside table.

James reaches out to her then stops and lies back on the bed.

'Why are you wearing my coat?' James squints up at her in the darkened room.

'It's raining outside.' He pulls the covers back and swings his legs over the bed, searching underneath with his feet, for his slippers.

'Your hair is wet. For goodness' sake, woman, why were you outside? You've already kept me off my sleep coughing all night and now you want to catch pneumonia.'

''S ok, soon my cold will be gone,' Ellie says as she returns to her concoction. A teaspoonful of the honey James brought in from the big hoose bees should be enough, she thinks. She strains the cooling liquid onto the honey and stirs.

James's plate of porridge and a brew of PG tips are waiting on the table when he shuffles into the kitchen scratching his head. He looks at Ellie where she sits nursing her cup. She knows he is mad at her but she cannot help smiling. She sips the brew and can feel her

100

throat ease. When the drink is cool enough she tips her head back and gargles for a minute before swallowing.

James looks at the book left open, the evidence of her early morning forage still scattered on the pages.

'What the hell is this mumbo jumbo you have been up to, Ellie?'

Ellie scowls. 'S'not mumbo jumbo.'

James scrapes his chair back and pulls a box out of a cupboard above the sink. It is the same box Green-apron tried to foist on her.

'I do not wish to drink your bitumen powders, thank you. I have my own cure.'

She holds up her cup and takes a swig and gargles hard before swallowing and smacking her lips.

'Ah, tastes good.'

'It smells disgusting.' James' brow wrinkles as he stares at his porridge bowl. 'You would be better turning you attention to perfecting Scottish cooking rather than messing about with this muck. My mother will be coming to visit us soon. Don't you want to put on a good show for her?' He pushes the book across the table as he sits back down to his tea.

'When is your mother coming? I will begin today to prepare the house for her.'

But James is not finished with his lecture, she can feel him revving up for another go, but she will not listen. She rises and moves to lift the baby from his cot.

'Ellie, you ask me to understand your life, but you have to try harder to fit in.' He pushes her book further from him. 'This nonsense does not help and you had better watch you don't poison yourself, Ellie – or someone else.'

The Pairty Line

'Wait tae ah tell ye this.'

'Whit?'

'Ye'll never guess who's jist been cairrtit aff tae hospital?'

'Who?'

'Phemie Wilson.'

'No! Whit fur?'

'Liver.'

'Anither yin, whit's happening tae this village?'

'Ah blame the cheap drink at the club masel'.'

'Ah suppose the bairns'll huv tae look efter themselves, eh?'

'Goad, they'll sterve if they huv tae rely on that big Carol leaving them ony grub.'

'They say the mother only fed them on broon sauce pieces onywey.'

'Aye, well, if that's true it's a wonder that lassie got sae big, eh?'

'Aye, right enough.'

'Dae ye suppose poor Phemie'll git help this time? She's no long hame fae the last stint in hospital.'

'Ah dinnae ken. Apparently they telt her if she didnae stop drinkin' she'd dee.'

'Mebbe they bairns wid be better aff withoot her, eh?'

'Aye mebbes. Och I'll huv tae go, that's ma door.'

'Well check it's no they Jehovases Witnesses. They've jist been tae me.'

'Dinnae you worry, ah ken how tae deal wi them.'

Chapter Twelve

The raspberry leaf is miraculous. As the day moves towards night Ellie's throat relaxes from the raging of a bush fire to the smouldering of an evening sun. The rain eases through the morning and after her midday meal, Ellie and Nat step out to the lane to gather more leaf. At bedtime her nose still runs but her throat is doused and the spirit who stabs at her brain has gone to sleep.

On Saturday morning James leaves early to visit his mother in Perth. His talk of his mother's arrival in their house has faded and Ellie holds back the words she wishes she could speak.

Every week the postman brings James thick envelopes which contain letters of white paper scrawled with blue ink; the handwriting slants backwards in the proud script of his mother. These letters he reads with a frown before he folds and places with care back in the envelope. They are never mentioned, never discussed and never found.

Ellie looks in his drawer, the one he keeps the prayer book in, she looks in his side of the wardrobe; she even looks in his fishing bag. This, she knows is wrong but like a child who puts her hand into a bee's nest to collect honey, she cannot stop herself.

'What does your mother say? When will she come see her beautiful grandson?' Ellie had asked when the first letter dropped on the doormat soon after her arrival in the witch's hat house.

'No, not yet,' he said without meeting her eyes.

'Why not?'

'Look, not now, Ellie.' He rose then and left the house and did not return until the light had left the sky.

She had tried once more – a month later when she asked to be taken to Perth to meet his mother. If she would not come to them, they would go to her. He had said then it was too early for her to meet Mrs Mason. That is what he calls her, as if she is still his teacher. Ellie now knows what "too early" means. Black is not the colour of a Perth bride.

Ellie will go to the nuns' graves and find sage. She will make a potion for Nat and see if that works better than the raspberry, but she cannot see how that might be when the raspberry is miraculous.

When she binds Nat to her she feels his cheeks are hot and her breasts tell her new teeth are cutting through his gums. That will be painful for him and for her. He is tight snug against her back but Ellie knows soon she will have to move him to a side sling, he is growing too big and his legs are becoming squashed like a bean pushing to break out of its pod. His feet remain unconstrained by shoes while he is in her wrap, but Ellie knows it will not be possible for him to run barefoot in this country; when he walks he will wear shoes.

She almost forgets her basket and scissors and has to return to the house to collect them from behind the back door. James has left the gate open again. Ellie has noticed that the gate in the walled garden has a spring that swings the gate shut each time it opens. Mrs Watson will help her find such a spring for her gate, she is sure. This one still makes a screech like a locust when it is opened. She will ask James to find oil to quieten it until it is fixed.

The morning rain has stopped and the blue sky is forcing fluffy white clouds down to the forest, pushing them between the trees, creating a cauldron of swirling moisture just outside her door. The path from the door is covered in damp cobwebs newly spun but this time she can take care and leave some of the craftwork in place. The song Ellie sings on the way to the meadow is the song her mother sang to her when she was a baby. She does not know she is singing until she reaches the chorus that tells the child to be happy and go to sleep for mother will keep it safe.

A prickle in her throat threatens to scratch open a wound. Ellie pats her pocket to feel for her own mother's last letter. Do the letters from Mrs Mason carry the same love Ellie's mother manages to place in each sentence, even though they are not written by her mother's hand but by the hand of the village scribe? Do they tell of the goings on in the village? Of the elder who has died, leaving his second wife to care for many children she did not bear? Or of the progress of a forest clearance which causes chaos to the lives of people and animals alike?

When she reaches the gravestones Ellie feels a shiver creep down her spine. A rustling in the bush makes her turn, expecting a wild animal to appear or maybe it is the silly dog of the priest. Something is not right, and then she hears a whimper, a whimper like the ones Nat gives her when she takes him from the sling and he has to unfurl his legs like a scorpion tail. Nat is quiet; he too is listening. As Ellie places a foot forward, a squat bird with a long tail of brown and blue and purple catapults into the air inches from her face and squawks loudly. Ellie jumps and places her hand up to her breast bone to quell the beat of her heart. The bird propels itself forward with a cackling echo, its flight low and short and Ellie wonders why it even bothers to fly. James has told her these birds belong to the estate and they are shot when the time is right, and she thinks these stupid birds are maybe not too hard to hit.

At the grave Ellie kneels and digs her fingers into the vegetation to clear the surface of another stone. The surface is rough with manmade marks. Many are too worn to read. Nat begins to chatter in her ear as she picks the pale green leaves of the sage bush. Above the chatter she listens, ready to run. The scissors in her basket fall into her hand, she is prepared.

The chat stops, Ellie hears something and senses her son hears it too. A whimper again followed by a sob and then a rustle and a gasp comes from the other side of the clearing.

'Carol?' A child's voice calls. 'Carol, where are you? What's going on?'

Ellie walks towards the voice but has to step over an old rotten tree before she can leave the clearing and go deeper into the forest. There she finds Mary, bending over, struggling to untie the shoe laces of both shoes which are wrapped round her ankles and tied together creating a binding. Mary looks up at Ellie. At first Ellie thinks she is going to smile but the face crumbles like dry earth and the girl releases a surge of tears. She falls on the damp moss, hiding her face in her lap. Ellie rushes towards her and sees that not only are her legs tied but there is a scarf dangling round her neck like a noose.

'What has happened here?' Ellie asks as she lifts the girl back onto the log and begins to use her scissors to open the laces.

Mary opens her mouth to speak but racking sobs escape her open mouth and she shakes her head and hides her face in her hands.

''S'ok, no need to tell just yet, let us take you home and clean you up before going back to Mummy.'

As Ellie helps the girl to her feet, she brushes ants from her own skirt then notices a colony scurrying, trying to repair their home. A fresh sapling twig broken from a tree lies beside the ant nest. This has been used as a weapon of destruction. It seems that whoever bound Mary had planned a greater punishment for her.

The Pairty Line

'Whit ur ye snifflin' aboot?'

'Ah, it's nithin', ah've jist got this awfy cauld, eh?'

'Whit ur ye taking fur it? Askit Pooders?'

'Naw, ah hate them things. Ah jist take a hot toddy, that's whit ma maw took and ma granny afor her. It works a treat.'

'Ma man ayeweys pits too much whisky in hot toddys.'

'Ma maw yaised whisky tae cure loads o' things. It makes a grand cure fur the tithic. A wee dod on some cotton wool and haud it tae the sair tooth. Ah yaised tae sprinkle it oan the bairns' dummys. It pit them oot like a light.'

'Aye, it dis the same tae ma man. It make ye wonder whit we'd dae without it, eh?'

'Aye, ah ken. Every three 'oors ah take ma toddy.'

'Every three 'oors, eh? Dis it no mak ye drunk?'

'Naw, ah jist go fur a wee sleep now and then. That helps the cauld tae.'

'Aye, well as long as it isnae thon Asian flu ye huv.'

'Margaret Menzies hud that, didn't she? She lost loads o' weight.'

'She could stand tae lose some, eh?'

'That's a terrible thing tae say aboot the pair wumman.'

'Whit? Dinnae you be sic a hypocrite, ah've heard you often enough oan aboot her.'

'Aye well, she goat the last laugh wi' her Marilyn Monroe figure.'

'Aye, ah suppose.'

Chapter Thirteen

On the way back to the witch's hat, while Ellie stops to wait for Mary, she pulls some leaf and places it in her basket with the sage. This, she is sure she saw in the book, will be useful when Nat starts walking and falls down and bangs his knees. She thinks that she will not have to wait too long to try it out.

Mary limps behind her sniffing. She has a smear of mud on her cheek and her eyes are large with ocean tears. She wipes the snot on her jacket sleeve then stares at it with a horrified look of one who has just desecrated a shrine. She wipes her nose again, this time with the butt of her hand. Ellie knows this is not the cold that she herself has been inflicted with but the result of the children's cruel torture.

'I'm never going to help that Eric Creighton with his sums ever again,' Mary states out of nowhere. 'Never, ever, ever, as long as I live. I hate Carol. I hate her, I hate her, I wish she would be run over by a train and squashed into the tracks, I wish the police would come and take her away and clamp a mask around her big ugly face and throw her in the dungeons.' Mary's voice is rising to the pitch of the crickets in the evening dusk. The tears begin again and Ellie wishes she carries with her a spare handkerchief.

Whatever happened in the forest, Ellie knows she will not have to wait long before the girl tells her story; she remembers the machine gun vocal she was given the last time this girl cried. As Sister Bernadette would say, she should bide her time, everyone knows plenty follows the drought.

Ellie is sure the girl will tell her when they reach home.

'Home,' she says it out loud to herself and smiles at the good sound and feel of it on her tongue. This is the first time she thinks of the witch's hat in this way, that is for sure.

'What?' The girl hurries to catch her up and Ellie thinks that perhaps her injuries are not so bad after all. This butterfly loves drama, she thinks.

'No 's nothing. Come, we are nearly there,' she says, unsure of the word, worried if she says it again so soon the thrill in her belly will disappear.

The girl stops and stands as if listening. Ellie hears a faint siren she has heard here before, like the President's police cars but with the different tone.

'Do you hear that?' Mary says.

'Yes, tell me what it is?'

'The ambulance.' Mary crosses herself and bows her head as she says 'Amen.'

'There must have been an accident at the pit. It's always the same when that happens. The ambulance screams along the top road. It's the only place it can be going; accident at the pit.' At this the tears dry and the brows of the girl furrow. 'Dad will be late home now and he promised to finish making my doll's house tonight.' Her lip pouts.

Ellie is sure the tear taps will turn again.

'Your father's work is important. This you must understand.'

The girl nods then shakes her head.

'Yes, but you should see my doll's house, it's perfect.

110

They had promised me this present if I was top of the class in catechism and I was but now it won't be ready for ages.' A satisfied mask slips down to show Ellie the pout again.

The girl looks at her and smiles the weak pathetic smile of an injured dog and then she remembers her limp and hobbles along the path.

The house is still warm from breakfast and smells of the burnt porridge. Ellie pushes the kettle onto the ring. She puts her basket on the table and begins to untie a knot at her belly. As she unwinds her binding, she reaches behind her in one move to swing her hammock into her front and lift Nat into her arms. The girl gasps.

'Oh, it's your black baby!'

Ellie laughs. 'Yes, my black baby, why so surprised, you never seen a black baby before?'

His chubby legs wriggle as Ellie holds him up in front of her face. A gurgle of laughter escapes Nat as Ellie rubs her nose into his belly.

'See, have a better look,' she says holding the baby out for Mary to take. 'You think you can carry my chubby baby boy?'

'Oh yes.' Mary tugs at his arms as if she were collecting yams from the barn.

'No, not like that, hold him under the arms. Sit on this chair and hold him.'

Nat stares at Mary and attempts a pull at her curls. 'Ouch.' Mary says as she tries to push the grabbing hand away.

'He likes to pull his father's hair too,' Ellie says as she shrugs her coat off and drops it on the chair back.

'Oh, look at your dress. "Red and green should never be seen, only on an Irish queen." That's what my Granny Gallagher used to say to me,' Mary says.

Ellie brushes her hand down her dress, this dress that reminds her of the mangroves and poppy flowers and makes her feel sick for home.

'What about an African princess?'

'Are you a princess?' Mary wrinkles her nose and looks round the kitchen. 'A princess should live in a kingdom.'

'I live in a kingdom.'

'No, you don't, you live in Hollyburn.'

'Is Hollyburn not in Fife, and is Fife not a Kingdom?'

Mary giggles, 'Oh yes. So you do, we both do.' The girl sighs and looks round the room then back to Ellie.

'I love your beads,' she says and Ellie puts her hand up to cover her *juju* and wonders what the villagers would say if they knew the real reason for such trinkets.

'My mum doesn't let me wear beads, she says it is wrong to buy trinkets when people are starving in the world,' Mary continues.

Ellie jams her tongue behind her teeth at the thought of the perfect doll's house. 'This is a charm given to me by my mother when my son was nearly born. To protect him and me,' she says.

'Like a St Christopher, you mean.'

'Yes, like a St Christopher.'

'Well, I have one of those.' The satisfied expression returns to the girl's face.

'Good, then we will all be safe,' Ellie says, too quickly.

'Sit here, sit here, 's more comfortable,' Ellie says, steering Mary towards the wooden chair with the new

112

red checked cushions she had finished sewing the night before.

The baby's black eyes screw up to slits and his face crumples like melting wax as he bawls like a construction truck horn. Mary looks as though the force of the bawl throws her hard against the chair back. She holds the baby at arms length as if he would hurt her with his noise.

'What is it, what have I done?'

'Nothing. He is hungry is all,' Ellie says as she relieves the girl of her obvious burden.

Ellie opens the buttons of her dress and eases her swollen breast out of her bra. She has begun to leak into her binding and can now smell the rancid odour of her stale milk. On her walk to the bathroom to wash her nipples, with her breast exposed and the screaming baby under her arm, Ellie is aware of the girl's eyes on her. When she returns Mary's eyes are focused on the floor as if examining for crumbs.

'What is wrong?'

'Nothing,' the girl whispers, flicking her eyes to Ellie's face and briefly to her breast before lowering them to the floor again.

As the baby's eager mouth latches on to her breast Ellie feels the satisfying tug of her union with Nat deep inside her belly. She wishes this other child would melt away, but there she sits, staring at them, with her cuts still to be cleaned and tears to wash away. When the child has gone, Ellie will bathe and wash away her alien stare.

She smiles at Mary. 'He is very hungry.'

'Is he eating you?'

A laugh rumbles in Ellie's chest and Nat shifts in his contentment.

'No, child, he is not eating me.' Ellie lifts her other breast which rests on her bare belly. 'This is my milk, Nat is drinking my milk.'

'Milk? Like from a cow? You can be milked like a cow?' The whisper escapes the lips of this ignorant child and Ellie can see behind the horror in her eyes, unthinkable thoughts and questions forming. Soon she collects these thoughts, sits up straight and looks Ellie in the eye.

'Does it hurt?' she asks and Ellie wonders how many more questions she has.

'Only when he nips me with his new teeth.' Ellie clamps down her teeth to demonstrate and watches the girl wince. 'Yes, little white pincers are bursting through his gums now. In future he will need to be careful; he is strong and has the bite of a crocodile.'

The crease on Mary's brow tells Ellie the inquisition is not over but the girl remains silent. The kettle begins to whistle and Ellie stands and pulls it off the ring before returning to her job.

Mary looks towards the window where a robin is pecking at the oats sprinkled on the sill but Ellie can see her eyes drawn back to the feeding baby. She sees the cheeks that a moment ago held tears now flush red as the girl turns to look at the robin again, then back at the little curly mop head gobbling up its dinner.

'You have never before seen a woman feeding her baby?' The wonderment in her own voice is even more extreme than the puzzlement painted on this poor child's face. The girl's flush deepens but she does not answer the question.

Ellie wants to prevent Nat from falling asleep just yet so when he stops sucking she stops his feed. His bottom

114

lip pulls forwards and he looks ready for another bellow but he stops when Ellie plops him on Mary's knee again.

'You play with him, he likes to play.'

Mary holds the baby in straight arms.

''S ok, you can hold him closer, he will not bite you.' Nat lifts his chubby hand up and tries to grab Mary's nose.

'Look, he likes you. That little boy there sees no one but me and his father, he misses my family.'

Mary lifts him up and bounces him on her knee as if she has suddenly remembered she has held a baby before.

'What's his name?'

'Nat. Short for Nathaneal. Means "God has given."'' Ellie lifts her leaf from the basket and compares it to the picture in her book. The book confirms her guess; she is learning these new ways well.

'I am named after the Virgin Mary.'

'Yes, it is a good name.'

After Ellie rinses the leaves she tears them into a tin basin before covering them with boiling water. A pungent aroma escapes the bowl and fills the room. She is aware the girl is watching even though she is cooing to Nat like a woodpigeon.

'Ugh, what's that horrible smell?'

Ellie rumbles her laugh, 'What? This? This is an old African medicine.' Ellie tears lumps of cotton wool off a pad from the cupboard above the sink and steeps them in the concoction.

'Africa, is that where you are from then?' Mary asks as Ellie kneels to dab the warm damp cotton onto the girl's wounded knee.

Ellie straightens her back and looks at her on the same level.

'Yes, that is where I am from.'

Tears have left tracks on the girl's face.

'You must wash your face before you go home.' Ellie did not want to speak about Africa.

Mary wipes her sleeve across her eyes but does not say anything.

'Why do I always catch you crying, Mary? Why is that?' She can see those eyes fill up again and see the little quiver of self-pity tremble on the child's lips.

'Don' know,' she sniffs, 'it's just this place.' She hugs the baby but sweeps the room with a roll of her head.

Ellie smiles but stares wide-eyed. 'What, my kitchen?'

Mary giggles, 'No, silly, Hollyburn.' She rests her chin on the top of Nat's head and he whips round and grabs a piece of her curls. Mary laughs, untangles the little black digits and examines them one by one.

'I have ten black babies at school. That's why Carol left me in the wood.'

Ellie is not sure what she is being told but says, 'Ten, that's a large family for such a small girl.'

'I am not small; I am nearly eleven.'

Ellie sits back on her heels to wait for it all to come out.

'Carol has nine black babies but they cost half a crown and she has been stealing empty juice bottles from the building site on the other side of the water pipe and taking them to the shop for the deposits. That's how she pays for hers but she was caught the other night and the police went to her door and her dad leathered her with a belt and her mum is ill, in hospital, with something that makes her sleep all day and now she doesn't have any money to buy the babies. I am already ahead of her with the stars table

116

and now I am going to beat her with the black babies and Mrs Jenkins will give me a prize.' The girl stops to take breath. She looks at Ellie.

'Carol is my best friend.'

'Is she?' Ellie asks. 'This girl, who tied you up and left you in the woods?'

Mary's head bows down. 'Yes,' she whispers. 'She was the first person to speak to me when I joined the school at Christmas. But she hates me to beat her at anything. That's all it is. And Eric Creighton is her cousin and he does whatever Carol tells him to do.'

'What did they do to you, Mary?'

'They came to my door this morning. I was playing upstairs, cutting Jacqueline Kennedy pictures out of Mum's *Woman's Weekly*. I love Jacqueline Kennedy, don't you? Mum made me a Jacqueline Kennedy coat and a hat when I was younger but they are too small for me now.

'Anyway, Mum came upstairs and said, "That Carol Wilson is at the door for you." Mum doesn't want me to play with Carol, she thinks she's common, and I heard her telling Dad that her mum has a problem. Mum wants me to play with that Kate Jenkins, but she's Mrs Jenkins daughter and I hate her, she's so perfect; she has pure white hands and shiny hair and smells of Imperial Leather soap all the time. Mum won't let us have Imperial Leather soap, she says it's too dear; we have to use smelly old pit soap. Kate is in my class too and Mrs Jenkins teaches her. Imagine having your mother teach you and having to call her "miss" all the time.'

Ellie nods. James's mother was his teacher and Ellie thinks when she overhears him talking to her over the

117

telephone, that his mother still expects him to call her 'Miss'. 'Yes Ma'am, no Ma'am, three bags full Ma'am.'

'So your mother, she says you were not to go out to play with this Carol.'

'No, she didn't stop me because we are supposed to love everyone, but she told me to be home by three o'clock, so I can get washed and changed and have my tea before Benediction.'

Ellie looks at the kitchen clock, two thirty; she will need to take her home soon.

'Carol said we would go to the woods to look for Flannel Foot's hideaway.'

'Flannel Foot?'

The girl's eyes widen. 'You live beside the forest and you don't know who Flannel Foot is?' Her voice rises to a monkey's pitch. 'He lives in a hideaway and in the middle of the night he breaks into people's houses and steals things. But he is so quiet because he wears flannels on his feet; no one in the village has ever seen him.' Mary looks out the window. 'Aren't you scared living here?'

Ellie shivers. 'The forest is a safe place. No one comes to this house, not even the painter of your wall.'

'The painter of my wall?' The question forms as the penny drops into the slot. Mary's face flushes again but she does not pick up that thread. This child has learned to be selective in her chatter, Ellie thinks.

'Oh, right – anyway, Eric came along. We went to Carol's den at the building site first then we walked over the pipe and we came into the forest and Carol showed me the graves. Do you know where the graves are?' Ellie nods but holds her tongue behind her teeth.

'And then they said that they knew where Flannel

118

Foot's hideaway was but they couldn't reveal it because he would find out they had and he would murder us in our beds before I had a chance to tell the police where it was. But they said they would take me there but I had to be blindfolded so I would never be able to reveal the location, ever.

'So Eric blindfolded me and they spun me round, and then they started laughing and spun me round again and then I fell over because I was too dizzy to walk and Eric kept shoving me with a stick and I fell in some nettles and stung my knee.' The tears spring back to her eyes and the self-pity finds its voice again.

'And then Carol says they would put a docken leaf on it and I was to sit on a log and wait until they found one. I could hear them scrabbling about on the ground, I could hear them giggling and then I heard another rustling and a singing.' She stops and sniffs and looks at Ellie. 'Was that you?'

'Yes, it was.'

'Well it must have frightened them because I could hear Eric say, "I've had enough of this, Carol." And Carol says, "No, it will be a laugh." And Eric says, "Well, you do it." I asked what was happening but they didn't answer me. Carol says, "Eric, wait for me" and then I think they left me.

'When I tried to stand up I fell over because they had tied my laces together, I took the blindfold off and you were there.' Mary smiles at Ellie.

'Thank you, you saved me from whatever they were going to do.'

'Ants.'

'Ants?'

'Yes, those naughty children had ruined an ant's home just so they could put them on you. I think this was their plan.'

Mary's face begins to crumble and Ellie holds her hand out.

'No, 's ok, they are gone, but please find new friends.'

'But Carol is my best friend ever.'

Ellie stands up and looks at the clock. 'Come, we must take you home.' Nat grumbles when she lifts him off Mary's knee and wraps him in his hammock.

'You have made a new friend here, no? This little boy, he likes you.' Ellie gives Mary her hand and helps to lift her up off the chair. 'How is your knee?'

Mary bends it forwards and backwards and swings her leg from side to side. 'It is still a bit sore but not bad. Thank you.'

'Good. Come, we hurry, you can tell me of this black baby family of yours on the way.'

As she closes the door Ellie notices the girl's reluctance to go.

'You come again soon, this time with no cuts or tears. You come for a cup of tea, my special tea, African tea.'

The limp is forgotten on the path as Mary skips ahead then turns to grab Ellie's hand. 'It will be quicker to go over the pipe.'

Ellie shakes her head. 'I cannot go over the pipe.'

'Why? It's easy. It's really wide and there is hardly any water in the burn just now.'

'I cannot go over the pipe and I do not agree that it will be quicker.' Ellie feels her voice change and coughs to clear the strange quiver that lingers there.

Mary shrugs. 'Suit yourself.'

They walk down the wide track which opens onto the road just before the church.

'Tell me, how does a little girl like you have such a big family of black babies?'

'Oh, it's great, the teacher gives you a card with a photo of a black baby on it and there are squares on the back and each time you pay a penny a square is marked. And when all the boxes are filled with pennies you are allowed to name the black baby in Africa and take the card home to show your mum and dad.

'I have ten black babies because Dad gives me pocket money and I only spend half of it on sweets and the other half on black babies.' She looks at Ellie. 'I don't have one called Nathaneal, I will call the next one after Nat. I have a Theresa, Bernadette, Agnes, Brigit – that's going to be my confirmation name, she's the best saint. I've also got a Joan and a Matthew – because some of the pictures are obviously boys, you have to take some boys.' She ticks them off on each of her fingers as she lists them. 'Paul, Clare, Margaret and Elizabeth. It isn't fair because there are more boy saints than girls so it is easier to get boys' names.'

Ellie stops at the road sign, her mouth is dry and she tastes the bile she is sure is rising from her bruised heart. 'I will leave you now; your friends cannot harm you here.' But the girl is not finished. Someone, something has given her permission to continue.

'Did you ever meet any of my black babies when you were in Africa?'

Ellie cannot speak. This is worse than the Society of the Holy Childhood. Was her own education paid for by

121

a small child spending half their pocket money to buy and own a black baby? Is this the value attached to her people, a trinket; a bauble to be collected and swapped? Why did the nuns keep this from her? Is this child making this up or could it be that some little girl, years ago had a card with 'Ellie' written on the back? Did part of this pay for her worn and patched uniform and the watered-down soup while the other part weighed down the young black fathers' pockets?

Ellie knows she had been fortunate to have been taken to the mission when she was small; her father never stopped reminding her it was one less mouth he had to feed and one more convert for the mission. She is grateful for her education but she was the one who was forced to leave her home for it. She was the one who worked hard for the nuns; she no longer owes a debt. This education should have come from her own, independent government, not from the charity of other nations who plundered the land, left it spent and threw it back into the care of a greedy few.

The restriction in her chest releases as she puffs up with anger; she wants to scream at this girl who now looks at her, expecting some sort of answer to her ludicrous question. She wants to slap that white face – hard.

'No, Mary, I did not know any of your babies.' She wants to hurt her, to tell her that the children in Africa have no knowledge of her indulgent pennies, but she cannot.

'And please do not call your black baby Nat, there is only room for one Nat and he is here, cuddled up to my back.'

Ellie's head is filled with cotton as she trudges home. She

wants to walk, walk as far as the river they crossed that first day when she arrived in this pathetic country; walk south as far as she can, catch a boat at the end of this 'civilised' island, pace the decks because she knows that she will not be able to stop walking. And once she is on her continent she will walk over desert and through storm and heat and drought and famine until she reaches her mother and she will be welcomed with kola nut and celebration and she will at last be able to stop walking and take her baby from his place at her back and they can be at rest.

But Ellie knows this is impossible because she has a husband who she has promised to obey and he is visiting his mother, a mother who has not yet set eyes on her own grandchild, because Perth and black do not go together.

With this thought Ellie decides to visit Mrs Watson, the only person who can give her some comfort.

The Pairty Line

'See that new pit manager? They say he's a right bad yin, like.'

'And how dae ye ken that then?'

'Annie Reynolds telt me, eh? Her man works the day shift and the Big Man there comes ower and sterts oan at the men afore they git intae the cage. Checking thir lamps and stuff. He says some o' them were "contravening safety regulations." He pulls oot wan eh the apprentices fae the line and sends him hame. Jist like that.'

'No!'

'Aye, and noo that pair laddie is doon a day's wages.'

'But is that no his job - the Big Man like?'

'No, it's no, it's the Overseer's job, eh. And that is Willie Harkle on that shift and he is no best pleased, ah cun tell ye, no best pleased at a'.'

'The manager's wife looks a right miserable bitch right enough.'

'Nae wunner, marrrit tae that.'

'That skinny she is. Could dae wi a guid plate o' mince and tatties in her.'

'Ah, but the Inglish'll no eat that, shairly, it's a Scottish bite.'

'Huv ye niver heard her speakin'? Ah heard her in the Dochter's surgery arguing wi' that sour faced receptionist. She's no Inglish at a', but she tries to speak proper like.'

'Where's she fae then?'

'Dinnae ken, sounded awfy like a teuchter tae me.'

'Aye well that explains a lot, eh?'

Chapter Fourteen

The main gates to the estate look as though they have not closed since before even Mrs Watson was born but the two stone lions perched on their pillars now stretch out welcoming arms to Ellie. She tugs to close the gates behind her but soon discovers they hold fast like a fence post stuck in concrete.

'Running away again, Ellie?' she mumbles to herself. As she trudges up the hard black tarmacadam she is reminded of the road to her home village.

When the President came to power after Independence, no one expected the first of his whims to be the building of a new road from the capital to his home town two hundred miles away. The area's small gold mine was to be developed and an airport was also deemed essential for the area. It was rumoured that the President planned to reclassify his newly rejuvenated home town into the new capital, the Gold Capital, even though many doubted the existence of bountiful reserves.

Ellie is not sure how it came about that this monster should be chosen for the particular honour of President, but his cruel reputation in her homeland gave way to gloomy predictions about the years ahead. The country was poor. Stories drummed through the forests and savannahs of rich oil finds in the delta. The colonial rulers had been reluctant to leave after that particular shock, but the wheels of independence had already begun to click and stutter and grind into place. Small groups of militia, opposed to the elected government, had begun to cause sporadic disruption in the surrounding villages.

The President's home village is the next one to Ellie's and the road is now complete. This she knows because the Fairbairns' estate has a stake in a mining operation there and James had been invited to attend the official road opening ceremony.

After Ellie married James she spent most of her days working at the clinic and waiting for the birth of her child. But she heard through her brother Matthew's letters that hundreds more migrant workers had to be shipped to this rural region. These workers had to be fed and housed and the surrounding villages were expected to accommodate this demand. Her brothers had farm land on which they grew yams and groundnut. The women maintained smaller patches of land to grow enough basic crops to feed their families. The villagers depended on these staple foods for their survival and yet when the road was planned no-one took into account the farmland, including her brothers', which would be churned up for the big black road to nowhere. The very land needed to feed the workers.

A vicious circle, Ellie thought. The salt river where women collected small shellfish to sell at market was dammed, destroying their living. The irony of this conundrum did not concern the President: he wanted his road and his mine, and the displaced population and the workers who died drilling, blasting and laying this gamble were of no concern to him.

On her last visit to her mother, just before she left for Scotland, Ellie witnessed the aftermath of this destruction.

She smelled the smoke from the cooking fires long before she expected to reach the villages. A line of grey canvas tents stretched to the horizon. Bare-bellied children scampered towards her holding out their hands for a treat from this stranger. She, a stranger in her own village, had not yet seen any of the familiar dwellings of her people, hidden as they were by the dense camp.

Her mother's house sits almost in the middle of the village, close to the chief elder's compound. Here she has lived with Ellie's elder brother Jacob and his family in a little shack with a corrugated iron roof for many years, ever since Ellie's father died of a dirty cut. When Ellie was sent to follow her brothers to a mission school at the age of ten, she had been sure that her parents would have a happy old age in the village.

Her second brother Matthew returned to the village with a desire to settle down and farm his own land. Once he had chosen his bride and claimed his land, his family had grown to a good size to keep him in his old age: three sons and three daughters. When the road construction began, Matthew was forced to uproot his family back to the village and their mother's home; they had nowhere else to go. Her mother's home was barely big enough for one family, never mind two.

Ellie felt her heart flutter as she neared her mother's home. Several of the older women watched her pick her way through the houses; some called a greeting, welcoming her back from the town. She saw her mother squat beside the cooking pit. Ellie knew she was about fifty years old but she looked like an old woman compared to the women of similar age in the town.

She thought of the fresh-faced nuns in the school with their superior carefree confidence, a result of a lifetime of blind devotion, faith and childlessness. How would they

127

have survived living her mother's life? The older woman looked up, saw her daughter standing before her, and a broad grin flashed across her face showing white teeth that would not permit the sucking of sugar cane. That smile transformed the face into the one Ellie remembered: the wrinkles wiped clear to leave an expression of beauty. Her mother unravelled her legs and straightened her back in the fluid movement of a butterfly taking flight as she stood to her full height. Years of carrying pots and firewood on the head had left all the village women with an imposing posture. Ellie felt her heart lift as she watched her mother glide towards her, as if the air around her feet elevated her six inches above the ground.

'Daughter.'

The hands that stretched out towards Ellie's were rough from working in the fields alongside the other women. She earned her keep and would not be a burden on any of her family. Ellie grasped these hands in her own soft, educated palms and allowed her mother's arms to hug tight and pat the small sleeping body of Nat strapped to her back. All the breath left Ellie's body and drifted above the scene of mother and daughter meeting after an unbearable absence.

'Mama.' Ellie hardly heard her own whisper as her language came home to her, but soon she was babbling to her mother in the tongue she was born with, her fine education forgotten for a time.

Matthew came to the door of the house and laughed when he saw his sister.

'Welcome, little sister.' She noticed he did not welcome her home. There was no longer a home for her here in her village. The President burned her bridge behind her and built his road on top when she left. She knew she had a new home to go to now, but she was overcome with sadness at the thought that Nat would never again see his motherland as she knew it.

The crunch of her wellies on the gravel brings Ellie back from her past. The big hoose lies just ahead of her and she tries to remember if this is where she intends to be. James will still be in Perth. She has no need to go back to the witch's hat just yet. The forest holds no appeal to her today. It can be left to the mythical Flannel Foot. She places her hand round her back and pats the bottom of Nat. Black babies - that is what Mary calls her country's children. She remembers the Mission Hospital and the boxes of supplies, the vaccines for the babies. Was it the exploitation of these Scottish children that paid for these vaccines? Did the President take his cut to help build his road? Ellie shakes her head; that is too impossible to believe. The church would not permit that.

Mrs Watson steps out the kitchen door cradling a large calabash bowl to her chest. She stops when she sees Ellie and looks back into the house as if she would like go back in. Instead she looks at Ellie again and says,
    'Ah'm jist going tae get some veggies fae the garden.'
    Ellie waits, she does not want this woman to dismiss her and this must have shown on her face because the older woman chews her lip and says,
    'Want tae come with me and then when we get back we can have a cup of tea?' she pauses. 'If you like, that is.'
    ''S ok, if you're busy.'
    'No, no, hen, ah can see you need tae talk.'

129

Ellie tries to take the bowl but Mrs Watson shoos her away like she would a curious cat. 'You can carry it back if you like, it's normally too heavy for me and Dod hates tae leave the garden.'

As they approach the walled garden Ellie notices the golden dog staring at her from behind an iron gate. His tongue hangs like wet washing from his mouth; his whole body is swaying in opposition to his tail. He is like a dancing lion. His face is broad and smiling

'Get ye back there, Boggie,' Mrs Watson says in a too loud voice.

'Boggie, here!' A harsh roar comes from deep in the garden and the effect on the dog startles Ellie. The smile disappears from his face and as he turns his worried eyes to Ellie, he seems to be imploring her to love him. His swaying halts and he crouches down and crawls along the path, almost on his belly.

Mrs Watson seems to read Ellie's mind. 'Don't worry, hen, Dod's not cruel tae him, he just needs a firm hand. He is a right daft dug that - just over recovering fae an operation, so he is; ripped his belly open on a gate while he wis barking at the bucket men. Just got his stitches oot the other day. No doubt Dod'll be worried he does hisel' some other harm.'

The man with the cap is sorting through some small brown plant pots with okra-sized seedlings in them. He nods to Ellie but does not say anything.

Mrs Watson says, 'Don't mind Dod, it's no' you, hen, he's just a bit shy.'

Ellie wraps her arms around her waist and touches her bundle who she knows is awake and content to listen to the exchange. She suddenly feels warm as she wanders past

130

plant beds, mounds of earth trenched up off the ground as they do in her country to prevent the rain washing the seeds away. Neat rows of seedlings poke tentative heads from the soil. The back wall is covered in thick stemmed vines trained up and secured. Mrs Watson hands her bowl over to Dod and joins Ellie on the path.

'It's a grand sun trap, eh? Gives us an earlier growing season than most, and longer too.'

'Aye, and ye'll be wantin' the new tatties soon enough, and ah've not long planted them.' Dod returns with the bowl which is filled with potatoes and greens. On top are some white flowers with small yellow centres, like fried eggs, two bunches, the stems of which Dod secures with twine.

Mrs Watson picks them up.

'Two today, eh?' she passes one out for Ellie to take. 'One is for you,' she says.

Ellie holds the flowers up to her nose; she inhales the delicate perfume with undertones of the sweet smell of earth and kindness. It acts like an adrenalin injection into her veins. She feels a lump in her throat and is sure she will cry had a whip not lashed her on the back of the leg; she spins round and there is the smiling dog wiggling his body and begging for a pat.

'Oh all right, one clap before we leave,' Mrs Watson says, grabbing a handful of the dog's ears and tossing his head from side to side. Ellie thinks the dog's ears will pull off, but his smile grows and his eyes close in what looks like ecstasy.

'Give him a wee toober yerself,' Mrs Watson says.

Ellie place her flowers on top of the brimming bowl and pats the dog's back while he is still asking for Mrs

Watson's attention. He responds immediately and lunges at Ellie, bashing his hard head against her knees. The feel of his warm velvet ears is soothing even though she continually has to remove her hand to prevent the lolling tongue licking it. She is not so sure the dog is clean and she had seen plenty bad cases from dog bites back home.

'Right, we better get this stuff back. Thanks, Dod. Ellie is going to help me back with the bowl.'

Ellie looks at the brimming bowl. Should she? She does not know if she still can. It would be a good test for her, but how would they react? She looks at Dod who is grabbing the dog's collar, and then she looks to Mrs Watson who has already been to Africa. Lifting the bowl to shoulder height is not easy, but as soon as she heaves it higher, on top of her head, she feels the weight transfer from her arms to her whole body. She adjusts the weight and walks towards the gates where she stops and turns her head round with ease. Mrs Watson is following as if this is the way most of the Hollyburn villagers return from the village shop.

'Thank you for the flowers, I shall not forget your kindness.'

Dod puts his head down but Ellie is sure he is pleased. Mrs Watson trips along behind Ellie. 'Well, my dear, this is a fine skill you have, you can come help me anytime,' the older woman says. When they reach the house she helps Ellie lift the bowl to the big table in the kitchen.

She hands Ellie the flowers again. 'There, aren't they just the job? He might be shy, that Dod, but he sure kens how tae please a lady,' Mrs Watson says while taking an electric kettle to the sink and filling it.

'Right, how about a cuppa,' she says. 'And then you

can tell me what's bothering you.'

Ellie thinks this is a fine idea and begins to unwrap Nat's bindings.

As the cup of steaming hot tea is laid down on the table for Ellie she can feel a hard stone lodge in her throat. Her lip starts to tremble, and even though she knows she must not in front of Nat, Ellie begins to cry.

'Now come on, hen,' Mrs Watson says, taking Nat from Ellie and giving him a piece of rhubarb dipped in sugar to suck. 'Tell me what's the matter.' She hands Ellie a Kleenex and places an arm around her shoulder.

Ellie can feel the strong grip of the woman who is old enough to be her mother.

'Is it true that the children here pay to own Black Babies?'

'Christ,' is all Mrs Watson says before falling silent. But the pressure on Ellie's shoulder increases.

'A little girl, Mary, was proud to tell me she has ten black babies and wants to call her next one Nat.'

A groan escapes Mrs Watson. With Nat hitched on her hip, she sits down opposite Ellie and takes her hand. The hand is rough, used to hard work.

'Look, Ellie, you are tae pay no heed tae that. It is only a device the church has tae get their bairns involved in charity work.'

'I was brought up in a mission. Was it these pennies that paid for that?'

'Ah dare say it wis, but only part of it. There are charities all over the world that feed money into Africa and India and all sort of places. Dinnae take it sae hard, you must have kent that the money wis coming fae somewhere.'

'But to be granted permission to give a name to these children.' Ellie can almost picture the card with her name on it.

Mrs Watson shakes her head. 'Ah know what you're thinking and it's just nonsense. The nuns would have given you your English name, no' a bairn.'

'My father gave me my name.'

'There you go then, what are you worried aboot?' She hands Ellie a fresh Kleenex and says, 'Come on now, drink your tea and think o' the lad here, he disnae want tae see his mum greetin', does he?' She stops and says, 'There's nothing else bothering you is there?'

Ellie thinks about the husband in Perth with the grandmother Nat has never seen and sticks her tongue to the top of her mouth to store these words away.

'No,' Ellie says, trying to smile. 'Thank you.'

'Any time, hen, any time.' She looks at the kitchen clock. 'Now ah must be getting on with the food preparations. The boys are due back from clay pigeon shooting, and they'll be starvin' and in need of a bowl of soup.'

Mrs Watson helps Ellie tie Nat to her back and hands over her flowers again.

'Dinnae you be worrying aboot the bairns in this village, they can be a pest but they're hermless.'

The Pairty Line

'Did ye see the fire last night?'

'Ah heard the fire brigade, eh. How, whit wis it?'

'They wee brats fae across the burn set fire tae the workie's hut on the buildin' site. Bloody hooligans, so they ir. They nearly burnt the hail place doon. It took the fire brigade an 'oor tae pit it oot, cause the hydrants wir sae far away. They hud tae tak the water oot the burn.'

'Thir right wee toerags, across that burn. Ah reckon the council deliberately pit aw the riffraff ower there.'

'It's cause they cannae git decent folk tae live there noo. Ah heard it wis they Taits that stertit it.'

'Aye well, it wid be, eh. Thir niver far fae trouble that lot.'

'Ah cannae unnerstand how that mither o' theirs allows it.'

'Can she stop thum? She looks as though she disnae hae her sorrows tae seek.'

'Her man's that smert tae.'

'Ah ken. It's a wonder he can stand tae live in the same hoose as the rest o' thum.'

'Thir must be something keeping him there.'

'Aye well, it isnae her looks that's fur sure.'

'That's an awfy thing tae say.'

'It's true. Dae ye ken how auld she is? Thirty five.'

'Niver! She looks ancient, at least fifty.'

'Aye well, that's whit a hoose fou eh hooligans dis tae ye.'

Chapter Fifteen

When Ellie ends her visit with Mrs Watson it is dusk. One bright star has put in an appearance but no more. She narrows her eyes to the gradual darkness as she walks away from the big hoose lights. The trees lining the drive seem to creep nearer to its edge. She remembers the sudden night of her home village, so like a blanket being thrown over the world.

The witch's hat will be out there in darkness and she now wishes she had left a light burning, even the small porch light would be better than the gloom she is walking towards. Here the nights are long but are growing shorter.

She makes out the widening path ahead and knows that her house is not so far away. At the sound of a crunch and a rustle in the undergrowth Ellie remembers Mary's story of Flannel Foot. She starts to whistle a tune she has heard played on the radio. Nat gurgles and blows bubbles to accompany her. Where is this Flannel Foot? If he exists, he has flown south for the winter following the migratory birds for sure. She wonders if the hut in the forest is his and will he return to it or is he just a folk tale? Does he have a home, or is he wandering to find a new one?

The rustling grows louder, and Ellie stops walking and shushes Nat by resting the flat of her hand on his rump. There is a movement on the path ahead, a shape with four spindly legs and head bent, grazing. It looks like an antelope, but Ellie knows this cannot be so. She makes out a slender neck and a flash of a white tail. Another beast, slightly larger, grazes beside its mate. She twists her body without moving her feet to let Nat see but she cannot quite make the revolution. She steps to the side and as she does, both heads dart up and then they are gone, crashing and leaping back into the forest. Their instincts seem highly honed even within the security of this estate.

Ellie sighs and Nat echoes in sympathy even though he did not get a chance to see the animals.

'Yes, they have gone, my son,' she says in her own language. 'Maybe we will see them again; maybe they will become accustomed to us before these villagers do.'

Nat rubs his forehead between her shoulders and Ellie stands for a moment to enjoy the massage her young son gifts to her.

Her husband is not yet back, there is indeed no light glowing from the witch's hat. Ellie unbolts and opens the kitchen door and gropes for the light but before she can move inside she jumps as a figure steps out of the darkness behind the coal bunker. She grabs the heavy torch from the back porch shelf and swings it round like a weapon while moving with her baby into the safety of the porch. She moves to slam the door when a black boot is forced into the space between the door and the doorpost.

'Wait, I'm a police officer, I need to speak to you, Mrs Mason.' The foot is wedged but Ellie can see fingers round the door frame trying to pull the door open. To her a uniform means trouble. Ellie's heart thumps as she slams the torch against the fingers and hears a swearing word uttered.

'Stop that, Mrs Mason! I am a police officer; you have no need to be afraid.'

Something in Ellie's stomach flips.

'My husband, something has happened to my husband?'

137

'Can you please open the door?'

Ellie opens the door and is confronted with the face of a boy in uniform who has red hot and weeping spots on his chin and cheeks.

'My husband?'

The young face wrinkles in a puzzle. 'No, there is nothing wrong with your husband,' he says, taking a notebook out of his pocket.

'I was just leaving when it was obvious there was no one here. I just thought I would have a look around, I haven't been into this estate since I was a wee boy stealing apples,' he says with a laugh in his voice. 'I shouldn't admit that, should I? It seems very secluded at night, aren't you frightened?'

'Only when I am crept up on.' Ellie thinks this boy is inflicted with the same verbal disease that affects Mary. 'What is the problem here, Officer?'

He coughs and Ellie almost expects him to bend his knees as she has seen comedians do when they imitate Sergeant Dixon of Dock Green but this boy's hat is flat and not pointed like Sergeant Dixon's.

'I am afraid we have received a formal complaint about you from Mr Gallagher.'

Ellie laughs, 'This is a joke, no?' She tries to recall the name — Mr Gallagher — but cannot.

'Mr Gallagher claims you have been enticing his daughter to your house,' he coughs again, 'casting spells and giving her poison potions.'

'Mary? Is it the child Mary that you talk of? I have spoken to the girl Mary, but that is all.'

The young man smiles and Ellie sees that he thinks this is a response of the guilty.

'He also says that you have undressed in front of this child and fed your baby in her presence.'

'What is this nonsense? I cannot feed my baby in my own house?'

'Has she been here? In your house?'

'I do not understand?'

'Has she been here? To this house?' he repeats slowly, making hand signals towards the house to insult her further.

'I understand your words, Officer, but not their meaning.'

The house is cold with the door still open. Nat is struggling on her back.

'Please come in, we will talk in here.' Ellie pushes the door and ushers the boy in. He looks reluctant.

'Perhaps you feel safer standing out in the dark forest,' she says.

He steps past her into her kitchen.

Ellie pushes the overhead light on and blinks at the brightness; she moves to the stove and rattles the ashes before shovelling in coal and opening the damper to boost the flames. She then checks the water level in the kettle before placing it on top.

'Sit down please, officer.' She notices the remnants of her potion still sitting there, with the bowl and the cotton wool.

The boy sits and looks at her plant book on the table but does not move to open it.

'Did you use an African spell on this child Mary?'

Ellie wants to laugh but knows she must not.

'Officer . . .?'

'Constable,' he corrects her. 'Stewart, Constable Stewart.'

'Constable Stewart. Why are you asking me these ridiculous questions?'

He stands up and squares his shoulders as if remembering his training.

'This is a serious allegation, Mrs Mason. Mr Gallagher informed me his daughter came home a short while ago. She was distressed, she said she had been in the forest and met you. You brought her back here and applied some African potion to her skin. She then began to quiz her mother about … about.' He coughed and went red. 'About breast feeding. Surely you understand why I have to investigate this. You are a …' He bows his head and Ellie can see his pink blush spread through his spots and thinks that there is something in her book to quieten the anger in his skin, but she knows she must not mention that now.

'You are a foreigner here,' he continues. 'A stranger. People jump to all sorts of conclusions at a story like this.'

'So the conclusions they jump to are that I abduct a child and poison her skin and her mind then walk her back home to the safety of her family? Is the child ill, has she come to some harm? Do women in this country not feed their children with mother's milk?' Ellie slumps against the stove, her legs feel as though they cannot bear her and Nat's weight a minute longer. 'This is ignorant nonsense.'

'She was distressed, and now her family are distressed.'

'She was distressed when I found her being tortured by her friends.'

Ellie sees her hands shaking as she pours boiling water into her teapot.

'What would you like from me, Officer?'

'Constable.'

'What would you like from me, Constable?'

'An explanation of your actions.'

'But you have already given me the explanation, Constable.'

'So what was this African potion then?'

Ellie sits down at the table and motions the boy to do the same. She will not play games with him, she is tired.

'The child had suffered an injury at the hands of her friends – non-foreigners.' Ellie finds it hard to suppress the bile in her voice.

'She is cut on her knee. I use the leaves of the thyme bush mixed with boiling water to make a poultice and to bathe the wound.'

Ellie pushes the bowl towards him.

The young boy sniffs the contents of the bowl. 'This is the African potion? My Glasgow granny uses thyme in her stuffing,' the constable says. 'Did you tell her it was an African potion?'

'Medicine,' Ellie says. 'It is African medicine. She is a child. I thought it would make the pain hurt less to tell her a little story. I wanted to turn her tears back to smiles. I see I am a stupid woman to do this. I did not think her parents would be stupid also.'

The boy stands and puffs his chest. 'I don't think Mr Gallagher would appreciate being called stupid by anyone. He is the pit manager and a respected member of this community.'

Respected enough to have his wall painted with bile, Ellie thinks.

'Mr Gallagher insists that you do not speak to his daughter again.'

Ellie cannot believe what she hears.

'I am a criminal then, to help a wounded bird? And what of this big-boned straw hair girl who Mary calls her friend? She will be forbidden to sit next to her in class, yes?'

'Mrs Mason, that is the wish of Mr Gallagher, I must advise you to pay heed.'

'Will that be all?'

The boy writes some notes in a small palm-sized notebook. 'Can I have your assurance that you will not talk to her and that you will not feed your baby in front of children?'

Ellie sits down on the chair and puts her head in her palm. Her baby is resting his forehead on her back, she knows he senses her pain and wants to make her better.

'You have my assurance.'

The constable scribbles more notes before snapping the book shut and dragging a dirty elastic band over it to hold it in place. He clicks his pen and stuffs it back in his tunic with the book. Job done.

'Thank you, Mrs Mason, I am sorry to have bothered you and bid you good night.'

Ellie opens the door but cannot find her voice. She watches him walk along the broken path. At the gate he stops and turns. She cannot see his face but she hears his message.

'You know, Mrs Mason, as a mother you should take more care.'

Ellie now knows that she has held her breath; at his words she gasps and chokes back her reply. What do you say against such hidden threats? She leans against the door frame and watches as he pulls a bicycle from behind the wall and pushes it along the track, back to the road.

She pats her son's bottom.

'When will this all end, Nat?' she says, before closing the door. Perhaps she should keep the door forever closed to the village. If the tortoise cannot escape from the vulture, he will lie still in his shell until the vulture has filled his belly elsewhere.

The Party Line

'Did ye hear aboot auld missus MacGoldrick?'

'Naw, whit's happened? Is she deid?'

'Naw, worse. She woke up in the middle o' the night, and there wis Flannel Foot rummaging through hir dressing table.'

'Oh my Goad!'

'Aye, ah ken. It's a wunner the pair auld sowl didnae hae a hert attack.'

'Whit did he look like?'

'She couldnae say. He hud a balaclava oan and ran away when she screamed.'

'It's ayeweys the same at this time o' year, just afore the clocks chinge he hus tae make the maist o the dark nights.'

'Eh? Onyweys, whit ur the polis daein aboot it? That's whit ah'd like tae ken.'

'Nithin', ah expect. They're too busy chasin' the bairns fae across the burn, eh?'

'Aye, no' like real police work, that's fur sure.'

'How ur your twa bairns fairin' these day?'

'No bad. Charley hopes tae get a stert in the dockyard, but they say thir's no much goan the noo eh?'

'Whit aboot the pit or the cooncil?'

'He's no goan doon the pit, Ah'm no huvin'it. And the cooncil's rubbish money, that'll be the last resort, but ah suppose it's better than nithin'.'

'And Shug?'

'Dinnae ask. A right waste o' space that yin. He'll be the death o' me so he will.'

'Och, he's only sixteen, ah'm sure he'll be fine.'

144

Chapter Sixteen

The flowers Dod had gifted to Ellie sit in a jam jar on the kitchen table but she cannot remember putting them there. When did she put them there?

'Pull yourself up by the ears, girl,' she says to the walls. Ellie sniffs the air; the perfume of the flowers fills the room with sweetness, diluting the foul taste of her last encounter. Ellie bathes Nat with the slowness of one in a trance. As much as she tries to enjoy his company and the feel of his soft skin, she cannot shake her mood. After she tucks him up into an early bed, she runs herself a bath and takes the radio into the bathroom with her. Her cold has almost left her, but she retains weariness in her body and cannot tell whether it is a remnant from the cold or a reaction to this place she finds herself in. Each dark morning when she drags herself from her bed, she feels as though she is preparing for a battle. Life should not be like this in this land of new opportunities for her.

Ellie found the radio while she cleaned the house that first week she moved into the witch's hat. It crouched behind the bread bin and looked as though it hadn't hummed a note since she was a baby. She had felt noble in her rescue of what would have been a precious object in her old life, and as she wiped off the grime and coal dust she took the same care she took with her boy. The music is different here. At home high life music fills the airwaves. Drums and trumpets thump out the beat for her generation. The nuns had allowed a radio in the refectory and although they had pretended to be disapproving of the music, Ellie often caught sight of a foot tapping time under the confines of a habit.

When she had twiddled the knobs of her latest find, Ellie was confronted with a dull click. She opened the small door on the back and found two leaky batteries welded to the connection points. James had taken it from her and cleaned it up, replaced the batteries and had it working in the time it took her to make a cup of tea. Sometimes he is most useful, this man of hers.

The morning is when she enjoys the radio most; while she empties the ashes out of the stove and cleans the kitchen. Some stations crackle and buzz, The Light Programme she finds has the best reception. She wiggles her hips in satisfied rhythm while she irons James's shirts with her fancy electric iron. Today, she sneaks the radio in to the steamy bathroom and tunes the dials through the static to Radio Caroline, The Pirate Station.

As she lies with her head resting on a flannel at the end of the bath and her toes jammed into the taps, she tries to visualise a small bobbing boat battling against high seas while the Disc Jockeys sway to and fro trying to hold the records still on the turntable, careful to place the needle on the groove. Maybe, somewhere above deck, the crew will be fighting off the swashbucklers who clamber abroad from their superior boat, intent on capturing the music and intent on denying Ellie her few moments of joy.

The bath is cooling so she runs more hot water but not too much because she must leave enough for James. Her mind slips back to the officer and she feels her blood tingle with the earlier rage. After she had closed the door on the youth, Ellie had wanted to go to the house by the road sign and hammer on the door. She wanted to ask the skinny woman and the rough man what it was that they thought she would do to their daughter; she wanted to ask Mary why she had turned against her when she thought she was her friend? But she did neither of these things because she is a coward, she knows this. She is a coward to leave her country when they struggle against a tyrant. She is a coward to leave her nursing when people continue to die of unnecessary disease. She is a coward to believe life here would be better, but most of all she is a coward to allow her husband's dismissal of her whenever she tackles the subject of his mother.

Her hand reaches under her ribs and tries to grab lungs and heart. She twists her thick layers of fat like wringing out a towel, twists and tugs, trying to rip the guts out of herself. She stares at the crack in the ceiling in the shape of an angel's wings dampening out towards the rose lamp, flaking plaster fringing the bottom of the floating dress.

She looks down at her belly, round despite her change in diet; it seems to be getting fatter. She traces the slivers of her pregnancy marks. Her thighs are now so wide they almost touch each side of the bath, wedging her in.

Hold Tight by Dave Dee, Dozy, Beaky, Mick and Tich bounces through the airwaves. 'Knocked off the top of the charts,' the Disc Jockey announces, 'by The Walker Brothers' *The Sun Ain't Gonna Shine Anymore*.'

When the smoky deep voice begins to sing Ellie feels a tear in her gut. She tries to hold tight to her emotions, but this song rips a hole in her resolve. Daft, this is what James calls her when she tells him she misses home. She is being daft. Daft; such a dismissive word.

She does not hear the rest of the words of this song. When she hears Bob Dylan's *Just like a Woman*, the cringe

147

of his cynical words brings her back to her situation. Is he singing on behalf of all men, for James? Is he singing to her?

She wipes the tears and her nose with the back of her hand, she has been silent for too long. She will not break. The smooth skin on her arms begins to pimple. The water holds only a few drops of heat. Her thighs feel cold, her nose is raw from the rubbing she has given it with the heel of her hand and her eyes are gritty with their own salt.

She hears the back door open and close and a shiver rattles her bones as if the draught has reached her in the bath. James is home from his mother's house.

The hot scent of vinegar drifts from the kitchen and she pats the dimples on her thighs calculating the addition from the chip shop feast she is now expected to eat. She wants to curl up on the settee with him, eat her chips and watch *Dr Who*, but she cannot move. She will need to tell him about Mary and the police officer, but she must find out about his mother too.

There is a soft tap on the bathroom door.

'Ellie? I'm home.'

She is expected to jump and welcome him, she wants to jump and welcome him, but something is holding her down in this cold bath. If she gets up she will have to tell him. She ducks her head in the water and remembers the time Sister Theresa kicked her into the deep swimming pool because she had refused to dive in. Deep water terrifies her, it always has. Witches float, Sister Theresa had told her, Satan will not let them drown. Ellie had touched the bottom then floated to the top but could not swim. As she thrashed the water she thought of Satan and wondered if he would not save her. One of the girls in Ellie's class grabbed her head and chin and led her to shallow water. Ellie never did learn how to swim.

In her cold bath Ellie holds her breath, pinches her nose with her fingers and squeezes her eyes tight. The water pulses in her ears. Her lungs burn, she lets out a few bubbles to release some of the pain in her chest but the burning contains it and sets a vice turning.

Some drops of water invade her mouth and when her fingers slacken their grip on her nose, a rush of lavender scented water sends the burning to the back of her throat and lungs before she clamps her mouth shut again.

She can hear the slapping she is making but cannot find the edge of the bath with her fingers. She swallows more water; she grabs again, her fingers slide off the side, and grip the bath and she heaves herself up. Her eyes open but the water is still all around her, a cough brings the burning to the back of her throat.

'Ellie, for God's sake what are you up to in there? Do you have the radio on? I thought I told you not to take it into the bathroom.'

A breath finds her swollen lungs, she tries to call out 'nothing' but nothing comes out of her mouth. She spits into the water and blows her nose into her hand and tries again.

'Just coming.'

Her heart is pounding in her throat.

'Just coming,' she repeats.

She grips hold of both sides of the bath and hoists herself out. The displaced water creates a wave that splashes out of both ends of the bath. The floor is already wet with her thrashing around; she mops it up with a towel and throws the sodden evidence of her foolishness in the

149

wash basket by the door. James will know nothing of this.

Ellie attempts to wrap a dry towel around her but it does not quite meet. It is one of the bundles of pit towels James brought her back from someone in the village. A present, he said. They are new but they are not as large as the threadbare bath towels she used at the mission. They will not last long, she thinks.

Folded pyjamas wait for her on the floor by the door. She notices that some of the bath water has splashed on one leg when she pulls them on. The soft flannelette hugs her but the cold wet patch of the material clings to her thigh and knee. She feels her left slipper is also wet as she slides her feet into them. It is like plunging into an ice puddle. Sidestepping along the short passage softens the squelching sound of the sole.

At the kitchen door she takes a deep breath and hopes her face and red eyes do not betray her. She pushes open the door and feels the warmth pass over her. James is sitting at the table. The stove door is open and the fire is cracking with fresh wood and coal. The vinegar smell is stronger here and prickles her nose. James's blonde hair looks shinier than usual and Ellie realises it is because he has turned off the overhead light and has illuminated the room with candles. Candles burn on the table and the window ledge.

James rises to his feet and hugs her. She can smell the outside lingering on his hair.

'I thought we could have a romantic dinner.' He smiles a shy smile. Ellie is tempted to ask why, he has not been romantic since Nat was born but the lump in her throat strangles her.

She sits down at the table and begins to cry.

'Oh no, what is it?' He grabs her hand and kneels down beside her chair. 'I tried to get home as early as possible but Mum had loads of jobs about the house for me to do.'

Ellie sniffs and wipes her nose on her hand again. She looks around for a hanky but cannot see one.

''S not that.'

'What then?'

She snuffles loudly and moves to wipe her nose with her hand again but James places his large white hankie with the blue embroidered J in her hand. Ellie looks at the hankie. She hates to wash and iron these, she can never get the creases out of the corners, but James prefers them to Handy Andies. She blows her nose and stares at the table. James pushes the chips towards her.

'I've been keeping these warm in the oven for you.'

Ellie takes one but it is already starting to cool and she sees the fat congealing around the edge like a crust on a fresh wound.

'What is it, Ellie?'

'They think I am a witch.'

James laughs a little laugh that is not quite filled with merriment, as if he too believes this but does not want to think about it.

'What rubbish is this you're talking about? Who thinks you're a witch?'

Ellie tells him about Mary and the boy policeman. She sees his fist bunch up and the blue vein on the back of his wrist starts to swell but he does not say one word until she is finished.

He stands up and takes a chip. 'It sounds like you have had quite a day. I told you not to play with herbs.'

Ellie feels her anger return. 'What do you mean about the herbs? You say this is my fault?'

But James does not answer her. He takes another chip and begins to chew.

'Is this the same girl who gave you the macaroni book?'

'Yes.'

James shuffles his feet and looks at her but does not come and put his arm around her as she wants.

'I wouldn't worry too much about the policeman. It sounds like it was just a stupid heavy-handed warning. He's probably a new recruit.'

Ellie feels her heart sink. Once again her husband makes excuses.

'What about Nat?' she says.

'What about Nat?'

'He said I was to be careful – as a mother.'

'Don't be soft, Ellie, that doesn't mean anything, it is just something policemen say.'

'What about the nurse? She says this too.'

'What nurse?'

'Nurse Lynn. She said I was to go to the doctor and register him. She said I beat my baby.'

James blows out a breath which fluffs up his fringe. 'She wouldn't say that.'

'She did say that. Why do you not believe me, husband?'

'I do believe you, but she's right, we should have got you both registered with the doctor. I'll take you next week.' He picks up another chip. 'I'm sorry I haven't taken much interest in your life since you came here. It is taking me a while to get used to you being here.'

The hands that lift Ellie to her feet are strong and sure.

'Ellie, no-one is going to hurt you or Nat, or accuse you of being a witch or take our baby away. I will make sure of that.' He takes her face in his hands and looks into her eyes. She can see her own reflection which makes her uncomfortable.

'I'm sorry,' he says at last.

'For what are you sorry, husband?' she says, even though there are niggles in her heart that all is still not well.

But he remains silent as if he does not know or does not want to tell her. The candles on the window ledge drip wax onto the sink and hiss. James turns from her.

'Where did the daffs come from?'

'Daffs?'

James points to the jar filled with white flowers with their yellow eyes staring around the room.

'Daffodils?'

Ellie smiles, she had forgotten the kindness.

'Dod.' The word sounds strange on her tongue. 'I have never heard of Britishers being called Dod?'

James pinches a corner of the tiny petal. 'Short for George,' he mumbles then turns to her. 'Have you been up to the house?'

She remembers the pleasure she took when she lifted the bowl onto her head, her neck felt strong and proud again. When she is sad she will revisit that memory and reignite the kindness. She will go back to the hoose soon, she thinks.

Ellie looks around her kitchen, she will take a present, what will she take? Tea, she will make some nettle tea.

'Dod is going to teach me how to make food for the

garden. Mrs Watson keeps her vegetable scraps and they go into a heap to rot, worms eat the food and it turns into food for the garden. This is clever, is it not?'

James pulls a petal off the flower and Ellie moves to take the jar out of his destructive grasp. James does not seem to notice.

'My mother has a compost heap,' he says.

Ellie sits in the chair opposite him and waits like a fisherman on the riverbank.

'When Dad was alive he would turn it for her, he would take out the top layer and then dig the bottom out. The bottom was rich dark earth that he would spread over borders to nourish them.'

The petal is thrown on the table. 'Mum still adds her scrapes each week but doesn't have anyone to turn it and spread it; it just sits in the corner rotting while paid gardeners stomp all over her roses and ignore what is there for them to use. She watches from the safety of her conservatory. She tries to tell them, but they don't listen. They are her gardeners, she pays them a fortune, but because she is old they take advantage of her.'

This is the most James has said to Ellie about his family since she and Nat arrived in this country, she believes. She is frightened to break the flow but knows she must ask him a question.

'What do you want to do for your mother? What do you do in this country for your family when they become too old to work on their land? Where is your motherland? Where is her village? Her village should help her spread this food compost.'

James sighs and moves to the window, to snub the guttering flame out. 'I am her family, I am her village.'

154

'If she came to visit her grandson, maybe she would not be so lonely.' Ellie cannot bite back her tongue.

James picks up the newspaper and flicks the overhead light on. The abrupt light makes Ellie blink. James throws himself into the chair by the stove; the chair with the new red cushions she made with some scraps of material her mother sent. Her husband has not noticed them and yet they have been finished now two days.

'Don't start that again,' he says. 'I've told you she isn't ready.'

'When do you go back to your mother's house?' Ellie asks.

'I need to go back next week, I need to persuade her to sell that house; the house and garden are too big for her.'

They sit in silence for a few minutes. James rustles his paper and pretends that they have finished their talk. Ellie struggles to find a word to say. Her husband loves her, she knows this, so why does she feel so alone?

After each word of the newspaper has been read, James stokes up the fire and leads Ellie to bed. Sister Bernadette had always told her never to go to bed on an angry word and although her questions remain in her and she is sure her husband will protect her, Ellie knows if her words spill now he will become angry and sullen. The questions will wait until another day.

She wants to believe they have found each other again and although she enjoys his body, enjoys the warmth she first felt when they shared a bed on the wedding night in her village, something gnaws at her bones and like a termite in wood, allows a chill through the walls of her soul.

It is Sunday and the house has the silence of the forest that surrounds it. Ellie looks at her husband sleeping beside her, content with the love-making of last night. She knows he will sleep for another hour if Nat allows. When Nat calls out James will lift him into bed beside him and she is sure they will soon be warm and snoozing.

There is just enough time to make the 9 am mass. Today it seems appropriate. Her strength has returned and she must display that she is not to be easily beaten.

She slips out of bed and dresses in her pink and orange outfit. As she captures her wayward curls in the matching scarf she remembers the black mantillas of the village women: so drab, so depressing. Outside, Ellie breathes in the moist air with the pleasure of a new day. The green shoots that yesterday had been piercing her garden have opened into bursts of yellow yolks nodding her on her way. The black bird with the orange beak is agitating around smaller buds of purple and yellow; his brown mate, somewhere out of sight, sings Ellie her now familiar song.

Ellie hears the woodpecker tapping in the woods. James has told her she would soon hear a cuckoo and this makes her sad because she knows what cuckoo mothers do to disrupt the family. The cuckoo tells you summer is on its way, James had said, be happy with that.

'Be happy with that,' Ellie says to herself.

Her feet drift along in light steps in the shoes she hasn't worn since the last time she went to church but then she had been driven. She is used to her red wellies; they make her feet sweat but are robust and comforting to her in the soggy ground of the forest.

As she walks her Sunday route up the winding road and through the gates with the lion guard, she begins to examine her motives for attending this mass. Is it to face her accusers or to ask the priest to appease her soul for her violent thoughts towards a misguided child? The spring in her step ceases as she see the cars file through the church gates. Groups of parishioners are walking towards her, families with two or three children, some laughing, others with their heads bowed watching their feet move one in front of the other.

One lady, stooped over a silver walking stick, seems to crawl up the road, and Ellie wishes one of the many cars would stop and offer her a ride to the door. Not one does. Some parishioners nod to Ellie as she approaches. She is the only one coming from the big hoose, and no one seems surprised.

As she walks through the church gates, she sees Mary with her father and mother, speaking to Father Grattan. He is shaking Mr Gallagher's hand while Mary beams up at them like a puppy waiting for a pat on the head. The girl Carol steps out of a car and marches towards Mary. Mary waves to her and then sees Ellie. The colour in the little girl's face fades from pale to ashen; she turns and scuttles into the church. Father Grattan moves from Mr Gallagher's side and exclaims,

'Ellie, so lovely to see you!'

She is aware of the change in Mr Gallagher's face, from simpering sainthood to murderous death. He grabs his wife's elbow and looks around, it is obvious he does not realise his daughter has already escaped. He seems confused; maybe he believes Ellie has magicked her away.

The priest clasps Ellie's hand in both of his. They seem to pull her towards him and away from danger. He looks tired; a cough is bubbling in his throat and he drops her hand to bring a hankie to his mouth and coughs roughly: it sounds like the rattling of bones in the sorcerer's bag. It sounds painful and Ellie thinks of the remedies in her book and realises that perhaps the priest is like Mrs Watson's sister, beyond the help of any medicine.

The girl Carol pushes between them and cheeks up to Ellie.

Garbled noises come from the girl like the radio station that needs more twiddling of the dial. Fast syllables with consonants and vowels of a foreign language seasoned with a few snatches of English.

'Pardon?' Ellie says.

The girl's eyes roll towards her forehead.

'Ah said, where's yer wee bairn the day?'

'Don't you be so cheeky, Carol. Mrs Mason will have left Nat at home with his daddy.'

'That his name then - Nat?'

'Enough, Carol, go and take your place – Was that your Die brought you here? Where are your mother and father this morning?'

At this the girl's eyes change from challenge to sadness and the priest coughs in regret.

'Tell your mother I will come and visit her tomorrow, would you do that, Carol?'

'Yes, Father,' the girl says, her shoulders slump as she slouches up the steps into the church.

'I shouldn't have done that – forgive me, Ellie.'

'I am not the one to apologise to.'

Ellie wants to walk up the middle of the church to be engulfed in the pageantry of the mass, but instead she tiptoes around the back pews and down a side aisle.

Coward, she thinks again. She shuffles into a seat which is not too close to the rest of the parishioners. A hymn she does not recognise is being played from the side altars by an elderly man with hair the colour of the flesh of coconut grown on the banks of the big river.

Ellie kneels and says a prayer of thanks for the health of her baby, her husband and her mother. She sits back in her seat and closes her eyes to wait for the service to begin and to listen to the shuffling and whispering around her. A sharp cough brings her back to awareness. A man the height of a palm tree and with a face of chiselled stone is standing by her side. Thick black-rimmed glasses cover inscrutable eyes. A large hand, nails chipped and soot-scarred, grips the bench at Ellie's side. She does not understand and her eyes must tell him that because he says,

'Yer in ma seat.'

Ellie looks at the empty benches to her front and back and side and indicates these to the man. He shakes his head.

'Naw, hen, yer in ma seat. Ah always sit here.'

Ellie slides her bottom along the bench a couple of feet and the man slaps into the seat she has just vacated, kneels down and joins his large scarred hands in prayer. She looks around sure that everyone is looking but all heads are lowered over hymn books or covered by black mantillas.

At the end of mass the priest leaves the altar and enters the sacristy while the final hymn is still being sung. Ellie is aware of the large man stepping aside. Past him squeezes Mary. She grins at Ellie before she sits down between the two adults. Ellie feels a panic in her breast. She does not want to speak to this girl. She does not want people to see. She looks to her right and left, where are her parents?

'Hello,' Mary whispers.

Ellie remains quiet, intent on her hymn book. She keeps her eyes fixed to the front and decides she will escape as soon as the hymn is over. She looks to the left – the old lady with the stick sits at that end, surely she will leave early? But when the hymn ends both the old lady and the large man kneel to say parting prayers.

Mary sits back.

'Hello, how are you?'

Ellie feels her mouth dry. Mary's tone is as if nothing has happened.

'Where are your parents?' Ellie asks, chilling her words with her caution.

'Mum wasn't feeling well. Dad took her home before communion but I had to stay because it is my last chance to beat Carol. I will get a gold star for going to mass last night and coming today, but it doesn't count if you don't take communion. Carol's mum has been ill and she hasn't been able to go all week, so I've beat her in the school Lenten Table.'

'And what is the prize for all this devotion?' Ellie could not help herself asking. Mary's brows furrow and her eyes worry.

'I'm not sure, but it must be good because otherwise why would everyone do it?'

'Maybe for the love of God?'

It appears by the look on Mary's face that this had not occurred to her.

'I'll come and let you know if you like. We are on Easter holidays now. I could come and visit you. I could

160

take Nat out for a walk.'

'I do not think that it would be a good idea. You should not come into the woods alone. You should not come to my house again. Your parents do not like it.'

Mary's brows wrinkle. Ellie senses the old lady move. She takes her chance and rises. 'I must go now. Please do not come to my house again.'

As Ellie leaves the church the old lady with the stick hands her two palm fronds fashioned into crosses. Ellie stares at these but can find no words.

'It's Palm Sunday, hen, these are blessed palms for you to hang up in your home.'

Palms transported here from the forests of home, just like herself.

When Ellie walks through her kitchen door, the smell of frying bacon rumbles her belly. Nat sits on his chair and beams a smile to water her legs. He looks so delicious she could eat him all up.

James stands tall at the stove wearing Ellie's apron tied twice round his girth. Ellie places the palms on the table, takes the spatula from James and waves him to a chair. She will not have her husband doing woman's work.

'You've been to mass?' he asks.

'Yes, I wanted to thank God for my healthy family and to rid myself of my selfish feelings.'

'What selfish feeling?'

Ellie does not turn to face him when she says,

'Sometimes I feel I want to go home.'

But she hears her husband sigh. What did she expect? It had not been her intention to utter these words, but they slip out her mouth like a fish caught by her loose grip that

161

tumbles back into the river.

'And do you feel better now?'

There it is. The dismissal.

Ellie turns and smiles to her husband. 'Yes,' she says as she buries the stone that sits in her chest deeper into her soul.

'Tell me about your mother? How is her health?' Like a scab she must pick Ellie feels both the pain and satisfaction of this question.

'She's fine.'

Ellie flips a fried egg over in the pan before sliding it onto the plate of bacon and placing it in front of James.

'Tell me what she said – about us, about Nat, about coming to see him?'

James drags his fingers through his hair.

'It's not easy for her, Ellie.'

'It is not easy for her,' Ellie repeats. Not easy for a woman to live where she has lived all her life, to breathe the air she was born into. 'In what way not easy?'

James dips bread and butter into the yolk but does not eat it. 'There have been no black people in her life. She has never met a black person before. She doesn't know what to do. We need to give her more time.'

'Tell me what she said about us?'

'Nothing, she said nothing, the subject didn't come up.' Her husband's eyes lower to the plate and he begins to eat.

'The subject did not come up.' Ellie keeps her voice low, quiet; she wants to shout but she does not.

'So we do not exist. Her son does not have a wife and a child.'

He lifts his eyes to let her see his struggle there. 'I

162

didn't say that.'

'You do not need to.'

Ellie begins to eat her food. She can live with this. She places a crisp piece of bacon into the outstretched hand of her chubby baby boy. Her bairn. The stupid narrow woman in Perth does not know the joy she is missing.

James does not allow the silence to last long. When he finishes his meal he coughs and says, 'I thought we could go out for a walk. A walk in the woods – you could show me all your haunts and then we could go and visit Dod on the way back, see if he has any spare seeds for your garden.

'Can we go for a walk to the village?'

'The village. Why do you want to go to the village? Nothing ever happens in the village on a Sunday, the shops are shut. It's dead.'

Ellie places her arms around her husband's shoulder and kisses the top of his head, and swallows back the tears that pool behind her eyes. Coward.

'I just want to show off my handsome family, is all. And the chip shop will be open, will it not? You could buy me my tea and we can sit in the park and watch the boys play football - green against blue, Catholic against Protestant.'

James wants Ellie to tie Nat to his back.

'Come on, Ellie, you always have him. He must get heavy for you. Let me have him.

''S not necessary. I am used to it, and I like to have him close to me.' Ellie picks Nat out of his chair and kisses his curls. 'You give my shoulders good rubs, do you not?' She says, nodding her head. Nat, her parrot son, mirrors

163

her nods. She ties him to her back and pats his bottom.

'Let us go.'

'Go,' Nat says.

James laughs, and Ellie thinks it is good to Sunday stroll with her family as she has read in the tatty British books of the mission.

The damp morning air has dried in the spring sunlight leaving a bright warm day. James wears corduroys and a long-sleeved shirt, but Ellie still misses the warmth of her country and covers her dress with a heavy wool cardigan. She has tried to put a hat over Nat's mop but he pulls it off and throws it to the floor so she leaves it on the kitchen table.

That morning on her way to church she had walked through the estate's main gates, but now she leads James to the track behind the house and through the gap in the wall, past the small hut and towards the nuns' graveyard. The hut looks different. The sacks are tidied and some of the rubbish had been removed. Like the cuckoo, the bird has returned.

James strides on ahead so she has no opportunity to show him. He does not seem interested. At the graves he stops and looks at the stones Ellie has previously cleared.

'It is the nuns' graves,' she says.

James looks at her. 'Who told you that?'

'No one, but look.' She points out the name of Sister Agnes.

James kneels down and with his thumb and finger scrapes back the moss from the sunken stones. There is a date: 1704.

'Well, I am afraid you've got that one wrong. This

graveyard is on unconsecrated ground. It was used for the burial of witches and suicide victims. Sister Agnes was probably the village name for an old woman who dabbled with herbs. A curewife.'

'I do not understand. What is "unconsecrated"?'

'Didn't your nuns tell you this? It is not blessed. People who do not deserve a Christian burial are here. I don't think they do that now.' He laughs. 'And of course we don't burn witches any more.' He winks at her, but she turns away.

''S not funny.'

'I know, but I still think that you are too sensitive to these things.'

'It is sad that women were treated this way. It is the same in my country. I will bring flowers for these poor souls who do not have a Christian burial. They should know that it is not so important.'

The path from the graves leads to the pipe across the burn. Two small boys aged about seven or eight are on the other side throwing boulders into the burn, competing for the biggest splash. The water is high and fast flowing.

'One day a child is going to fall in there and be killed,' James says. 'They should fence it off. In fact, I think a child *was* killed here a couple of years ago. I don't know if that's true, and it's better not to ask. Everyone is related in this village.'

'I do not like it here.'

'No, I know what you mean: it's creepy. Come on, let's go.'

The boys ignore them, but Ellie hears a parody of a chimpanzee's call as they pick up a small track and leave the waterside. She looks to James, but he makes no indication he has heard; only the tightness in his jaw tells her that he has.

The small footway doubles back and takes them past a house.

'Father Grattan lives here,' James informs Ellie.

They walk down a short gravel track and enter the main road just before the road sign. Ellie can feel the blood in her veins pulse harder when she sees Mr Gallagher standing on the banking just above the painted wall. He is hacking back a bush with a large pair of scissors, and Ellie thinks a machete would be better for a job such as this.

'Good afternoon,' James shouts.

'No,' Ellie hisses to him.

'Shsh,' James says, batting away her protest.

Mr Gallagher turns round with a smile; it reminds Ellie of a crocodile basking on a riverbank. This is the first time she has seen this man with his smiling mask pulled over his face. He looks at James, and when he looks at Ellie his smile remains, but a slight shift in his eyes betrays him.

'Well, hello there.' He puts the scissors down on a sack, bounds down the banking and jumps the wall, all in a couple of strides.

He holds out his hand to James.

'Mick Gallagher. And you are the factor of the Broomfield estate.'

James takes his hand. 'Yes, that's right. James Mason. And this is my wife Ellie.'

Mr Gallagher takes Ellie's hand in his cold limp grasp, shakes it once and drops it like a stone before saying,

'Yes, I think I have seen you at Mass.'

Ellie's tongue is stuck behind her teeth.

'And who are you, young man?' The crocodile puts his hand up to stroke Nat's hair and Ellie shrinks back.

'This is our son Nat,' says James. 'Say hello to the nice man, Nat.'

Ellie cannot prevent the snort that escapes her nostrils. James' eyes flick to hers then back at Mick Gallagher.

''Ya,' Nat chuckles.

'Ho, do I detect a Fife accent?' the Gallagher man says. 'It doesn't take long. My daughter Mary is already talking like a native.'

Ellie sees his face colour and backs away. She will not go on with this farce any longer. 'James, I think we should go, Nat is restless.'

'No, he's fine.'

'No, no, don't let me keep you,' the crocodile says. 'I have work to do anyway. I don't want the little woman to catch me slacking from my Sunday chores.' It seems that the man has also had enough pretence.

'There, he seems nice enough,' James says to Ellie when they are out of the sight of this hypocrite.

Ellie kicks a stone hard into the road. Tall grass sprouts and reaches high from the kerbside. She grabs it and picks it to pieces, scattering the remnants onto the pavement.

'Well, didn't you think so?'

She continues to walk. Where had 'the little woman' been, when they were having their pleasant chit chat? Hiding in the house? Ellie knows one of their windows looks along the road and she can feel the woman's eyes watching them behind those damned net curtains.

'You forget, husband, that this man accused me of

poisoning his daughter. He set the police on me. Rather than hobnobbing with him, I would have preferred if you punch his nose.'

'For God's sake, Ellie! I think there must have been a misunderstanding. He was perfectly civil and polite.'

Ellie looks at the road ahead of her.

'I do not think we should go to the village now. It is getting late and Nat will need some dinner.'

'But I thought you wanted to go for a fish tea?'

'I do not have much appetite. In fact I feel a little sick. I think I should go home. You can go for some and bring them home if you like.'

'They'll be cold before I get home.'

He takes her arm; she wants to shake it off. She wants to shake him, why can he not see?

'Come on, Ellie, we'll go home and you can have a rest. I know what will cheer you up: we can have some of your famous macaroni for tea.'

The Pairty Line

'Did yer man tell ye? Thir's a new dance band at the club.'

'Naw, ah niver knew. Ur they ony guid?'

'Fantastic. They play aw the auld stuff but also Jim Reeves and Perry Como.'

'Aw, ah luv Jim Reeves. That "Ah luv you because" it's beautiful.'

'Me an' a'. It's such a shame he's deid, nae mair great tunes fae that yin, eh?'

'Sad. Ah huvnae been tae the club fur ages, is the dancing still the same? Ye ken, the same auld show-affs struttin' thir stuff.'

'Oh aye, that Jenny Middleton tryin' tae look swell wi' Charlie Mathews.'

'Ah dinnae ken how Jock Middleton pits up wi' it – imagine huvin' yer wife paradin' aboot in another man's airms.'

'But Jock's no interested in the dancing. It wid take him away fae the games room. Ye ken how darts mad he is.'

'Aye, ah suppose so. Still, ah must try tae get back; git a babysitter this Seterday and come an' hear the Jim Reeves songs.'

'Dae ye think yer man'll want ye tae come?'

'He's like Jock Middleton, as long as ah dinnae expect him tae dance he'll no mind.'

'Right, ah'll see ye there, then.'

'Yer oan.'

Chapter Seventeen

When they arrive home, Ellie feels no better. She unties the sleeping Nat from her back, lays him on the playpen mat and covers him with a blanket.

'I think I will go for a bath.'

James looks at her as if he has not seen her before.

'No, Ellie, sit down. I need to talk to you. We are tiptoeing around each other like frightened rabbits.'

She sits on the chair with the red cushions that James has not yet noticed. As Ellie unbuttons her cardigan she is surprised to notice that her hands are shaking. What is she afraid of? That James will grant her wish and send her home? The door to the rest of the house lies open and Ellie's feet itch to flee to the bathroom and the safety of the warm bath where she can dissolve her fears. Or perhaps he will tell her that he will take them to Perth. What does she fear most? Coward.

'Do you know that I have hardly seen you smile since you arrived here?'

Ellie shrugs; she does not know where this is leading to.

'When was the last time you smiled?'

His voice is so low and searching. Ellie shifts in her seat. She wants to go for her bath, she wants to be clean. But she knows the answer to his question.

She lifts her head and faces him. He has worry in his eyes.

'This morning when I rescued the mess you were making of breakfast.' He will let her go if she does not show him her pain.

'Last night you mentioned we hadn't been to the doctor yet to register you and Nat; I think we should go tomorrow.'

'You think I need a doctor?' She cannot hide her surprise. Or is it disappointment she finds in her voice?

'I don't think it would do you any harm to have a check-up. You have had a cold and have been a bit down. You probably just need a pick-me-up.' He stands and holds out his hand to help her up. 'Now go and have a quick bath to make you feel better before we have our meal.'

Once more Ellie is dismissed, and the bath, that moments before seemed so attractive to her seems like a punishment for her cowardice.

The lady at the front desk glares at James when he tells her that he wants to see Dr Wishart and he does not have an appointment.

'Is it an emergency?' This time she attacks Ellie and Nat with her vicious eyes.

'Yes, it is.'

She raises a pencil thin eyebrow. 'Well, you may have to wait for as long as an hour for a space in the diary. I haven't had any "no shows" yet today.'

'That will be fine, as long as we can see him.'

The chatter Ellie hears from the front desk ceases as soon as she and her family walk through the open double doors into the waiting room. Most of the seats are filled, but one man rises and motions for Ellie to take his seat and for James to take the vacant seat beside her.

'Ah should be next onyweys, hen,' he says.

Two women to the right of Ellie start to speak to each other. At first Ellie cannot understand their words but like with the radio she soon tunes in to the garbled noise.

'Ah cannae get ma telly tae work. Ah missed Sunday Night at the London Palladium.'

'Och, that's a shame, it wis that gid last night tae.'

'Thanks a bunch.'

A black door opens and everyone's eyes turn to watch a small woman with a walking stick shuffle out.

'Mr Mathie for Dr Wishart,' the poisonous receptionist calls from the office.

'Ye see? Ah wis right.' The man who gave Ellie his seat nods to her before he begins to limp towards the black door. Everyone watches his progress, but before he reaches the door, Nurse Lynn barges from another door and holds her hand up to the man.

'Just a moment, I need to ask the doctor something.' She leaves him standing halfway between his seat the doctor's room.

One of the women beside Ellie clicks her mouth and says in a loud voice, 'That is the height o' ignorance. See that wumman, she should git the sack fur aw the trouble she causes.'

Ellie turns and looks at the speaker and finds the woman looks right at her.

She nods to Ellie, 'Pure mischief-maker, so she is.'

'I know,' Ellie says. And looks at all the heads nodding in agreement with her.

James places his hand around her wrist like a handcuff and squeezes.

'Don't say any more,' he whispers.

She does not understand. Why must her husband

always keep her in shackles?

When Nurse Lynn comes out, the man continues his painful journey in to see his doctor, and the woman beside Ellie says to her friend,

'That Bill Mathie's not long fur this world, ah reckon, Bella.'

'Whit is it? Dae ye ken?'

The woman whispers something that Ellie cannot make out, but she hears several intakes of breath.

It is only when the Bella woman is called and leaves to see a doctor called Hurry that Ellie understands why her husband has stopped her from speaking. As soon as Doctor Hurry's door has closed on Bella, the woman next to Ellie addresses the man who sits opposite her across a table scattered with magazines.

'It's a right shame, thir always the last tae ken.'

'Is it still goan oan then, Isa?'

'Aye, Bella's man is niver done sniffin' roon Tess Mitchell. In fact, no jist sniffin', Shug, no jist sniffin'.'

'It's a pure shame, so it is.'

James rises from his seat and moves to the table between them breaking the eye contact of the two gossips. The time he takes to rummage for a magazine seems longer than necessary and is enough to halt the conversation and the waiting room falls into silence.

When 'Mr Mason for Dr Wishart' is called, Ellie is sure she hears several clicking noises from the busy mouths in room.

She had expected Dr Wishart to be an old man but he is not.

James shakes his hand and says, 'Thanks for seeing us without an appointment.' He signals to the door.

173

'They're not too happy out there about us being taken so soon.'

The doctor laughs a gentle laugh. 'Don't worry about them; give them something to gab about. Most of them are here every week, I'm sure they only come for the blether.'

'What a beautiful baby.' The doctor holds out his arms and takes Nat onto his knee. 'What can I do for you?'

James explains about Ellie and Nat's recent arrival and about the nurse's suggestion they should be registered. He coughs and says,

'I also think my wife may not be too well.'

Ellie can feel her heart quicken and her skin begin to bristle like a cat backed into a corner. Is she not here, does she not have a voice of her own?

The doctor looks at Ellie over his glasses.

'In what way not well?' he asks her.

'She cries a lot and thinks everyone hates her,' James says.

Ellie can feel heat in her blood. Her head bows; she does not want this man to think she is possessed by some evil spirit even though sometimes she feel she has been.

'I see,' is all he says, before turning his attention to Nat. He delivers Nat back onto Ellie's lap and asks her to undress him. He looks at the notes on his desk.

'I see here in the nurse's report a mention of a rash on Nat's hand - has that cleared up?'

'Yes,' Ellie whispers.

'And a bruise?'

'Is a mark of birth.' She points to it.

'So it is,' he says. 'Sorry, she should have known.' He sounds Nat with a stethoscope that Nat tries to grab, but the doctor is too quick for him. Dr Wishart then takes his temperature and examines his eyes and mouth. He returns to his desk, makes some scratches with a pen and then asks Ellie to dress Nat again.

'Well, Ellie, you have a fine healthy son there,' the doctor says. 'Breast-fed, I assume?'

'Yes,' Ellie whispers again, but she feels a small smile pull at her cheeks. The doctor looks at James. 'You should be proud of your wife. She has given your son the best possible start.'

'Yes, yes, I am,' James says, but Ellie thinks he does not sound so sure and would prefer to throw the blanket over them again.

The doctor writes some more then stands and takes the baby from Ellie and hands him to James.

'Take Nat into the waiting room, James, while I examine your wife.'

Ellie can see her husband's reluctance, but he submits to the doctor's request.

When the door closes, the doctor does not return behind his desk but sits in the seat James has just vacated next to Ellie.

'Now, Ellie, I am just going to give you a quick look over and ask you a few questions, it shouldn't take long. How long have you been here, in this country?'

'Three months.' She finds her voice is leaving her, and is replaced with tightness in her chest.

'And how has your health been?' he asks as he looks in her ears.

'I had a cold last week, not bad.' She takes a deep breath to quell the quiver in her throat. She wills this doctor to stop being nice to her. She is sure she will cry and does not want the people in the waiting room to see her tears.

'What did you take for your cold?'

She can feel herself stiffen as he rubs the stethoscope with his hands to make it warm.

'Did you take anything for your cold?' he repeats. She wonders if he has heard of the police officer's visit and of the accusation.

'I take herbs.'

'Really?' he says as he listens to her chest and her pounding heart.

He sits down beside her again. 'What herbs did you take?'

'Raspberry leaf and sage.'

'And did it work?'

She nods, 'Yes, I am better.'

'Good,' is all he says. A small wrinkle appears in his brow, making him look older.

'How do you feel in yourself?'

'I do not understand.'

'Do you miss your home?'

'Yes.'

'What do you miss about your home?'

'My mother.' The pressure in Ellie's chest makes it hard for her to breath. She wishes this doctor would stop asking her questions. She wants to go home to her kitchen.

'What do you find hardest about living here?'

Ellie looks at his kind white face and considers lying, but knows this is wrong. She swallows and says, 'All the white faces. Everywhere, white faces.'

'Yes, I can see that would be a problem.' The doctor says. 'Do you ever get depressed, Ellie?'

'I do not know.'

'Your husband said you cry a lot. Do you cry?'

Ellie nods her head before she gives him his evidence.

'Do you often feel tired?'

Again she nods.

The doctor rises and begins to write something in the notes and then on a prescription pad.

'When was the last time you left Hollyburn?'

Ellie stares at the doctor and shakes her head. And he mirrors her.

'It cannot be easy for you, being here. I'm giving you something to make you feel better.' Then he scores it out and says, 'But you probably won't take it, will you?'

'No.'

'Well, you find your own herb and eat plenty greens.'

He holds out his hand to help her out of the seat.

'I have a baby clinic on the last Wednesday of every month. I would encourage you to bring Nat.' His smile warms her. 'It would be good for you to meet others, and you would be a good role model to the mothers here. They think breast-feeding is a waste of time.'

'Goodbye, Ellie. Make an appointment to come back in two weeks to see me again and we will see how you are feeling.' He shakes her hand. 'Try to get out of the village more.'

Ellie expects the doctor to ask to speak to James again, but he does not.

As she leaves the waiting room with her husband and baby, Ellie hesitates at the reception desk. The doctor told her to make an appointment.

'What did the doctor say?' James asks.

'He says I am fine. I need to get out more, is all. Eat more greens,' she says as she walks away from the desk knowing she does not lie to her husband.

177

The Pairty Line

'Whit dae ye hink is wrang wi' her?'

'Ah dinnae ken, but she wis a hell o' a long time in wi' him.'

'Dae ye hink oor doctors will ken aboot foreign illnesses?'

'Goad knows. She certainly looked happier comin' oot than goan in.'

'My, but that's a bonny bairn she's got. Eh?'

'Ah ken. How did you get oan onywey?'

'Och, the usual. Ma doctor hus ye in an' oot afore ye've a chance tae git yer coat aff.'

'Ah ken whit ye mean. Mine hus the prescription written an' hondit tae ye as ye come in the door.'

'Thir jist no interestit.'

'No wi' the like o' us, but ah bet that wee black baby gits lots o' attention. Eh?'

'Dae ye think he could huv some horrible African diseases tae pass oan tae oor bairns?'

'Mebbes, ah'll be keepin' ma bairns away fae um onywey.'

'Ah'd hardly ca' you're bairns bairns.'

'Disnae metter how auld they ir, they'll ayeways be bairns tae me.'

'If you say so.'

Chapter Eighteen

In the living room there is a gramophone that looks like a piece of furniture. A shiny front door with one handle pulls downwards with a soft *shoof* to reveal the turntable. Sad memories of the Reverend Mother's study are evoked by the smell of beeswax polish that fills the room each time the gramophone door opens. Sometimes when Ellie is alone, she will sit in the living room and stare at this marvel, then temptation will grab her and she will open the door to capture those familiar feelings again.

Reverend Mother's study was the only room in the mission school that did not smell of little children. It was the room you were sent to receive special news. Ellie had only been in the room three times. The first was the day she was told her father had died. She had not cried; she had asked to go home, but this was not permitted; it was too expensive. The mission would never survive if it paid for very child to return home when a family member died, the Reverend Mother had told her.

The second time was when the Reverend Mother had tried to persuade her to take her vows. That time did not last so long because the nuns already knew she had made up her mind. The third was when the Reverend Mother informed Ellie of her new home at the clinic up river. She would leave her home of ten years the next day and should be grateful she had this opportunity.

The dial beside the turntable in the gramophone has 33, 45 and 78 stamped round the edge like a cooker dial.

In this house most of the records are heavy plastic and scratch out with the thick needle the music of Bing Crosby and Ruby Murray. There are a few lighter records too: Tchaikovsky and Mozart. To play these it is necessary to lift the gramophone arm and twist the needle to the other side because a thinner needle is needed.

Ellie has played all the records she could find in the house, including Andy Stewart's *A Scottish Soldier* and *Donald Where's Yer Troosers* - songs she has never heard on the Pirate Radio or even the Light Programme. She wants something she can dance to. High life music from home or music from America, the music she hears from the Pirates, that is what she wants.

James arrives back from an evening meeting at the big hoose just after nine. He bundles into the kitchen carrying a packet from the chip shop even though she has given him a tea of jollof rice before he left for his meeting. He kisses her and dumps the packet on the table

'Wait till you see what I've brought you,' he says, pushing the packet towards her and going to the cupboard for plates. He unwraps the packet and reveals two golden crispy tubes.

'Spring rolls - they are Chinese and the chip shop has just started cooking them. Old Giuseppe said he got the idea when his daughter brought a 'Chinkie' back from the town.'

Ellie stares at the food.

'Have you not had your meal? Am I a bad wife, do I not feed you enough?' Ellie says. The jollof rice was good and filling, and yet here he is stuffing himself to busting with grease.

He munches into the golden rod. 'I was a bit peckish, that's all. They are lovely, try some.'

'No, thank you, I am getting fat; I need to eat less.' Ellie ignores her husband's grin. He received one of those white envelopes from his mother that morning and Ellie wants to ask what it contained but pushes her tongue behind her teeth. Their silence ticks in time to the kitchen clock.

He shoves the packet towards her. 'Come on.'

She can see the vein in his head throb which makes his smile false.

'Have you been to the village today?' he says, trying to stir the atmosphere.

'Yes, I go after lunch time now, when the housewives nap and the shop is quiet. I do not frighten little children. Is that not good?'

James munches with his head down and does not answer her. Once she thought he was brave but now he is back in his own environment, she can see that he is not.

'Where can I buy a record?' she asks with a straight mask.

He stops chewing and stares at her with the second spring roll raised to his mouth.

'What?'

'Oh, you hear me now.'

'Don't start, Ellie.'

It is always 'Do not start, Ellie, do not be daft, Ellie' with him. He can never face an argument. This is the man who embraces Sister Bernadette's rule of never going to bed with an angry word between them, a rule which only seems to work one way as she remembers the many slammed doors when he storms off to bed at a single mention of his mother. This is a rule which has served him well in avoidance, she thinks.

'A record, I want to buy a record to play on the gramophone. I am bored with Bing Crosby and Troosers.' She sees a tick of a smile at her attempt at a Scottish accent.

'There is a record store in town, tell me what you want and I will go and buy it.'

'No, I go next week – on my own and on the bus.' She is satisfied at his shocked face. 'The doctor says I am to get out of this village now and again. For my health.'

'On the bus? Come on, Ellie, are you sure? You haven't been on a bus before.'

'You forget I travel all over my country on rough tracks and dried-up river beds. You forget that you met me when the valley bus broke down and you and your henchmen helped pull it from the ditch that your construction lorry ran us into.'

'You mean winch man, not henchman.'

'I know what I mean. I will go on the bus to town and then maybe I will take your son on the bus to Perth to visit his grandmother. How will she like that?' Her tongue slips, even though her vow was to not mention his mother.

He looks at her, then away, and she knows by his flickering attention that he suspects she is serious.

'Look, Ellie, about my mum. I've already told you, she just needs a little time.'

'Time?' She hears her voice rise and she forces herself to lower it. 'Time, James? We have been married for two years.'

'Yes, but she didn't know. I thought it best not to tell her until just before you both moved over.' His face colours, he knows this is wrong.

Ellie can feel the heat boil up in her chest, her fists clench and unclench on her lap. She lays them on the table, pressing hard to prevent her from hitting this husband of hers.

'You did not tell her when Nathaneal was born? What is wrong with you? You did not rejoice, as all new fathers do? You hid behind distance. You tell me this now?' The force of her anger robs her of breath. She pulls back her shoulders and sits erect, her neck stretched taut like King Cobra. 'I cannot believe you are telling me you did not inform her about this marriage, about your baby until a few months ago.' She grinds her teeth, she can hear the growl in her voice but that is what she wants.

'Tell me, James, if you had not been sent back here, when were you planning to tell her? When Nat was in school, when he was himself married? Does your mother have claws or perhaps she has poison on her tongue? What are you afraid of, James?'

He pushes back his chair and stands up.

'This is nonsense, Ellie, she knows now and that is all that matters. She just needs time to adjust. Now I am going for a bath unless you have used all my hot water.'

Now it is his hot water. He forgets she is the one who cleans out the ashes, fills the coal scuttle from the bunker outside. It is she who heats the water while he is visiting his mother and goes to buy chips. This is no different from a woman's life in her fatherland.

'No, you are not running away this time.' Ellie stands to block his way. Even though she is much shorter than he, she is heavier. He towers above her and places his hands on her shoulders.

'Ellie, please don't …'

'No,' she says, 'I want you to promise to stand up to this woman.' She can feel the grip on her shoulders tighten. The breath she has been holding in her chest is slowly releasing. 'Take Nat to see her. Not me, I do not matter, but take Nat.' She places her hand on his chest and feels his heart beating through his shirt. 'Please take Nat.'

His eyes are downcast like a woman's and she cannot see the truth in them when he says, 'OK, I will speak to her next week and arrange something.'

With his hands still on her shoulder he moves her gently to the side of the door and escapes to his bath. All energy leaves Ellie's body as she sits down at the kitchen table, lays her head on her crossed arms and prays that her husband keeps his word.

The Good Friday dinner dishes are clean and stacked, James has taken the Fairbairn boys to afternoon mass, and Nat is down for his nap. Ellie will sit quietly by the fire and write a letter to her mother. She has not heard from her family for a while and is becoming worried with the deepening political troubles in her fatherland. The phone rings. Ellie expects it to be the hoose calling. They are the only ones who call. Often it is Mrs Watson to ask James to fetch her some provisions from town, or the Fairbairn boys demanding James to take them to a friend's house or back to boarding school. But the boys are with James so it must be Mrs Watson. Ellie has grown used to her chats with Mrs Watson and rushes to answer the phone before it rings off. She will 'pass the time of day' with her friend.

'Hello.'

There is almost silence, just a faint insect buzz. Ellie wonders if it is the party line. When she first moved into the house James had tried to explain to her that they shared a telephone line with someone in the village. When the other party uses the line, James cannot. Sometimes when he has to make a call he picks the phone off the cradle, listens for a minute then slams it down again.

'Blast! They're on the party line again.'

'Who are "they"?' Ellie had asked.

'I don't know, but they can sure blether.'

'Can we hear what they say?' Ellie was intrigued with the idea of eavesdropping on the villagers.

'Yes, but they sometimes know when you have picked the phone up, they can hear a click or something, or your breathing. They'll shout, 'get off the line.' Anyway, it isn't polite.'

At first Ellie is too scared to try, but long days with only Nat to talk to had worn her fear to curiosity. After her incident with the policeman she had kept her head in her own world. But she knows that the longer she stays in this house the harder the temptation will be to resist listening again. She now knows when they are on the line listening to her blethers with Mrs Watson; she hears the click of the phone.

The first time when she tries to phone the hoose to see if James is there she hears the voices chattering. As with the voice of the big girl Carol and the women in the waiting room, Ellie knows it takes a minute to tune in to the jumbled sounds. She picks up the word 'toe'; she tries harder to make out more words. A lady tells another lady about her sore toe and having to go to a toe person with a name she could not pronounce. Once Ellie deciphers the words she feels guilty; she waits to be told to get off the line, she wants to be told to get off the line, but they do not.

She puts the phone down quietly with a resolve not to try again but her conscience is not so strong and the devil on her shoulder tells her this would not be so sinful; she will listen again.

But this time it is not the party line. There is no chattering, no voices to tune into and the phone rings in her house, the call is for James, of this she is sure.

'Hello,' Ellie says.

No one speaks, no 'get off the line' even though Ellie can hear breathing.

'Hello?'

She hears a click and then a burr of the dialling tone. She replaces the phone and it rings again five minutes later. This time Ellie picks it up and waits. She holds her breath because she can feel who this is.

'James, is that you?' a woman's voice says.

Ellie swallows the poison that has risen to her throat and rearranges the words that spring to her tongue.

'No, 's Ellie. Who is calling, please?' The intake of breath Ellie hears from the other end of the line sinks to the bottom of Ellie's heart for she knows her suspicions are correct.

There is a pause.

The words, 'Kindly ask my son to call me when he has a minute,' rasp across the miles like a whip crack, followed by a hard click. The cold air that travels down the line from Perth causes Ellie to pull her cardigan round herself and she wishes her son would wake soon so that she can hug him tight and feel warm again.

The light hangs strong in the sky until early evening. James told her at breakfast of his plans to fix the gate when he gets home from Mass.

'Hallelujah!' Ellie had exclaimed. 'A bigger miracle than the one expected in two days time.'

James suggests that he also build a sand pit for Nat; he could play there with a bucket and spade when the weather is warmer. Ellie does not understand what this sand pit is, but if his father thinks it will be good, Nat can have it. But not yet: the gate still squeaks on its hinges.

At the sound of this squeaking gate, Ellie rushes to open the door and meet her husband. He stops on the doorstep as if slapped. He has been in a pleasant mood lately and does not grumble too much about the African food she prepares although the various macaroni dishes are still his favourite. He even eats pepper soup without comment now, but the spices Mrs Watson gives to her do not sit well in her husband's stomach.

Her thoughts are heavy when she sees the wary look cross his face. It seems he knows her mood before she does.

She can see the forest circle them and wishes they could stay in seclusion forever. Never leave and keep James and Nat locked in her care where no one can harm them. Even the crocodile mother knows to seclude her family from danger. These are purple thoughts, romantic thoughts. Rubbish. The telephone has brought the outside world to her and reminds her of the flea that has been hiding in the folds of her skin and has been nipping her since she came to this country. This grandmother: the wicked grandmother. Her thoughts transfer to words without her bidding:

'The wicked grandmother has phoned. She has commanded you to phone her.'

James's eyes narrow only a little, but she sees the change. Two spots of colour flood to his cheeks like a drop of blood in a saucer of milk.

'When?'

Ellie signals to the house with her head. 'Now.'

She sees his frown.

'Why didn't you come and fetch me?'

Ellie pulls the top of her head to the sky.

'Fetch you from where? I said 'just now,' did I not? When do I have the chance?'

James smiles apologetically. 'Sorry, it's just that she hasn't been well recently.' He moves past her and kisses the top of her head. 'Sorry,' he says again.

Although she is tempted to follow him and listen, she does not. She steps into her garden and tries not to think about it.

One small moment passes before she notices the figure walking toward her. Mr Winski.

She has seen little of him since the day she had witnessed his pain, but she knows he still goes into the woods two or three times a week. Today his head is down and his feet drag fresh shoots from their roots. His black work coat hangs loose over his back as if he has lost weight, and he has a duffle bag draped over one shoulder. His eyes are still tinged with coal dust like he wears women's makeup.

The miners return from one shift at around three o'clock. This she knows because she has met a group of men trooping off a bus at that time. She had expected some to shout at her but the white faces with the black-rimmed eyes looked past her as they hauled themselves into the bookmaker's opposite the post office or into the

Miner's Welfare Club next door to it. Others scattered in different directions but none crossed her path. There is a back shift and a night shift too; often when she is lying in bed at night she will hear the ambulance siren far off in the night and she will remember Mary's prophesy and wait for James to come home at lunch time to tell her of an accident. Often it is only a bursted finger, sometimes it is more serious.

'Good afternoon, Mr Winski.'

Mr Winski lifts his head and adjusts the duffle bag round his back as if he does not want Ellie to see. He stands straight, clips his heels together and bows his head in salute to Ellie.

'Afternoon, miss,' he says.

'How are you?'

He seems surprised that Ellie wants to speak to him. She wants to delay his delivery into the woods as long as possible. She does not want to return to her kitchen to hear her husband's cowardly talk and imagine this man's real pain.

'No bad, aye, no bad.' The words are slow and hard to come. This English language does not come easy to him, she can tell. She resists a smile at the small tinge of Scottish accent and hopes this will not happen to her.

His feet sift from side to side and he moves the duffle bag to the other shoulder. He looks at his watch and then behind him as if he believes he is being followed. Ellie steps off the path and lets him go, hoping his agitation will leave him.

'Goodbye,' she says.

He clicks his heels again and passes without having to utter another dreaded English word.

The Pairty Line

'Goad's truth, ma shooders ur killin' me.'

'How come?'

'Och, ah've been huvin' tae cairry heavy shopping bags back on the bus fae the toon. Ah wish the Co-op wid stert thir hame delivery again, eh?'

'Huv they stopped it like?'

'Aye, did ye no ken? Stopped it last month so they did.'

'Well, of course ma man takes me shoppin' in his car on a Seterday morning.'

'Lucky you, eh – ma man cannae drive and refuses tae learn. Says we've nae need fur a car.'

'Why dae you no learn yersel'?'

'Me? No' me. Ah couldnae.'

'How no? Oor Mig's jist past her test and said she wid teach me.'

'Naw, ah'm too auld.'

'Yer thirty-nine.'

'That's whit ah mean – too auld.'

'Ah wonder if the black lassie cun drive.'

'Dinnae be daft, they jist huv camels owre there.'

'But whit aboot thon first black polisman in Ingland I wis reading aboot? Ah bet he cun drive.'

'That's different, the polis wid huv hud tae teach hum oor wey eh daein' things.'

'Aye, ah suppose.'

Chapter Nineteen

The company at the hoose proves too tempting for Ellie. Each afternoon at two o'clock she straps Nat to her back and visits her friends for a cup of tea. Dod shows her how to plant and care for potato plants but warns her not to plant them before Good Friday. Now Easter is behind them she can spend more time in her own garden.

When Ellie mentions to Mrs Watson of her plan to visit the toon, Mrs Watson offers to look after Nat.

'It'll be better the first time you go, jist so you can suss oot the place like.' The older lady says.

Ellie is not so sure.

'He has never been without his mother or father,' she says.

'Well, it's aboot time he got used tae it.' Mrs Watson takes him from Ellie and throws him in the air; Nat squeals with delight. 'There, you see, he'll be fine. You'll only be gone a couple of hours, and if ah have a problem ah can always get James tae come and calm him.'

Ellie knows where the bus stop is because she has passed it many times on her way to the shops. On her early visits to the village, the women standing at the bus stop would stare at her as she passed; now they nod. She has not disappeared back to the jungle as they had wished, and they no longer care. In the afternoons she will often encounter the children from the small school who need to travel home to neighbouring villages. James had explained to her that most of the villages have their own

Protestant School but Hollyburn's Catholic School serves a number of villages in the area. These children, who are supposed to be brought up to love thy neighbour still yell at her and make monkey sounds.

The bus timetable, hanging behind scratched and 'fuk the pope' painted glass, tells her the service into Aucheneden runs every twenty minutes. The bus to Ellie's home village ran once every five days or so to coincide with the market days.

Today Ellie is the only person waiting at the bus stop. She checks in her shopping bag for her purse, she checks in her purse for her money. The pound and the ten bob note curl around some change. Some of this is the money Ellie has saved from the housekeeping James hands to her each week. There are normally a few shillings left over which she stores in a jam jar under the sink. Ellie intends to post some of the money to her mother, but today she will spend a few pennies on herself.

When the bus rounds the corner she steps forward and puts her hand out as James has told her to do. The bus is travelling so fast she expects it to drive past her but then sees the indicator flash and the bus stops with its back door beside her. A lady the size of the chief's wife, wearing a black uniform, looks down at her from the bus platform. The driver sits in a cab which is separate from the passengers and Ellie does not understand how she will pay for her trip. The lady in the uniform puts her hands on her hips.

'Well, are ye comin' on or not?'

Ellie steps on and sits on the first seat she comes to, a long high seat beside the open door. The seat faces across the aisle to another row and she notices the rest of the seats are in pairs and face the driver's cab.

'But who do I pay?' Ellie says.

'Ye pay me. Ah'm the bus conductress.'

The conductress stands in front of Ellie and jingles a brown bag which must contain coins. 'Where ye off tae, hen?' she says.

'The toon.' Suddenly Ellie can't remember the name of the town everyone calls "The toon" and she hopes this lady knows what she is asking.

'One shilling, thruppence,' she says as she whirls the handle of a silver machine. Out of the machine curls a paper ticket which she tears off and hands to Ellie in exchange for a half crown. She throws the coin in her bag and shakes it, banging it on her huge thigh as she hunts for change. As Ellie is given her change, she notices the woman's hands are dirty from the coins.

When the transaction is finished the large conductress heaves herself, one buttock followed by the other buttock, up onto the seat opposite Ellie and smiles at her.

'How you finding Hollyburn, hen?'

'I find it fine.'

'Aye well, they're a right lot in these villages. Don't let them get to you.' The bus stops at the top of the village and two women in matching coats and head scarves step on.

'Hiya, Rose,' one says to the conductress. They nod towards Ellie then climb the stairs to the top deck. Rose sighs then heaves her bulk up the stairs after them. Ellie watches the village disappear with a strange mix of panic and joy. She wonders how far it will be until they reach the next stop. It isn't far; they arrive just as Rose returns

193

to her seat. Two women get on and Rose asks for their money and hands out their tickets before they climb the stairs. 'Saves ma legs,' she tells them.

'Aye, don't let them get to you,' she repeats as she sits back on her seat, signalling upstairs with her eyebrows. 'They're all the same in these wee villages.'

Rose cradles the money bag on her lap and settles herself back in her seat

'Aye, ah remember my brother Bert, when he wis in the army; he wis stationed in Egypt and brought a fine young lass back wi' him. You should have heard the stooshie they made at home. That wis years ago mind, but ah don't see much change. It's a' one to me what colour yer skin is. Ma mother taught us to respect everything in this world. Mind you, she wis a very unusual wummin for these parts.'

Ellie does not know how to reply and when Rose picks up her newspaper and starts reading she realises she does not need a reply.

The bus passes many fields with grazing black and white cattle and waving with grain Ellie guesses might be wheat but she is not sure. Out in the open she is struck again by the many shades of green, the lushness of this country. Very few people board the bus but everyone who does says 'Hiya, Rose' to the conductress, and each time she has to go upstairs she sighs her sigh. Ellie is surprised at how much available room there is downstairs. In her country this bus would be bursting with bodies.

'Nae offence like, but see the next time ye come on ma bus, goan sit up the stairs.'

'But it seems like you do not like going up stairs.'

'No, but it's 'cause you're doon here that they're aw

goan up there. Like ah say, nae offence, hen, but it would help me oot, eh?'

Ellie assures her there is no offence taken.

Houses appear in continuous rows, and there is hardly any gap between larger buildings. The bus stops beside another school and Ellie watches the children hanging and swinging from the school railings, shouting at the bus.

'Where dae ye want to get off, hen?' Rose asks.

'I am going to buy a record.'

'Are you now? Ah love that Cliff Richards myself. Ah widnae mind cuddling up tae him. You want to go to Russell's. Get off at the next stop, cross the road and walk up the wee lane; it's at the other end.' She points out the window and rings the bell. 'When ye come back the bus stop is right at the entrance to the lane.' She points across the road. 'There. But ye might want a walk roond Woolies first. Ah always have a walk roond Woolies even when ah don't need anything. Their back door is just across the road fae the record shop, just afore the High Street.' She ushers Ellie off onto the pavement.   'Mind noo. Up the stairs on the way hame.'

Cars are orderly in the toon. A blue boxy one stops to let her cross, but she is forced to stand in the middle of the road until a bus passes her going in the opposite direction. A horn blasts quite close to where she stands.

The lane is called Cobbler's Lane, which she knows to be accurate because she can smell leather and soon stands looking in a shop window filled with odd shoes and tatty handbags. There are also cobbles on the ground, just like the ones in the Dickens books she read at the mission school. She finds this strange in this modern town. The cobbles feel hard and knobbly against her thin soles and she realises that since coming to this country she has rarely walked on their hard streets.

The music store sits tucked into the corner of the lane, with only a small window looking out onto the street. Ellie opens the door and feels she has walked into the Tardis of *Dr Who*. There is a counter on one side which leads to a set of steps onto another floor. Along the opposite wall are racks of records. A girl with long hair tied in thick plaits flicks through one compartment as if searching for a name in a stack of index cards. Flick, flick. The girl pulls one out. Its gaudy cover means nothing to Ellie. With a flip of her wrist the girl reads the reverse side before slotting it back in its place and resuming her flick, flick, flick.

The room smells of the old rags Ellie used for polishing the chapel floor at the clinic. She walks across dusty wooden boards and is reminded of the first flat she shared with James after they were joined in marriage in the eyes of the British colonial administration and in her family tradition.

She grabs a wobbly handrail as she climbs four steps into the back of the shop and gapes when she sees an arrangement of musical instruments. A drum kit, three guitars, silver and gold trumpets and saxophones. Another set of index trays, this time filled with sheet music stacked for flicking, lie unobtrusively in the corner.

'Can I help you?'

Ellie jumps and checks her mouth does not drop open like a child given a gift.

A man, younger than James, with straight, dark mopped hair in the style of The Beatles' John Lennon stands beside Ellie and waits for her answer. He presents her with an honest look, not the false smile of Green-

196

apron. He merely waits to see what she requires. A serious young man, Ellie thinks.

'I am looking for a record.' She detects a small quiver of his lip. 'A record they play on the pirate's radio.'

'The hit parade you mean? Do you want to buy a single?'

'I think so. The Walker Brothers, *The Sun Ain't Gonna Shine Anymore* is one that I know.' The words 'ain't' and 'gonna' lump out of Ellie's mouth, she cannot speak this American speak. It is not the correct Queen's English that was beaten into her at school.

'Are you sure you want that one? It's been in the charts a few weeks now and folk are becoming sick of it.'

'Oh.' Ellie does not know what else to say. All she knows is that she would like to buy a record.

'What about Tamla Motown?' the young man asks. 'Look at you, you're black, this is the music of your homeland, slave music. How do you feel about that?'

How did she feel about that? 'What is this Tamla Motown?' is what Ellie says but what she wants to ask is: 'How do you know about slaves?' This young boy is the first person here, with the exception of Mary, who looks her squarely in the eye. He calls her black and is comfortable calling her black because that is what she is.

'Listen to this.' His serious face animates with the joy of a toddler. 'It's a bit old too, but this is going to be a classic in years to come.'

The boy leads Ellie to a booth that protrudes from the wall by about a foot, its insides are covered in small white dots smaller than her fingers, but even so, she cannot resist the compulsion to press her fingers into them and look at the dotted imprint left on her fingertips.

'That's the soundproofing.' He places cups over her ears and jumps back to his counter. Ellie holds onto the cups thinking they will fall but they are joined together. She leans against the dotted wall and looks into the shop. The young girl who flicks and flips records has left her alone with the shop boy who now looks up and sticks his thumb up at her.

A piano sounds in her left ear followed by a guitar in the right. Deep men's voices and one high voice begin a 'do, do, do' harmony then the high voice smoothes into a lyric. Ellie can feel tightness in her chest; she thinks she will choke, the skin between her shoulders begins to tingle, and her foot starts to tap without her permission. She feels hot and cold at the same time when she hears the tears in the singer's voice. Ellie does not know the name of this emotion but it is close to sadness and joy welded together, like the tears in the song, how can this be so? The words hold meaning but the music reaches into her core and puts down roots. Then it stops before the end; she does not understand but the boy is signalling to her to take the cups off.

'Wait a minute, that's far too sad for you, you look like you'll be greetin' in a minute,' he says rummaging through the rack of single he has on his counter.

'*Hold Tight* by Dave Dee, Dozy, Beaky, Mick and Tich?'

'Yes, I know this *Hold Tight*,' Ellie says.

'Yeah? No, maybe not.' He searches again, 'Or what about this, you look like a woman who knows her fashion. *Dedicated Follower of Fashion*. He lays it on the counter then resumes his search, stops and holds up a record. His joy transmits to Ellie. 'Yes, of course,' he says, almost

198

to himself. 'This has just been released and is just the thing for you,' he says, placing a disc on the turntable and miming for Ellie to replace the cups over her ears.

'Here we go,' he says. 'I bet they have pretty flamingos where you are from?' Bouncy guitars begin to play. Not only does Ellie's foot tap, but her shoulders and hips begin to sway. When a flute plays, the boy pretends he is playing along as he sways in time to the music. He signals for her to take the cups off. She shakes her head; she does not want the music to stop. The boy takes them off for her and she hears the music now fills the whole store. Her feet shuffle her out of the confines of the booth and propel her round the shop floor in her own dance. With her eyes closed Ellie tries to enter another world but she feels as though her feet take her off the ground and will soon tip her over.

She is breathless when the music ends, she wants to feel this way forever.

'I told you this was for you.'

'Yes, yes, I will buy it. Can I buy it?'

'Of course you can,' the boy says as he takes another record from a shelf and puts it in a bag.

'No, I want that one.'

'Yes, but this is a shiny fresh one. You don't want the shop version, it's all scratched.' He hands the bag across the counter towards her and smiles, 'And the next time you come in here I want you to have an upbeat song in mind. None of this sad stuff.' Then he laughs, 'Although they are good. That will be seven shillings and thruppence please.'

As he takes her money and opens the till he asks, 'Where to now?'

'Excuse me?' she says, placing the record in her shopping bag.

'Where are you off to now?'

Ellie looks to the door, not wanting to leave, but as she checks her watch she sees she has spent over an hour in this shop.

'The bus conductress suggested I might like a walk in Woolies.'

'It's just round the corner.'

'Thanks.'

So there are people here who do not stare - the conductress and now this boy. Ellie decides she likes this toon.

She walks in the direction the boy indicated for Woolies and crosses another cobbled street. Broad steps lead up to six glass doors and a red and white sign above the door reads "Woolworths". Ellie sees a young man with oily hair crouched against one of the doors. The hand he raises to his mouth holds a burning cigarette and not only are his fingers tinged yellow but his knuckles are painted with markings of blue and red in the shape of a spider's web. They are similar to the tribal tracks scored on some of her countrymen's faces.

He looks at her with narrow eyes as if daring her to talk to him. He coughs roughly and spits a pebble of shiny phlegm onto the step beside his sharp-toed shoes. When she begins to climb the steps, she sees him slide his back up the wall until he reaches his full height; he presses his back against the building as if willing it to consume him.

Ellie stops two steps below him because he looks like a rat caught in a corner and she does not want him to flee.

'I am looking for Woolies.'

He swallows and says, 'Ye've found it.' He nods his head towards the door. So, Woolworths and Woolies are the same thing. Now she knows this for sure.

First she notices the smell of rubber and then the sweetness of candy and paper. The lights are bright against the early afternoon gloom and unidentifiable tinkly music plays everywhere at the same volume but, unlike the music store, this music induces sleep rather than dance. Silver moving stairs in front of her climb to an upper level where she can just make out people walking and chatting. Ellie walks past bins of rainbow-coloured sweets and counters filled with different types of biscuits. Her teeth tingle at the thought of all this sweetness and increases when she sees towers of coloured boxed Easter eggs, mugs with foil covered eggs and loose chocolate eggs piled and toppled on top of each other. A sign hangs from the ceiling: 'Easter Eggs Half Price.'

Some shoppers gape at her as she walks towards the moving stair, others pretend she does not exist and bustle past on their way about their business. The moving stairs seem to speed up as she approaches them. She can tell by the way the other customers grab the hand rail and jump on that this is new to them too. An old lady with a stick hesitates at the bottom, places her stick on the step then pulls it away. She does this four times before saying 'Och, tae hell wi' it,' and turns and walks out of the shop.

Ellie takes her turn and grabs the hand rail, jumps on and glides up to the next level. At the top of the stair she waits until they disappear into the floor before jumping off, almost losing her balance and colliding with the cluster of people waiting to jump onto the downward-sloping stair.

The upper level of the store smells of wool and string and earth. Rows of plastic bowls, buckets and mops jostle with crockery and pots. At the back of the store Ellie sees the familiar black jacket of Mr Winski with his neat-haired wife beside him. Their heads are bent forward intent on something. Ellie can see across to the wall beside them where a tall rack is filled with green packets. As she walks towards it the green packets come into focus and she makes out different pictures on each one. Seeds. Not just for vegetables but for flowers too. Ellie steps up beside the Winskis.

'Hello,' she says.

They both turn with shy smiles. He bows and clicks his heels together; she nods to Ellie.

'Hello,' Mrs Winski says. Mr Winski's lips part to smile but they do not quite make it.

His wife holds up her seeds. 'We plant vegetables. Dese wans will be best.'

Carrot and parsnip and cabbage.

'How is it you know how to grow them?' Ellie asks.

The older lady points to the sky. 'Weather not so different where we from.' She then points to Ellie hugs herself and shivers. 'You will be cold, no?'

Ellie pulls her coat tight over her shoulders and mimics Mrs Winski. 'Yes.'

Her husband says something to her in their own tongue. She scowls then nods.

'We must go,' she says, pointing to her husband. 'He has to start dat night shift at dat bloody pit.'

He bows once then spins around on his heels, and they leave her with the rows of seeds and no clue.

The bus stop for her return journey is directly opposite the stop where Ellie got off. As she rounds the corner from the cobbled street, she sees her bus at the stop and people boarding. She twists her shopping bag strap around her hand and begins to run. No passengers are left on the pavement and the bus begins to move just as Ellie reaches out her hand to grab the metal pole. Someone from inside the bus shouts, but the bus pulls into the road and Ellie only just stops herself falling into the gutter. Twenty minutes to wait until the next bus is better than five days.

Beside the bus stop is a café. The windows are steamed over, but Ellie can make out the rows of seats and tables scattered with little gold ashtrays and salt and pepper pots. It tempts her, but as she steps forward to open the door, she is halted by a big woman with black hair who rams in front of her.

'Come on, Lily,' the woman says, pulling her friend with her. 'Let get wan o' thon frothy coffees afore oor bus comes.'

The other woman with hair the colour of James's but with black showing in her parting, screws up her nose and looks at Ellie, slowly from the roots of her hair to the toes of her feet.

'Aye well, it's better than staunin' oot here onywey.'

The Pairty Line

'Obscene, that's whit it is.'

'Whit?'

'They Wilsons huv only gone and got fitted cairpits.'

'Git away wi' ye, they niver huv?'

'Aye, awe owre the hoose. Who'd huv thocht it o' them? That wumen cannae keep her bairns fed and shod. The St Vincent de Paul ur ayeweys taking other folk's cast-offs tae them and yet they can afford tae dae away wi thir lino.'

'Ah've niver seen a hoose wi' fitted cairpits.'

'Huv ye no? Aw, thir great. Soft and bouncy, they say thir easier tae keep clean than a square. Eh?'

'How dae ye ken that like?'

'Well, when ah heard the news ah went roond tae the Wilsons wi ma Freeman's catalogue tae see if she wantit onyhing on tick, and she asked me in.'

'That wiz a bit brazen o' ye, wiz it no?'

'Listen, they could huv won the pools or ony hing, eh?'

'And did she want ony hing?'

'What do you think?'

Chapter Twenty

There is a scuffing noise coming from outside the kitchen window. Ellie stops pounding the nettle leaf that has been drying in the airing cupboard and listens, but it stops. She reckons she has enough leaf to make nettle tea to last a whole month. Once she clears the nettles from around her compost heap she can make more and have room to plant the squash seedlings Dod has given her.

No more words have crossed her table about James's mother since he threw her the scraps from the urgent telephone call. There was in fact no urgency. The call had been to tell James that he had left his scarf behind. Ellie thinks this is a fine excuse. It was only at the end of the call that his mother mentioned she had spoken to her solicitor about her pension and could James come up and help her sort it out – he could collect his scarf at the same time.James had finished the call by saying he could not come up this weekend, he was spending time with his family. He had put the phone down and sat in silence. Even though Ellie wanted to ask why he had not suggested he take Nat visiting, as he had promised, she decided it was best to leave him with his thoughts so she busied herself shining the stove top to sparkling even though this was not needed. As she cleaned and sang her *Pretty Flamingo* song to herself, she felt the strong arm of her husband circle her waist. He bushed up her curls with his hand and kissed the back of her neck.

'I had better make a start on the sand pit.'

Ellie puts the dried leaves in a tall black tin and picks

up her sewing; she will finish her skirt soon. The clothes she had brought here are now too tight for her. She feels constricted and trussed up around her stomach.

The week before, a box arrived for Ellie from the Fairbairn's estate. Her mother had sent a parcel of fabric. That wily woman now knew the best and cheapest way to contact her daughter. Mr Funny-hair quizzed her as to the box contents but she would not let him know. When she saw the size of the box she said,

'I will ask my husband to collect it. This will not fit on my bike.'

'Fair enough, hen.'

When she had opened the box her breath caught as the colours burst onto the kitchen table; mango flesh, ripe red berries, a noon sky and the ocean pooled in the bay. And now these colours are almost formed into a garment to brighten her day.

The back gate squeaks, and Ellie sighs. Her husband the Factor is not so handy. She hears the scuffing at the kitchen window again and wonders if James has come home early.

Giggles, she hears giggles. Ellie thinks of the skinny woman scrubbing the wall and jumps to catch the perpetrator but before she can reach the door a tiny knock sounds from the other side. She opens it to find Mary standing with her fist in mid air ready to knock again. Beside her lurks that big girl Carol.

Both girls step back and gape at Ellie as if they did not expect her to answer. The girl Carol reacts first and prods Mary in the back. Mary jumps and, taking a deep breath, launches into speech:

206

'Oh sorry, but please, Ellie, can we please take Nat out for a walk in his pram, please?'

What is this they are talking about, walking with a pram? What is this pram? Ellie thinks these girls have teased her enough and begins to close the door.

The girl Carol steps forward. 'You know, missus, a wee hurl out in the pram.' The girl makes a pushing motion. Ellie feels her face warm at her own stupidity. On her trip to the shops she had encountered many little girls push babies, trundling toy baby carriages, but she has also seen older girls pushing full-sized carriages. This is a little girls' pastime in Hollyburn, she thinks.

Both girls stare at Ellie.

'Why are you not at school?' she says to them.

Mary sighs, 'I told you at church – remember?'

Ellie wonders how it is that two little girls can make her feel so stupid; this is not the way it should be.

The girl Carol slumps her shoulders. 'Easter holidays. We are off for two weeks now.'

Ellie nods but remains silent. When she still does not answer the original question the bold Carol moves forward again as if to step into her kitchen. Ellie moves to block the door.

'Come on, missus, let us take yer bairn out for a hurl?'

Ellie does not know how to answer; it is as if these children have put a spell on her. She looks over their heads and sees Mr Winski coming up the track, past the gate. When he sees the children, he stops. He glances at his feet and turns to walk back the way he came, but before he does, he lifts his hat to Ellie and she raises her hand in a return greeting. Both girls spin round and watch Mr Winski walk off back towards the village.

'See him, he's weird. Dae ye ken 'um?' Carol says.

'Yes, but he is not weird,' Ellie says.

'How weird?' Mary asks.

The Carol girl laughs.

'That's the Pole. Ma da says he's weird and he's such a baby. He's ayeweys greetin' at the pit. But dae ye ken what they did tae him?' She starts to laugh so hard snot falls from her nose, Ellie begins to feel sick, but thankfully the girl wipes it off on her cuff.

'Just fur a laugh they pinched his pit piece wan day and wouldnae gie him it back and wouldnae gie him onyhing tae eat, then somebody did. Ma da says he's always mooching aboot and he never gits the hard jobs tae dae on account o' the fact he cannae speak proper Inglish. But he can understand it, ma da says, he's just thick as a plank, that's what ma da says, everybody kens that. But everything they dae tae cheer him up fails because he's such a miserable foreigner.'

Mary looks at Carol. 'My dad says he just doesn't understand the way people speak here.'

'And whit wid yer da ken aboot it?' Carol says. 'Your da is niver doon the pit even though he's suppose tae be the manager. He should be getting that Pole sortit oot.'

Mary's face turns the colour of flame. But Carol is not finished. 'If he cannae un'erston plain Inglish he shouldnae be here, he can bugger aff back tae Pole Land

Both girls seem to have forgotten Ellie standing at her door. She is aware that the heat is leaving her kitchen and she wants to get back to her sewing. Then Ellie remembers something she has been wondering about since Palm Sunday.

'Who won the prize?' she asks.

'Whit prize?'

But Ellie sees Mary's smug grin and knows the answer. Carol casts her eyes down.

'Tell me, what was your grand prize?'

The smile slips.

'A Mars Bar.

Ellie knows what this is: *"A Mars a day helps you work, rest and play."* James had brought one from the chip shop one night. More inches to add to her hips. Very tasty, but Ellie feels a cheat prize for six weeks' devotion, or is it six weeks of bribery and deception?

Mary seems to feel the need to qualify her prize: 'It's not just about the prize; it is about the taking part.' Ellie can hear an adult voice in that comment. 'Anyway, I had given up sweets for Lent so it was great to get it.'

'Is that no whit Easter eggs are fur?' Carol asks. 'Tae make up for aw the weeks wi' nae sweets ah mean? Ah dinnae see how a Mars Bar wid make much difference.'

Mary drops her chin. 'Well, I thought it was nice to get it anyway.'

Carol lifts her face and looks straight at Ellie. 'Ah'm gonnae win the black babies onywey, who cares about a stupid Mars Bar, eh? Ah huv much mair black babies than she hus.'

If it wasn't for the gormless expression on Carol's face, Ellie would suspect that these girls have come to taunt her. Carol's eyes show no shame or irony. The girl Carol is stating a fact. Mary on the other hand lowers her head further and toes at a weed growing in the crack between the step and the path.

'Come on, missus, gonnae let us take the bairn oot for a hurl in the pram?'

Ellie grips the door, she wants to close it and return to her home colours.

'Nat does not have a pram, and I have already told Mary that she should not come to this house again.'

Carol spins on Mary who has managed to break the weed from its stem and is spreading its seeds all over the path now.

'He does not need a hurl; he has a garden to play in,' Ellie continues. She almost closes the door and then remembers her manners.

'But thank you for the offer, girls. Good day, girls.'

As the girls turn with heads held high, Ellie is reminded of the warning her father used to give his children: 'If you show kindness to a monkey once, he will live in your yard until he has destroyed your home.' Ellie hopes this is not also true of little girls.

She watches them walk up the path and squeak the gate open. The encounter leaves her numb, not mad as it would have done a few weeks earlier. Is this because she is now becoming used to these villagers? Perhaps the doctor is correct and she just needs to get used to being away from her homeland and out of Hollyburn more often.

Before she returns to her kitchen Ellie fetches a small can of bicycle oil from the shed and smears a couple of drops on each gate hinge; she moves the gate back and forth, no squeak. She stands for a few minutes and looks towards the village. The fact that Mr Winski cries too does not make her feel better. Ellie wants to follow him, she wants to tell him to go to the doctor and for the doctor to tell Mr Winski that it is OK to feel sad.

The Pairty Line

'Huv ye goat yer coal delivered yet?'

'No. Ah'm gettin' ten hunner weights next week. How, like?'

'Coont it goan intae the coal hole then, eh?'

'What fur?'

'Ah goat ten hunner weights last week and ah'm shair ah'm short.'

'Short?'

'That's whit ah said. Ah'm shair that Eck the Bleck is skimming some and selling it buck-shee.'

'Dae ye reckon?'

'Aye, ah reckon he's pittin' in only nine bags instead o' ten.'

'He widdnae dae that.'

'Wid he no? Listen, he thinks that cause we git it fur nithin' we widdnae miss a bag or two, eh?'

'Aye, but he's been deliverin' pit coal fur years, if he sterttit that he wid lose the Coal Board's business.'

'Jist coont them goan in, is aw ah'm sayin'. If ah'm right oor men'll sort it oot fur next time.'

Chapter Twenty One

Rain comes in the night, and Ellie prays the seeds she has planted directly into neat earth rows in the garden have not been washed away. In the morning, after the rain, there is sunshine. Dod has shown her how to sow some seeds in pots and grow them into seedlings on her inside window ledge.

Ellie takes her tender strawberry seedling plants from the ledge and positions them on the coal bunker to catch some rays. She can almost taste the fruit on her lips as she finishes washing her hands. James whistles in the bathroom and when he returns to her kitchen, he announces he has to make a trip to buy a piece of machinery for the estate. The only place it is to be found is in the City of Glasgow.

'Why don't you and Nat come too?'

Ellie does not need to be asked again. Almost before the words are out of her husband's mouth she has a bag of Nat's provisions packed and their coats on.

'How long will it take to get there? Will I need to make a picnic?'

'Yes, that would be nice, and you better pack an umbrella, it always rains in the West.'

Ellie looks puzzled. 'But it always rains here.'

James laughs. 'No, it is dry here.'

'It is always raining. Every season is rainy season in Scotland.'

James picks up an umbrella from the door stand. 'But not today. So we take one then?'

'Please remind me to take my seedlings inside when I return,' Ellie says as she straightens up the little pots. These babies still need her care.

They have driven only a short distance when they are prevented crossing a bridge by a queue of cars stopped by a small red light. The bridge, smaller than the Forth Road Bridge which was opened by Her Majesty Queen Elizabeth, is swinging open in the middle, like a gate from a gate post. A mighty shipping vessel pulled by four smaller boats sits low in the middle of the river.Five cars queue in front of the Landrover. Huddles of car people stand on the verge to watch the big boat being pulled through the bridge gap.

When the boat is clear the spectators return to their cars, but it is another five minutes before the bridge swings closed, and still the traffic is not allowed to proceed.

'We're going to be late and won't have much time for sightseeing,' James fusses.

'This does not matter. This river is wonderful.' Ellie hugs her son. 'Is that not so, Nat? Look, Nat, look at the ship.' Nat giggles and points, 'Sip, sip.'

When the red light switches off and a green light glows they cross the river. The sunshine of the morning is replaced by a grey, grey sky and soon the rain lashes down on the windscreen.

The fields are similar to the ones they have just left, but Ellie feels a loss when she crosses the bridge, as if she is treading on someone else's territory. After an hour tall block buildings appear on the horizon ahead.

'We will be there soon,' James tells her, but she has already guessed this. The streets begin to crowd round them. Black four-storey buildings, all with sad eyes and gashes for mouths, line the pavements and welcome them to Glasgow.

'How can these house dwellers bear to live so close together?'

'Tenements,' James says. 'Most people in this city live in houses like these.'

'Where are their gardens?'

'They have no gardens as such, only small back yards.'

Ellie looks for grass and trees and sees only patches of them, scarred and chaotic. Thick smog hangs around the buildings. High industrial chimneys choke the air; a fire seems to burn in every house, discharging smoke from every chimney. When Ellie first arrived in Hollyburn, she hated the smell of newly lit coal fires in the morning, it smelled dirty compared to the wood smoke she knew best; she is now used to that. But here the houses, so packed together, belch out smoke that forms a blanket over the entire city.

'How do they breathe?'

'They don't – well, not properly anyway.'

Ellie wraps her arms around Nat and holds her handkerchief up to his nose. They drive past a park. A small deer runs across the road and James brakes hard to avoid a collision. Even though the park is surrounded by a high metal fence, Ellie can see inside to a lake with small boats floating. Another of those red lights forces James to stop the car again right beside the park gate. Through this gate Ellie can see a dog chasing a ball and grabbing it with its teeth. Little boys run after it shouting, trying to get their ball back. The boys wear the same blue or green jumpers they wear in Hollyburn, this is a Scottish uniform, she thinks. Ellie is almost sad when the green lights up and James moves the Landrover forward.

He turns into a major road that stretches ahead of them for miles. At least three church spires pierce the grey sky. The pavements are crowded with people dodging each other's umbrellas. Colour splashes from the shops and the brightly coloured clothes of the many pedestrians make Ellie's eyes ache. There are people with black faces, brown faces, pink faces, white faces walking the same streets. If this is Glasgow she wants to stop and step out among its people.

Ellie spots two Asian women drift along; their cool turquoise and coral dresses escape under drab brown outerwear, like butterflies struggling to escape the pupa. If only Ellie could stop and buy some material of such colours. Gold jewellery hangs heavy from pierced ears. The rings and bangles swing with pride as each step is taken; their sparkle lights up the dull day.

James glances toward her. She knows she gapes, but cannot stop. This is why her husband brought her to this street, she is sure: to show her she is the same as others in this country. She is not the only black face in Scotland.

Shop windows display drapes of materials in the style of the Indian trader women who peddled wares to the clinic in the town back home. One shop has a table weighed down with fruit and vegetables bursting with life and spilling onto the pavement. There are yams. She is sure. She sees yams. She has not tasted yams for six months.

'Stop! Please stop.'

James pulls off the road into a side street and parks. When Ellie steps onto the pavement her legs tremble. The air catches her throat; she can almost taste coal dust and feel grime on her teeth. She clutches Nat tight and turns the corner into a wide street.

At the shop front she hands Nat to his father and touches the vegetables she has not seen for so long. The vegetables are past fresh but there are yams and cassava of her village and also many other things she could only find in the markets. An old man in a dirty white dashiki nods to her as she hands him the yam and her money.

'Where are you from?' she asks him in English.

'Sierra Leone,' he says, handing her back her yam in a brown paper bag. Ellie waits for him to ask where she is from but he does not, he turns back to his assistant and begins talking in their own tongue.

Her eyes roam the busy shelves of the shop but the crammed space means there is no room for the likes of her, and soon the old man ushers her out of the door to make way for a male customer; a regular by the way they converse and one who knows what he wants to buy.

James meets her at the door, puts his arm around her shoulder and kisses her forehead.

'Come on,' he says. 'Let's go for that picnic before the rain gets any heavier.'

He drives only a little further and parks beside an austere building with "BBC" emblazoned on the side wall. Ellie wonders if she will see that lovely Andy Stewart, for she is sure he works at the BBC.

She stares at the gate, not daring to take her eyes off the place, someone she will recognise might come through the gate.

'Come on, starstruck.' James leads her across the road and into a park.

Tall trees sprout through grass lawns and form a

canopy over their own territory. Benches line hard paths and bushes arrange themselves in order of height to create a neatness Ellie has only witnessed near the big hoose. James propels her to a rectangular glass building. When they walk through the door Ellie gasps at the heat, and she realises she has forgotten how comforting heat can be. She smells the damp humidity and the tangy earth.

But the heat is not as welcoming as her African heat; this heat has no sun. There is still a grey sky above this city. This heat, which is captured and held in a building in Scotland, is oppressive and claustrophobic. Plants tower over her blocking out the dull daylight trying to penetrate the glass walls. The plants are the plants of her African back yard and beyond. Nat struggles in James's arms and begins to cough. He does not like this, Ellie thinks.

She sits down on a bench and closes her eyes and tries to feel home. But where is her mother's voice calling her from the river and the scratching of the chickens in the yard? Ellie cannot resurrect these sounds from her memory. She hears the harsh voices of two women discussing how long they wait for a bus. She hears the sound of the hose a worker is directing towards these fragile foreign plants. She hears her own inner voice reminding her she is in another world and this world is now her home.

The Pairty Line

'Whits the matter?'

'Och, ah'm fine.'

'Ye dinnae soond fine – ye soond – different, eh?'

'No – its nithin'.'

'Dinnae gie me that, ah cun hear yer aboot greetin'.'

'Och, ah micht as well tell ye. Yir gonnae fund oot sin enough onywey. Ah'm goan intae hospital tae get ma left breast aff the morra.'

'Oh goad, ye niver said ye hud a problem. When did ye fund oot?'

'Jist this morning, the biopsy report came back and Dr Hurry wants me in right away.'

'Ah goad, ah'm right sorry. How long will ye be in fur?'

'No long, a couple o' weeks.'

'Oh goad, ah'm sorry.'

'Aye well, ah'm sure it'll be fine.'

'Aye, it'll be fine.'

'Aye.'

Chapter Twenty Two

When Ellie wakes next morning, a cold dread enters her body. Dod had warned her to return the little plants to the warmth of her kitchen. This she forgot to do, but she cannot imagine what harm could have befallen them overnight. She creeps through the silent house and opens the back door. There they are. Small green seedlings that yesterday erupted from their pots to catch the sun now fall limp and shrivelled. She cannot understand why this has happened and mourns for the death of her plants.

'The frost has killed them,' James tells her. 'Sorry, I should have reminded you.'

The letter she received from her mother had distracted them both. Mrs Watson must have slipped it through the door yesterday; it was waiting for Ellie when she and James returned from Glasgow.

The news is not good and is told in short statements with no detail. There is fighting in the eastern part of her country, and Matthew has left his wife, children and mother to go and fight with the militia against the President's men. Jacob has gone to work in the mine to earn money to feed them, but the new road is being blockaded and it is difficult to get to market. What food they have in the fields is hardly enough to feed their own children and they have a whole village to feed. Her mother thanks her for the money she sends, this has helped.

Ellie feels she should be there to help them, but here she cannot even keep some small plants from being killed.

The forest is chilled even though the sun shines

through the trees, casting slats of light on the path for Ellie and Nat to follow. The day is still and silent, as if the birds are awaiting their arrival before they begin to chant. Ellie wants the silence to persist, to punish her; her anger is directed towards herself: if only she had taken her plants inside when they returned last night but she was too consumed by anticipation of her family's troubles. She had no cockerel to sacrifice towards the protection of plants as her father and brothers used to do at the beginning of the growing season. This, she is sure, will be a problem in her country this year.

How will they survive? The letter of her mother is warm in her mind. What can she do for her family? James has told her not to worry; her brothers know best, she would only be an added burden. The best they can do is to send provisions to the estate. Her family will be well looked after. The family maybe, but what about her country?

She looks around the lush forest and knows that her sorrows are nothing compared to others. She can search for new plants to grow in her garden. Plants, not from a packet, but from the earth where they have been living for centuries. It is her own stupidity that causes her pain and the thought of her embarrassment when she has to explain to Dod what she has done.

Childish laughter moves through the trees from the plot of the nuns' graves. Ellie shakes her head; even though she knows the truth of this burial ground, she cannot rid herself of the name she has given it.

The two girls, Mary and the big child, Carol, sit in the clearing with what looks like a chess board between them, on the board is a tumbler on which both girls balance their index finger. The tumbler is gliding between letters Ellie can see scratched in bold red around the edge of the board.

Carol notices Ellie first and jumps to her feet. She grabs Mary's arm and tugs her also to her feet. They look as though they have broken all the eggs in the yard.

'What are ye spyin' on us for?' Carol says as she grabs the tumbler and the board, which Ellie now sees is an upturned Kellogg's Cornflake box, and stuffs them in a duffle bag.

Mary wears a mask of horror over her pink face.

'I am not spying,' Ellie says, 'but why are you playing with the spirits?'

Their feet shuffle the earth and their eyes are downcast.

'It's just a game, Ellie.' Mary holds her head up but her arm is still gripped by Carol.

'Yeh, you must have played wi' a ouija board sometime,' Carol cheeks, at the same time moving backwards away from Ellie, dragging Mary with her.

'Carol just wanted to contact her Airdrie grandad, that's all. He died last year and she misses him. Don't you, Carol?' Mary nods as if inciting agreement from everyone.

Ellie shakes her head. 'This is nonsense; you must know to never do this — tinkering with the spirits. What would your parents say if they knew? You have no idea what you are doing.'

She can see by the smirk that now appears on Carol's face that her words have fallen among the thorns, never to be picked up.

'My village has a sorcerer, but believers and non-believers will not cross him. He knows how to talk to the sprits, little girls do not.' Even as the words leave her

221

throat she can feel them lose their bite as they fly to the girls ears.

The big girl, Carol, steps forwards at this and seems to have forgotten her escape.

'Dae ye ken him then? This sorcerer? Does he put spells on people? Is it true that ye're a witch?'

Ellie wishes to cut her own tongue out. She should not have mentioned the sorcerer.

'It is all nonsense. It must be ignored. Your priest will not be happy.'

'You've changed yer tune, one minute it's aw sorcerers and now it's the priest. Make yer mind up.'

Ellie wishes that the priest had caught the girls when he was out walking his dog. He would have burned them alive if he had.

'Go home, little girls, and play with your dolls.'

'Voodoo dolls, ye mean?' Carol says, digging Mary in the ribs. Mary giggles.

Ellie can feel her feet itch to be away from these silly children. They are more dangerous than the spirits they are playing with.

'Go home, you do not belong in these woods, your parents will not like it.'

Carol stands in front of Ellie, and for the first time she realises that this child is almost as tall as she and looks much stronger.

'Why can't we play in the wids if we want tae? We've played here afore you came and we'll play when ye're gone.'

The way the words spit out of this child's mouth hits Ellie like a threat.

'You dinnae even belong here,' Carol finishes with a

swing of her bag. She plumps back on the grass pulling Mary down with her.

'Come on, Mary,' she says. 'We'll finish oor game. Ah'm not takin' a telling fae that black witch.'

Mary is now nodding in humble agreement, and Ellie's blood is so hot in her veins that she forgets to point out to the pair that Mary and Ellie had arrived in this village about the same time. But she does not know how to answer the challenge either so she walks away further into the forest where she knows they will not follow her for fear of the fabled Flannel Foot. While these silly girls are not afraid of spirits, they are afraid of a mythical creature called Flannel Foot given to them by their parents to scare them away from the depths of these woods.

Giggles follow Ellie into the deep wood, but she knows she is free of their physical presence. How could she have imagined Mary could be her friend? Carol has control over part of the girl and her parents control the rest. Ellie witnessed a spark of defiance the day Mary wiped the ashes from her brow, but that spark flares and dies under the slavery of conformity. The girl needs to learn to break free. Despite Ellie's desire to help she knows it is too dangerous for her and her son. She will keep her head down. The birds are quiet again and the air is filled with expectation. A Harmattan-like chill breezes over Ellie and she shivers.

She tries to forget the encounter and thinks of her task. The baby is quiet behind her. She knows he does not sleep by the small grinding noises he makes with his new teeth. He talks to her and his surroundings in his own language that she understands is full of love and reassurance.

Some of the seeds Mr Winski had suggested Ellie buy

from Woolworths had survived the frost but were babies still. They will not be ready for harvest until two new moons have passed. Mrs Watson's book describes to Ellie a good salad weed called burnet, and Ellie remembers the picture and knows where she can find some.

The forest is leading her on with its silence and peaceful embrace, gaps appear between branches exposing footways she has not noticed before, opening wide and saying, 'Come in, Ellie, we have food for you in here.'

She passes the log where she encountered Mr Winski's pain. From here she can see the grass surrounding the site is overgrown but parts have been trampled as if walked on where it never has been before. Perhaps a large animal. She has noticed a red and white sign on the road next to the church, showing a deer running. Ellie thinks these deer live in this forest as well as in the estate.

When she reaches the flattened grass she sees that an animal would not disturb so much foliage. A curtain of tall bushes with large purple flowers frames a path of broken and bruised branches. The path beckons Ellie, her instincts tell her she must be careful, but the devil on her shoulder urges her to go on. She ignores her instincts as she has many times in the past. Maybe she will find a new plant she can add to her potions. But as Ellie proceeds through the bushes she wishes she had not listened to her devil. The hair on her arms prickle and itch, and her mouth is dry with fear.

She places her hand around her back to reassure Nat that she is okay, but she can feel the rhythmic breaths of his slumber. Branches grab at her hair, often catching and refusing for a moment to let her go. She wants to turn back, but her feet continue to move her forward. She hears a squabble of the crows, and when she pulls back a branch many black wings flash upwards before settling on a tree.

She sees the feet first, suspended some inches from the ground. Black work boots polished to army standard, with smart heels that had clicked together when she last saw them. This is why the forest led her here. A latrine smell reaches her nostrils before the smell of death. As she walks to the tree, a cloud of buzzing flies lift from the suspended corpse. Ellie does not want to look at the face of this poor man, the crows will have feasted on their delicacy of eyes and the flies will have filled the cavities with their next generation.

It is not as if she has not seen a hanging man before, but she has never seen a ripe one. The swollen face brings the memory back to her. An elder in her village threw his cloth over a tree and hung himself when the gods refused to give him a good harvest. These things were common when she was a girl, despite the church's teachings.

Ellie is surprised she can look on this sight without horror. What she feels is sadness that Mr Winski has chosen to end his torment in this most final of ways. She hopes that when his remains are put safely to rest, he too will find peace.

Before Ellie leaves the site she bows her head and recites a prayer without knowing whether it is appropriate or not in this situation. She notices the duffle bag lying beside a log. The ground before the log bears a trail of damaged earth; this log has been dragged from another place. This log he used to stand on to bear his weight until he chose the moment to take control of his life and his

225

death and kick it away. The duffle bag would have held the rope, this she now knows. He had passed her door with this bag before.

How many times had he walked past her door on his mission and returned home unable to complete it? This is no lynching or cry for help. This time there is no aborted attempt; he did not intend to be found or stopped. Her medical training tells her he has not been dead long, perhaps a day. Ellie knows she cannot cut him down and James has returned this day to Glasgow. The priest will know what to do next, she will fetch the priest, but she does not want to leave the corpse – it does not seem right. He hangs so still and yet Ellie knows as soon as she turns her back the crows will resume their feast.

Two rustle in a nearby tree, waiting. They always wait in pairs, these black scavengers. She wishes she were taller, stronger, to be able to reach and cut him down. When she was a young girl she could climb trees like a warrior. Her limbs had been long and thin as the tree itself. But she had stopped growing before her first bleeding time, and her thin limbs were filled with fat and could no longer carry her up a tree. Also, she did not want Nat to see. Even though he is too young for understanding, the sight is not good.

Her baby fits so neatly into the curve of her back. Like one of her limbs, often she forgets he is there, were it not for the occasional massage he makes with his forehead between her shoulders.

'Farewell my friend, I will get someone to look after you.' She is nearer the big hoose, but she knows the priest's help will be better. He might even be able to give the last sacrament, if that is permitted for someone who has committed such a mortal sin as to take their own life. She is certain Mr Winski's troubled soul has long left his body behind, but it would be a comfort to his wife.

The thought of his wife fills Ellie with a sense of urgency. She must be worried to sickness. Ellie picks up the hem of her skirt and runs through the woods. She arrives at the nuns' graves in minutes and arrives so abruptly those little girls have no opportunity to hide their evil game again. Ellie does not stop to admonish them, let them call up the devil if they please for he has already done his worst today. The priest will deal with these children if they remain. That would be punishment enough.

'What is it, Ellie?' She hears Mary's voice.

'Nothing — no, the baby is ill,' she calls back, for she does not want them venturing where they should best avoid.

Ellie runs to the crumbling house at the edge of the wood where she knows the priest lives. The peeling paint door she hammers on is opened by a man-woman. Ellie recognises her from the church as Aggie Aitkin, 'the housekeeper.' She is normally found bustling around the edges of the altar steps, no doubt wishing she were a man and permitted to step where women are forbidden. Ellie thinks she is halfway there; she looks like a man with her wire-strength grey curls and sprouting face hair.

'The Father, he must come quick.'

'Father Grattan is busy just now.'

'Tell him, tell him he must come with me now,' she pleads, but even as the words leave her throat she can see the pursed lips of one who loses her water when she coughs. This man-woman is not going to help her.

Ellie steps back into the path and shrieks as she used to call her father from his yam field. She does not know which room the priest will emerge from but she knows her call will bring him.

Somewhere in the house a dog barks.

'For goodness sake!' The man-woman tuts. 'Such an exhibition. Ah'll fetch him,' she says before closing the door against Ellie's presence.

In less than a minute the door opens and the priest steps out while shrugging on his jacket. 'What is it, Ellie?'

'You must come with me.' Ellie is aware the man-woman watches. She does not want this news to race through the village like a bush fire.

'There has been an accident in the woods. You will need your knife.'

The priest's eyebrows rise to his hairline then join in worry. He knows, she thinks. Maybe this happens in these woods before.

Father Grattan turns into the kitchen and grabs a packet of cigarettes and a box of Swan Vestas from the counter and a pen knife from a drawer by the door.

'Let's go, show me the way.' Then he turns. 'Aggie, phone for the doctor.'

'And the constable,' Ellie adds.

'Is that right, Father?' the man-woman queries Ellie's command.

'Yes, get the police, we'll be back soon.'

The girls leave only a patch of flattened grass which Ellie does not point out to the priest. They will receive their punishment elsewhere.

The birds scatter on their arrival at the hanging tree. Mr Winski looks almost the same, but the white mark a bird has left on his polished boot turns Ellie's sadness into tears.

'Poor bugger,' Father Grattan says. 'Look, I'm not going to be able to cut him down on my own, Ellie. Can you go back and fetch the police and the doctor and bring them here? I will wait and keep the birds at bay.'

This time Ellie is content to leave Mr Winski in good hands.

The thoughts of her husband's broken promise to take Nat to Perth, her family's plight and the dead seedlings have faded with the intense pain Ellie feels for Mr Winski. As she sits at the kitchen table and relays the day's events to her husband Ellie feels numbness she has never experienced before. Her husband's face shows shock but little compassion. He does not even want to try to understand this poor man's horrors.

'There is nothing you could have done to help him. He was always a bit weird, everyone knew that.' And with that the subject is dismissed. Weird. This word, used by children and men.

The Pairty Line

'Did ye hear aboot the Pole?'

'Aye, fund hingin' in the wids, been missing fur days apparently. Ye cannae help but wonder aboot these foreigners eh?'

'Awful business, but did ye hear who fund um?'

'It wis that big coon, wisn't it? A bit o' a turn up that, eh?'

'Can ye hear sumthing?'

'Aye, possibly, whit is it? The pairty line?'

'Thur ayeweys listenin' in these days – get aff the fucking line, ya nosy bitch.'

'How dae ye ken it's a wumman?'

'A jist dae.'

'How're ye feelin onyweys?'

'Aw right, guid days an' bad days, ye ken?'

'It must be hard. How's yir man taking it?'

'Well, that's another story, eh? — Did ah no say git aff the fucking line?'

'That them gone then?'

'Ah think so. Look, ah'm away fur a lie doon – ah'm fair worn oot.'

'You dae that, hen, ah'll ca' ye later.'

Chapter Twenty Three

Every day Ellie walks up the estate path to the church to look for an intimation of Mr Winski's funeral. It does not appear. She does not know what happened to his body that day after the constable was sick in the bushes and Doctor Hurry pronounced the body dead. The authorities sent her home and told her 'her services were no longer required.'

'Could you ask the Father about Mr Winski's body?' Ellie asks James at breakfast.

'Look Ellie, this is none of our business. You should forget it. I bet the villagers have, it will be like the newspaper in the chip shop - old news. They will have moved on to someone else to talk about.' He reaches over and takes her hand. 'You just have to hope it isn't you.'

'What if he has to be buried in unblessed ground?'

'I don't think they do that any more. We don't live in the dark ages, you know.'

Images from her dreams follow Ellie into daytime. The shoe with the white bird-dropping comes into focus before the feet begin to swing. Often Ellie wakes in the night and smells the familiar smell of death. It is a dream, she knows this, but the smell of death remains in her nostrils, and each time it occurs she rushes to Nat's room to check he is still breathing.

What worries her most in these waking hours is this poor man's burial. She hopes he has been taken to his motherland. He should be buried in his motherland.

If Ellie were to die here on this foreign ground, would James take the trouble to transport her back to her land? She must remember to ask him. It would be good to have the warm red earth cover her body. With these thoughts Ellie feels the tightness in her chest and the smell of mother replaces death, and she does not feel well again until she is in bed and turns her body to cradle into James's back, to feel his warmth and try to be safe.

In the weeks after the incident, the few times Ellie is in her garden, when a shadow passes over her, she looks up expecting to see Mr Winski walking by, lifting his cap and clicking his heels. She knows that in her time at the witch's hat house she exchanged only a few words with him, but in that time she felt a kinship.

Each day brings warmer weather and yet Ellie finds it harder to raise herself out of bed in the mornings. James wakes first and expects his porridge to be on the table. She drags herself from the covers and pads through to the kitchen. The baby is chattering to himself in his cot, he is such a good boy, she will leave him there for a little while longer, he does not seem to mind his wet nappy too much.

After she watches James leave the house she crawls back into the cooling bed and pulls the covers over her head. Often it is not until Nat is screaming that she can summon enough energy to stand and face the day. By this time Nat's nappy is so heavy with urine it hangs to his knees. A nappy rash blazes hot and sore all over his bottom and although she smothers this with cream, it does not clear up.

This laziness must stop, Ellie tells herself every day.

Almost two weeks after her terrible discovery in the woods, Ellie sits in her chair with the red check cushion and stares out of the kitchen window while the baby naps. The robin still visits the window ledge in the hope of a scattering of oats but Ellie does not just neglect her family, she has not put any oats out for days. This little bird will desert her soon, she thinks, if she does not do something. She only has to rise from her chair and go to the cupboard and step out the back door, but her arms are too heavy to lift herself and her feet are nailed to the floor.

The sky is blue, it has not rained for over a week and although the kitchen is cool, Ellie knows that it will be warmer outside. She thinks about her plants and it occurs to her that she has not been out of her back door for over a week. The weeds are sure to be taking advantage of her neglect.

The gate creaks; James has still not fixed it, and the oil she used has dried. She has lost the will to ask him again, it can hang from its hinges for all she cares now.

There is a tap at her door. It will not be Mrs Watson because she is overseas with the Fairbairns. It will not be Dod, he never disturbs her. Like a spirit from the forest, he leaves his gifts for her on the coal bunker.

The knock sounds louder the second time, persistent. As if whoever stands on the other side of the door knows Ellie is in here and will not take no for an answer. Ellie presses her palms into her chair and hoists herself up.

A head appears at the window, a small neat head with searching eyes. It is Mrs Winski. The heart in Ellie's chest thumps louder than it has for a long time. Since that terrible day Ellie had not thought about Mrs Winski; she had been too busy feeling sorry for herself. Now here is the widow at her kitchen door and Ellie does not know what to say to her.

She tries to remove her own mask of self-pity but does not know if she succeeds. She opens the door and is confronted with a woman who smiles but cannot hide the sadness in her eyes. Mrs Winski holds out a tray of seedlings to Ellie.

'I bring you strawberry plants,' she says. 'Too many dat man of mine grows – he want to give you some.' She pushes the tray towards Ellie. 'Dat was his wish. Please take.'

Ellie prises her shaking hand from the door frame and takes the tray from Mrs Winski then looks past the older woman, out into the garden as if expecting Mr Winski to appear. Then she remembers her manners.

'Please come in. Would you like a cup of tea?' Mrs Winski follows Ellie's gaze and looks round at the garden. She bends down and plucks one of the many mature weeds that have invaded the cracks in the path; she looks at it then rolls it between her finger and thumb before putting it in her pocket.

'Is a nice day,' Mrs Winski says. 'Why we no' sit out here?'

Ellie bows her head and says, 'Yes, you are correct, Mrs Winski, why not sit out here?' She puts the tray of seedlings on the coal bunker and turns back to her kitchen, 'I will get you a chair and put the kettle on.'

How to start a conversation with this woman? Ellie rehearses many beginnings but she should not have worried because as soon as she returns with chairs, Mrs Winski starts to chatter like the gaudy birds of home.

'Thank you for looking after my husband,' she begins. 'Dat must have been a shock.'

'I am sorry for your pain.'

'You know, first I want go back to Poland. Dat is what we should have done when this trouble start but Marek, he did not want go back. He was stubborn man, dat man of mine; he did not want fail his family here.'

'You have family here?'

She shakes her head. 'Not now.'

Ellie can hear the kettle boil but she does not want to leave this story. Mrs Winski takes a white ironed handkerchief out of her pocket, she picks off the dead weed and flicks a speck of earth from the cloth and returns the weed to her pocket.

'Dat was not so clever, eh?' Despite her heavy accent Ellie detects a hint of Scottish in her voice. She winds the handkerchief round her finger, her eyes remain dry.

'We came over five years now. The mines in Poland are dangerous, poor paid. We hear new mines open in Fife, Scotland. Marek and I, we marry ten years already.' She looks at Ellie and shakes her head. 'No children. But Marek, he has two younger brothers, Brunon and Borys. Much younger than us, like our own, they were. Marek, he want better life for them. Better than he had. He take them here, for trade apprenticeships. Here they earn apprenticeships.

'One, Brunon, he electrician, Borys a fitter. They go college, one day a week. Imagine, not one, two of our family in college. They learned good English. Marek, his was not so good but they teach him well. They make rule with him: he must speak English before nine o'clock at night. After nine we speak Polish. Boy, was dat man of mine silent before nine.' She laughs. 'And after nine we struggle like hell get word in sideways.'

Ellie becomes aware that the kettle still boils. If she does not rescue it soon it will boil dry. But she cannot leave Mrs Winski while she is staring into her memory.

'Great storyteller, dat man of mine. He know such history of his country. Such bloody history too. His favourite saying would be "Anna, if we can survive our bloody history we can survive anything."' She stops and dabs her nose with her handkerchief.

'Let me make you some tea.'

The widow remains in her position with her handkerchief round her finger, staring at the garden. Ellie hands her a mug of nettle tea and waits for a reaction, for she is sure this woman will approve.

'He laugh lots – after nine. He would sing folk songs and tell of horrors in war. The boys were not born until after but inherited dat hardship.' She shakes her head. 'We thought we take them to safety.'

'What happened?' Ellie follows Mrs Winski's gaze but cannot see the painful images that reflect in the older woman's eyes.

Mrs Winski takes a sip of tea and nods her head. 'Is good, you must give me recipe.'

Ellie remains silent, she is good at waiting.

'Did you know dat luck is bad for miners go under ground on Christmas Eve? Men don't come, even when they should.' Mrs Winski begins. 'Dat pit manager, he knows shift will be short staffed, so he ask young boys who already work dat day shift to stay work back shift – 'work a doubler' is called. They are keen, those boys of mine. Marek, he been sick and not go, he was one of those the boys making up work for.

'They were both working in same area, this not usual,

236

but this night it was way it was. Brunon, he became electric, all men stood back, Borys try help. The men there say they try stop him but he go to his brother and he become electric too. They are taught not touch electric people but his brother is hurt and he is tired. Both die.' She stops talking then, and heaves breath into her lungs as if she has been underwater. Still she sheds no tears.

'Marek, he blame himself. He should have been there, he could have saved at least Borys. He would not have let him touch his brother. He sink into blacker hole than the one he works in.

'The men they try help Marek.' Mrs Winski smiles and turns to Ellie, 'They are good people here. They help, they bring gifts, they say prayers, they put flowers on grave, but they cannot speak to Marek in his own voice, cannot comfort him. I, who speak his language, cannot comfort him. At work they make jokes with Marek, include him in their games, this does not work, so they give up, they have own troubles.' The woman's voice becomes quiet and Ellie can hear tears in her breath. 'I blame him too – sometimes, not always, I cannot help, but never say to him, not out loud.' She beat her breast. 'In here I blame him and he know. Guilt is like rust, eat you while alive.'

Ellie remembers the story the girls told her of the men in the pit bullying the Polish man; did they have this wrong? Was it really just their way of trying to help him?

'He sink lower, he no' go doctor. I beg him go home Poland but he wants stay. Too proud to go home, he believe our family will call him coward. So we stay.' Mrs Winski shakes her head. 'I do not cry now, I have no tears left. Past months I watch dat husband of mine fight his way through each day. He walk in woods.' She smiles at Ellie, 'He like you very much but he worry for you. He say you look unhappy, he know what unhappy is, he say you should tend your garden more, you look like gardener, like him.' She points to the tray of strawberry plants sitting on the bunker. 'He know you look after these well.'

Ellie feels tears roll down her face.

'Do not cry for him, his pain is gone.'

Mrs Winski takes hold of Ellie's hand and examines it in the same way Mary did on their first meeting, but the older lady does not remark on her colour. 'He is right, dat man of mine, these are gardener's hands, Marek know these things. He also know you could not help him. His torture is over, he is at peace.'

'I am so sorry,' Ellie says. She hears Nat chattering, awake from his nap. She must go to lift him but is frightened this woman who has lost so much will be hurt at the sight of her baby.

'Is dat baby awake?' Mrs Winski asks.

'Yes, but he is good, he will play.'

'Please, I will like hold baby, if dat okay.'

When Nat sees Mrs Winski he holds out his arms to her in welcome and blinks his eyes at the older woman.

'Look at dat, this baby flirt with me,' Mrs Winski says.

Poor baby, Ellie thinks, he is so sociable and I give him no company.

Mrs Winski takes him and kisses each of his fingers in turn, then sits him on her knee and points to the red breast bird who is nosing for some food.

'See robin, now where his wife is?'

'What will you do?' Ellie asks. 'Will you go back to Poland?'

'No, there is nothing there for me.' She kisses the top of Nat's head. 'I stay here. I have friends here. I clean church every Friday, I go Woman's Institute, I sometimes go to bingo in club.' She picks the weed out of her pocket and rolls it round in her finger. 'I grow vegetables and wins everything at the village show.' She puts the weed back in her pocket. 'I am well.'

She hands the baby back to Ellie and looks hard into her eyes. 'Are you?'

At first Ellie can feel that familiar tightening in her chest but when she takes a deep breath it is as if she is breathing in the refreshing wind that blows off the big river.

'I will be well.' She points to the plants. 'I have strawberries to plant.'

Mrs Winski squeaks the gate open then turns. 'You speak good English,' she says. 'Dat is a good thing, I thinks.'

The Pairty Line

'Ah'm fed up hearin' aboot fitba'.'

'Ken whit ye mean – it's a' ma man can talk aboot these days.'

'It's bad enough the noo, whit's it gonnae be like wance the World Cup actually sterts? Ah'll no get a look in wi' the paper, nor the telly.'

'They buggers at the BBC 'll cancel everything onyweys.'

'It's they smarmie Inglish commentators ah cannae stond.'

'Mebbes we should huv a pairty fur awbudy that disnae want tae watch fitba'.'

'Whit team is yer man supportin'?'

'Brazil.'

'Ur they no aw blackies?'

'Naw, thirs nae blackie countries playin' this time.'

'Why no' like?'

'They aw took the huff.'

'Whit fur?'

'God knows.'

'Well, who's oor blackie gontae support?'

'She better no' support Ingland.'

'She'll no' dae that – ah'm shair.'

Chapter Twenty Four

Since the day of Mrs Winski's visit Ellie has remained out of her lazy bed after seeing James off to work. By nine o'clock each day she has Nat fed and dressed and ready to play in his sand pit in the garden while she tends to her crops, then they will take a trip into the forest to collect free food.

James had built a sturdy deep sand pit for Nat in the small patch of land in the garden Ellie had not yet cultivated.

'Come on, Ellie,' James had said as he hammered wooden stakes into the ground. 'You can't claim the whole garden for your vegetables.'

James had always thought a sand pit would be fun for their son, but when Ellie saw the delight her small boy took in filling up cups with sand and emptying them out, a wave of homesickness over took her. In his motherland Nat would have played in the compound with the other children, watched over by the many grandmothers while Ellie went to the fields with the younger women to tend her crops. The sand would not be boxed in; it would be the dry red earth he sat in, the earth of his motherland. Then she remembered the heat and the flies and the many times when the crops failed and she had to agree with her husband this was better.

It is still too early to go back inside. Nat's cheeks glow with health after their foraging trip to the forest. Today has been a good day. Although Ellie has begun to harvest some crops from her vegetable patch, she still enjoys her trips into the forest to search for native food. But there is one place, however, that she cannot revisit. The sight of the hanging man is too fresh in her brain and the memory buzzes round her head like so many flies.

She breathes in the fresh air as she stands at her kitchen door; the air is sweet here. Why had it taken her so long to notice that? Nat can stay out a bit longer with his cups and spade, she thinks. She checks round the garden to ensure there are no dangers for him. Here is safe. In her country a mother would not leave her child alone in the yard. Danger is everywhere, not only from snakes but from the rabid dogs that roam free, but with so many other children to play with a child is never alone.

Ellie places her small son in the sandpit and checks James's latest handiwork, the shiny new catch on the gate, before going into the house to change out of her wellies. The basket of fungi she has just collected needs identified; Mrs Watson's book lists many species, along with their uses and harms. Ellie knows she must get this right. She begins to read the first page then decides she can do this later, these fungi are not like leaf; they do not wither and die as soon as they are picked. This can wait, she has a small son who already spends too long on his own and has no one else to play with.

Ellie closes the book and is just moving to the open door when she hears Nat bellow. The noise comes not from the sand pit where she left him, but from the gate. Ellie tumbles out of the door to see the blonde-haired scarecrow girl run away from her with arms stretched out in front. Clutched in her grubby hands is Nat. His face crumples into an indignant yell. The newly fixed gate lies open behind them.

'Nat!' Ellie shouts. 'Carol! Stop!'

Ellie plucks the hem of her skirt into her fist and with speed she has never known her heavy body to possess, she runs. Her sandals sink into the ground, wet seeps between her toes, damp and chilling, but she soon forgets this when she sees where the child is headed. Carol does not run back to the village, down the track, but turns towards the woods. Ellie almost catches her at the nuns' graves but a tree root reaches up and grabs her toes, and she falls. Her hand scrapes the earth and her arm collapses underneath her. She picks herself up and starts to run again but the girl has reached the other side of the clearing. Despite the pounding in her chest, Ellie feels her heart almost stop; she now knows where Carol is taking Nat.

'Oh God, no! Please God, no!'

Ellie is sure the girl cannot successfully cross the pipe carrying her son. She has watched children perform this dare before. They wobble enough without a load, and this girl holds her baby.

It has rained bits and pieces all week, and the burn is flowing high against the bank.

'Please, come back.' Ellie tries to keep her voice calm but can hear her own desperation. 'Please, he is a baby. You will drop him.'

The girl looks round but does not falter. Ellie tries to make her legs go faster but despite the girl's bundle and her heavy frame, she is nimble in her Wellington boots and her feet are not hampered, like Ellie's, by a long trailing skirt and sandals. The gap between them widens. Ellie watches in horror as the scruffy child steps onto the pipe.

'No!' she screams.

243

Her resolve to stay calm dissolves and is replaced by the acrid smell of her fear. She sees the girl does not have a proper grip of Nat. The water foams brown as in the cataracts of the salt river of home.

Ellie begins to pray. To pray for something she knows to be impossible, she prays for the Carol girl to clear the ten or so feet across the pipe. The girl is almost halfway across when Ellie reaches the water's edge. To follow would be what any mother would do, but Ellie stops and stares down at the foaming water and tries to push down her fear. The girl moves Nat under one arm and Ellie can see he is too heavy for her. He begins to struggle.

'No, baby, do not struggle!' She shouts above the roar of the water. She realises she has made a big mistake when she sees his neck twist, his head turns this way and that, trying to locate the source of her voice. He is slipping from the girl's arms. The girl hitches him up and steps over the middle section. Nat now sees Ellie and struggles harder, and suddenly he is free from the restraining arm. Ellie witnesses the terror in her son's eyes as he tumbles towards the water. The brown foam engulfs the black curls.

Her breath has disappeared with the run; she must find breath. Ellie hears her own screams in her head but like in a dream she cannot hear the sound coming from her mouth. She thrashes down the banking until she reaches the burn, but he is gone. She clambers the bank and runs, following the flow. His clothes snag a branch that holds him; Ellie reaches to grab, but he is gone again. Like a rag doll he bobs towards the pool that swirls and holds the water for a few minutes before it continues underground and on to the village.

Like the pool the Sister kicked Ellie into when she was a child, it looks deep. Ellie must catch Nat in this pool before the burn widens further and disappears under ground, then he will be lost. The pool is shallow at the edge. The water drags Ellie's skirt as she wades into the pool. She splashes forward to grab Nat. Water covers his head, she can't reach him, she must go deeper, she begins to scream as hard as she had when they took her from her village to go to school, as hard as her depleted lungs will allow. Her fingers touch his sleeve, she grips, and then it is gone.

A dark figure flashes past her, pushing her back towards the bank. Through her screams she hears a splash. The priest thrashes the water out of his way and with one movement grabs the baby and shakes him out. He kicks his way to the other bank and lays the baby on his front. Ellie feels the wet fabric of her skirt seep into her bones; she is on her knees, by the water's edge. The priest coughs and spits as he pumps two fingers against the tiny body. He then turns him on his back and begins to breathe into his mouth. Waits and breathes again.

Ellie rocks back and forth on her knees, clutching the *juju* that hangs around her neck, chanting 'Please God, do not take my baby. O Virgin Mary, you watched your son die, do not let my son die too.'

She shivers, even though the sun has come out fully from behind clouds and opens the flowers. She wants to cross the water but cannot; she continues to kneel on the other side and watch the priest. He lifts his head a little, as if waiting. A faint squawk drifts over to her side and then she sees a tiny chubby hand reach out and touch the priest's face. Ellie collapses her head into the earth and wails thanks to the Virgin Mary for saving her baby. When she lifts her eyes again, the priest stands with Nat cradled in his arm.

'We need to take him to hospital,' he shouts across the pool, motioning for Ellie to move further along the bank away from the noise.

'Is he fine?' she says, her throat and lungs hurting; she has screamed too hard.

'We need to take him to hospital,' the priest repeats. 'Go to my house and wait there.'

Even though Ellie knows that the priest will take longer to reach the house, she trots all the way. She should have been braver; she should have done more to save him herself. The priest had looked anxious; what if Nat were still to die and she had not lifted a finger to save him? What would his father say then? He would be sure to beat her and she would deserve it; she would welcome it; she would hope that he would beat her to death.

The paint-peeled door stands closed against Ellie. She looks towards the forest and wants her baby in her arms but does not know which way the priest will come.

'Please make him well,' she prays in her own language. 'If he lives I will be a good Catholic and go to church every Sunday. I will be a good wife and will never complain again.'

She will not move from this spot until the priest brings her baby but she is there only a moment when the big man-woman comes out of the paint-peeled back door.

'What do you want? Get away with you.' She waves her arm as if chasing the cattle from her vegetable patch. 'Shoo! Go home now.' The words are strong, but her eyes stare white. She looks like the old women in Ellie's

246

village when the sorcerer comes to collect his provisions.

'Shoo! Go away!' she says, waving a dish towel at Ellie.

'No!' Ellie screams at her. 'I wait for Father!' Ellie says as she turns from the man-woman's frightened stare and walks in the direction she hopes the priest will come then she stops and runs back to the house. 'I wait for Father.'

His hair is almost dry by the time he steps round the house.

'Nat has a nasty cut on his forehead and he is still coughing up water. He should be fine but we need to get him checked out.'

Nat's head is cuddled into the priest's collar and his hand holds the lapel in a tight fist. Ellie has to prise his fingers apart to release the grip. When she has him in her arms she can feel his heart beat fast as he sobs into her neck.

'Oh poor baby, my baby, what have I done to you? You must bawl for me again.' Ellie kisses his head.

'Aggie, can you please phone Mr Mason up at the house. Tell him we need him to come here immediately. And bring a blanket down from the airing cupboard; this child must be kept dry.' The words only just make it out of the priest's mouth when he begins to cough hard. He takes a soggy handkerchief from his jacket pocket and covers his mouth. Ellie does not like the sound of that cough and knows that a swim in the river is not the best medicine.

'Come on. Let's get him into the house until James comes. '

Father Grattan leads Ellie through the back door into

a small kitchen with a white enamel cooker. When the brown and white dog bounds in from an inside room, Nat whimpers and digs his head further into Ellie's neck. The dog capers around the priest's feet and jumps up on his wet clothes.

'Get down, ye daft brute,' he says, grabbing the dog's collar and pushing him to one side.

The priest places a light hand on Ellie's elbow and leads her into a sitting room lined with books, more books than Ellie has seen in her whole life. It smells of the priest; stale cigarettes and damp dog hair.

'You must get out of these wet clothes,' the priest says.

'No, 's fine, just my skirt.'

Aggie Aitkin comes back into the room and hands a rough grey blanket to Ellie. 'Mrs Watson says Mr Mason is out to the town at the moment. I have left a message for him to come here when he gets back.'

Nat begins to shiver as Ellie removes his clothes.

'I will take you. James can come to the hospital when he gets back. I'll go and change and get you an overcoat to put on.' He throws a bunch of keys at his housekeeper, almost hitting her on the head.

'Aggie, bring the car out of the garage for me, please.'

The old maid jumps from her sentry position by the door. 'Yes, Father.'

Ellie has no idea ordinary women can drive. The only women she knows who can drive are nuns. She has never seen a Hollyburn woman drive and yet here is this old dame, able and willing. She must be a man after all. Before Father Grattan collects her and Nat from the front room she hears him speaking on the telephone. She wants to go and grab it off him, she wants him to hurry. They

248

must get Nat to hospital.

The interior of the black car also smells of stale smoke and is beginning to make Ellie feel nauseous. The priest's overcoat she wears is covered in dog hairs; her wet skirt is bundled up beside her on the seat. Nat had been sick over the coat in the priest's house but with the help of Aggie Aitkin Ellie managed to wipe most of it off although the smell clings to her and she knows this is not helping her. Nat has fallen into a daze on her lap and she is not happy with the dull colour of his skin. She wants to pinch his cheek to wake him and to bring back her giggling lively baby boy.

'How far is the hospital?'

'Not far, in the middle of town. Don't worry, we'll soon be there, we'll go straight to Emergency.'

A couple of ambulances are lined up in front of double doors. The priest draws up behind them and jumps out of his side to open the car door for Ellie.

'Hey! Ye cannae park there!' one of the ambulance men shouts.

When the priest stands, exposing his dog collar, the man holds up his hand.

'Sorry, Father, didnae realise.'

The walk through the double doors into the warm waiting room drains Ellie of all strength, her mouth fills with bile and her legs begin to buckle. She clutches the priest's sleeve to prevent herself from falling over in a faint.

There is an assortment of a dozen or so white people scattered around the seats; some read papers, some stare at the wall. There does not seem to be much illness in the room; everyone has limbs and there is little evidence of blood, but they all have the same grey unhealthy complexion of the Hollyburn villagers.

Behind a counter sits a woman in a black suit. When they approach the woman looks up at the priest and with a bored expression says, 'Yes, can I help you?'

The priest holds Ellie's elbow. 'We need to see a doctor quick.'

'My boy, he fall in the river.' Ellie cannot find her tongue.

'Your boy, he fall in the river,' the bored woman repeats. She pushes her wheeled chair back and reaches into a tray behind her, pulls out a sheet of paper, then with her feet shuffling she moves herself and her chair back to the counter and shoves the paper towards Ellie.

'Fill this in.'

Ellie looks at Father Grattan.

'My boy is very ill. He needs a doctor. His head is cut, he is not speaking.'

'Fill in the form and then we will get someone to look at him.'

'I don't think you understand, Miss, this boy almost drowned, I had to perform CPR on him.' He places his hands on the counter. 'Mrs Mason will fill your forms in shortly. This boy is a British citizen. Get a doctor now.'

The bored woman looks up at him and tries to maintain her ambivalent stance, but Ellie can see her eyes waver.

'Take a seat.' She rises and disappears through an inner set of double doors. She returns a few minutes later with a nurse in a blue uniform who takes Nat from Ellie. Nat does not object because he still has not woken from his stupor. But when Ellie rises to go with him the nurse holds up her hand.

'No, I'm sorry but you must fill in the paperwork.

250

Then you can come through.'

Ellie looks at the paper. 'I do not have a pen.'

Father Grattan makes to take the paper from her. 'It will be okay, Ellie. I will help you fill this in.'

'I do not need help, I just need a pen.'

The bored woman from behind the counter holds one up.

Ellie finds her palms sweat and pinching the pen between her fingers is like trying to pick an angel fish from the fisherman's basket. She rubs her hand on her skirt and concentrates hard on her handwriting. Her eyes fill with tears when she writes in the boxes: nationality and place of birth. She falters at the part that says name and address of doctor. She looks at the priest and he takes the pen and fills in the box for her.

He takes the form and hands it to the woman. 'Now take her to her baby.'

The same nurse returns and leads Ellie through the double doors.

'How is my baby?' Ellie says to the girl as they walk along the corridor.'

'He is with the doctor.' The nurse replies in the same bored voice as the woman at the desk.

She holds back a curtain and ushers Ellie to a bedside. Nat's face is covered with a clear plastic mask. His naked body looks so small and dark on the long white hospital bed.

'Will he be alright?' She looks, for the first time, to the man in the white coat standing beside the bed. His face is black. Not as black as hers, but he is unmistakably African. Egyptian, possibly.

'Can you heal your little brother?' Ellie says, but

before she even has time to embrace the warmth she feels at this fellow's presence the doctor shouts at her,

'He is not my brother! This is an NHS hospital, woman, not a black African village market.'

Ellie steps back. Her face stings with force of his words, she cannot find her voice.

He turns back to Nat.

'What has happened to this child?' He sneers the words.

'This is my child, he needs help, I used to be a nurse; I know.'

She forces the words from her mouth, but they are small, insignificant and stupid. She is back in her country where the men treat their women like shit. Beat them if they do not work in the fields from sunrise to sunset, beat them if they ask for some money to buy clothes and pencils for their children, beat them because they are bored during the rainy season. She is back in the mission hospital where doctors are kings and male porters and toilet cleaners are treated better than trained nurses. She is a Black African back in her own continent, where prejudice against skin colour is everywhere. Here is this lighter-skinned doctor treating her like an animal. Nowhere is she safe from such treatment.

When she speaks again to the doctor it is with eyes cast down and in a small African woman's voice:

'He fell in the Hollyburn river and the priest fished him out.'

'How long was he in the water? Did he stop breathing? Did he always maintain his pulse?' He touches the head wound. 'Did he lose consciousness?'

'I do not know. I was on the other river bank. The

252

priest saved him; he gave him his own breath.'

The doctor's eyes seem to burrow deeper into his forehead. 'Well, why am I wasting my time talking to you? Where is this priest now?'

Ellie nods towards the curtain.

'The waiting room.'

'Then go and get him,' he shouts.

Ellie shrinks back from the words but does not move. She holds tight of Nat's hand. 'No, I do not leave my baby again.'

The doctor stretches his back and rises in front of her like a cobra. 'Do as I bid, woman. Do you want your child to live or die?'

'He is not going to die. Look, he is alive, you are a doctor. You can keep him alive, can you not?'

'Go and get the priest, I say.'

The curtain opens and a small grey-haired woman with spectacles perched on her nose steps into the cubicle and pulls the curtain back behind her.

'What is going on here? I can hear you bellowing all over the ward.'

'She will not go and get the priest from the waiting room.'

The older lady peers at Ellie. 'This lady looks as though she is concerned for her child. Call a nurse to fetch the priest or go and get him yourself.'

The old lady glowers at the man with murder in her eyes.

'Go on then! What are you waiting for, man? I will stay with them while you get the priest.'

The old lady walks round the table and pulls back the eyelid of the sleeping child then checks his pulse. As she

253

does this she smiles towards Ellie. 'You have a beautiful boy here.'

Ellie looks at the closed curtains; her voice dries up again like a river bed between the rains.

'Don't worry about him; he is the same with all women here. I expect he is worse with you because you're African too.' She gives a little chuckle and pats Ellie's hand.

'One day all women will be able to stand up to the likes of him. You just need to get into a position of power first. I know it's harder for you but that day will come too, I am sure of it.' She looks at her watch. 'Although I doubt I will live to see the day.' She nods toward Nat. 'I am sure he will be fine. He's had a bit of a shock and we will need to keep him in overnight for observation. They bounce back so quickly, little ones, don't they? My two boys were never away from the emergency ward when they were wee.'

The black doctor returns with Father Grattan and James and the old lady disappears behind the curtain as if she had never been.

James pushes towards the bed. 'Will he be alright?' he says as he puts his arm around Ellie and she leans in further to him feeling his warmth.

'He will be fine, sir,' the doctor says. 'We just need to establish the history of the accident. Perhaps you can take his mother for a cup of tea while I discuss with the priest what happened because the mother does not seem to know.'

James scowls at the doctor but does not say anything as he takes Ellie's hand and tries to lead her through the curtain.

'I am not leaving.'

The doctor sighs.

James pulls his back straight; he is taller than everyone in the room. He darts through the curtain and returns with a chair, which he places at the other side of the bed and guides Ellie over to sit down.

'We will sit here quietly if you don't mind. My wife wants to stay with our son.' James looks down at Ellie. 'I will get us some tea,' he says, almost as a question, and all Ellie can summon is a nod.

The Pairty Line

'Whit aboot that wee pickaninny bairn nearly droonin', eh?'

'Ah ken, that bloody Carol Wilson should be locked up.'

'Is she no too young fur that?'

'They could pit her in Borstal – imagine, stealing a baby. There's no telling whit she might dae next.'

'That pair wee black wumman must huv been oot her mind wi' worry.'

'And her no' able tae swim tae. She couldnae even try tae save the bairn. Imagine whit she'd huv been like if he'd really droon'd?'

'How come she cannae swim?'

'Nane o' thum can, the blacks like. Huv ye niver noticed at the Olympics or athletics – nae black swimmers.'

'That's weird, how's that then, eh?'

'It's thir noses, thir too wide, cannae pit thir heids under the water. If they dae their noses fill up and they droon.'

'Well, ah niver kent that. Thir no' like us at aw ur they?'

'Naw, but still nae reason tae steal thir bairns jist the same.'

'Jessie MacIvers telt me she's planning tae go doon the road and ask the wee black lassie if she wants tae pit ony o' her veggies in the village show.'

'That'll be fine as long as she disnae beat Duck Donald.'

'Oh, bit whit a laugh it wid be if she did. We'd niver hear the end o' it.'

Chapter Twenty Five

The day after the accident James and Ellie sit at the kitchen table and wait in silence for the visitor who is due to call. The house is too quiet without Nat. The doctors are not happy with his breathing and because his arms are painful with the wrenching he received from Carol, he is kept under sedation until the swelling of the joints has settled down. James phoned the hospital that morning and was told to call back the next day, he may be discharged then.

Ellie looks at her husband and sees him as he is. The man who sits opposite is not the man who rescued her from the dusty road, he is not the white man who strolled into her village and told her brothers that he wanted to take their sister into his own world. As the West African sun dipped below the horizon of her life, her husband transformed from the proud eagle soaring above all other animals in the land into the fickle hare that scurries from one situation to the next, never stopping or bothering to deal with his life. The promise James made to Ellie only weeks before has been hidden in the back of his mind and she knows he will never resurrect it as long as he has doors to slam and his work to hide behind.

The day before as she sat by Nat's bed and listened to the exchange between her husband and the doctor, she realised that they were both similar. At first she had thought the doctor would sympathise with her. She thought his prejudice of her darker skin would be diluted amongst all these white faces, but this was not the case. He had treated James with respect and Ellie as a cockroach on the ground to be stamped on. And James, her husband, had appeared not to notice.

During the night Ellie had listened for Nat crying out for her, even though she knew he was not there. She relived the moments by the burn and reminded herself that she had overcome her fear. She had almost had Nat in her grasp before the priest plunged in. But she had left it too late; she should have been braver and crossed the pipe. If they had fallen in they would have fallen together but at least her son would not have had to endure that terror alone. Like the rushing of the river, the last few months had been tumultuous for her, but not for Nat. He has thrived in this country. What life would she be taking him to if she returned to her fatherland? A life of war and hunger and corruption? Unlike the crossing of the pipe, Ellie cannot leave the fate of Nat's future until serious damage has been done; she must decide soon.

Constable Stewart has a small red flush to his cheeks when James ushers him into the room and points him to the seat with the new red covers while Ellie puts the kettle on.

'Why isn't the sergeant dealing with this?' James demands, his voice deeper than normal.

'The sergeant is on his holidays, I am afraid I have been left to deal with this serious matter.'

'Well, do you have any news for us?'

'About the abduction, Sir? Yes, I do.' He takes the small note book with the dirty elastic band out from his tunic pocket.

Ellie's throat dries. What information does this book already hold about her life, about the time when this young boy had told her to take better care of her child?

Does he now think that she has allowed this terrible thing to happen?

He looks at both James and Ellie before taking a sip of his tea. Ellie wishes he would get on with his tale.

'After you called me yesterday, Mr Mason, I went to the residence of Carol Wilson. I don't know if you are aware of this, but the girl's mother is in hospital at the moment. In fact, she has been in and out of hospital for years with alcohol-related problems.'

'Yes, I know, is very sad,' Ellie says.

James and the Constable frown at her in puzzlement, and she feels her face heat.

'I don't care about this,' James says. 'Is the girl behind bars? My son is still in hospital, and I want to know he will be safe when he returns home.'

'Yes, we detained her yesterday, sir.'

'Why did she steal Nat?' Ellie asks.

'She said she wanted a black baby to help her mum get better.'

Ellie's hand shoots to her mouth. She is going to be sick, she is sure.

'Apparently every time she got a black baby at school she named it Phemie after her mum. She would take home the little card the teacher gave her with the baby's name written on it and her mum would be better for a while. Her mum would tell her she was clever and next time she should get a boy and call it Thomas after her granddad who died two years ago.' The Constable is still shaking his head. 'But since her mum has been in hospital she has not been able to give Carol her black baby money.'

'Where is Carol now?' Ellie asks, for despite her initial hatred of the girl she cannot help but feel her pain.

259

'She's locked up in a secure school in Airdrie. Her maternal grandmother lives nearby so she can act on behalf of the girl's mother when the time comes for her to go to court.'

'Where is this Airdrie? I have heard of this place before.' Ellie asks.

'It is a town in the West of Scotland. Many of the miners in Hollyburn migrated here from towns in the West of Scotland when the pits closed over there,' the constable says.

'So Carol returns to her motherland,' Ellie mutters. Even the girl Carol is a foreigner in Hollyburn it seems.

'Eh? What's that, Mrs Mason?'

'The Motherland – the land where your mother is born. In my country, when a person dies they are taken back to their motherland to be buried.'

'Aye, I suppose in that case you could say she has returned to her motherland to be sorted out. But the main thing is she is off our streets and your son will be safe from any further problems.'

'Good riddance,' James says. 'That's what she deserves. She almost killed my son.'

'She will be without her mother; this is an even harder punishment. At least she will have her grandmother.' Ellie can feel James bristle beside her but she does not care: she only speaks the truth.

Nat recovers well once his sling is off and his cut heals, but his eyes do not shine as they once did. They dart worried looks to the door each time he hears a sound. He often crawls into the corner and prefers to play in his playpen or cuddle into Ellie as she sits in the chair with the red check cushion. He is now too big for her back sling; now she ties him to the side of her hip. His first steps are taken just in time to help pick the first crop of strawberries at the beginning of July.

As Ellie washes the crop and takes the white husks from the inside, she hears voices drift in through the open door. Through the still air she makes out the voices of children playing in the forest, and for the first time since the day Nat was stolen from her Ellie thinks of Mary and wonders if she has made new friends, better friends. For even though Ellie kept her promise to the Virgin Mary and now attends Mass every Sunday, she lies in bed late, cuddled into James and attends second mass to avoid seeing Mary and Mr Gallagher. She even has her own seat that the parishioners leave free for her. It is the seat beside her friend Mrs Winski.

The strawberries are for supper and there are plenty left on the plants for Monday when Mrs Winski will call in for a chat and a cup of nettle tea. Many times in the past Mrs Winski has invited Ellie to her house in the village, but Ellie makes excuses and Mrs Winski does not press her. There will be plenty time for Ellie to visit but that time is not yet here.

When all the strawberries are cleaned, Ellie sits down in her chair, and Nat toddles to her knee. She picks up a book she has read to him a hundred times. James left early in the morning to visit his mother in Perth. The kitchen is tidy, the food is prepared for the evening meal and it is still not yet lunch time. Ellie knows she smiles more often these days but a stone weighs down her heart.

She looks at her son and hugs him tight. How is it such a small person can give her so much joy?

'I know, Nat, let us go to the town,' she announces. 'We can get more books there, at the library, and if the library has closed doors, I am sure that Woolworths will have some. We can begin to build our own library.' She lifts him high above her head and he giggles. 'You and I are going on an adventure, Nat.'

The sun has been shining for four days now. Ellie looks at the blue sky clear of clouds. She dresses Nat in pale blue shorts and white shirt. As she pulls on his white socks she rubs and admires his beautiful skin. The brown Clarks sandals she and James had bought him in the Co-op shoe shop feel snug on his feet. He grows so fast. She stands him on the kitchen table and examines her boy; he is no longer a baby but a little boy. A little boy who nearly died.

Ellie ties him to her side but before she leaves the house she writes a note for her husband and leaves it under the bowl of strawberries on the kitchen table.

The bus stop is crowded with huddles of women and the big boy Ellie recognises as Eric Creighton. When Ellie approaches the bus stop, the woman Bella, who had been gossiped about in the doctor's waiting room, puts her hand out and touches Nat's head.

'How's yer wee boy now, hen?' she asks. 'Hus he got ower his fright in the burn?'

Ellie smiles, 'Yes, he is fully recovered now, thank you.'

'Ye must huv goat a right fright, him fawin' in the water and aw that cairrie oan wi' the Wilson lassie?'

'Yes, we did,' Ellie says, 'and how are you? Have you recovered from your operation?'

The woman touches the front of her coat and nods.

'Early days, hen, but ah'm no bad the noo. A bit jiggered noo and again, that's all.'

One of the other waiting women shuffles up beside them. 'This ye aff tae the toon wi the wee man then?'

'Yes, we are going to the library or Woolworths to buy a book.'

'Ah, books is it? Ah'll bet the wee fella' ll be a right clever thing when he gets tae the primary.'

'Yes, I hope so.'

The bus trundles along the road and pulls in short of the stop. The boy Creighton jumps on in front of the women and dashes up the stairs.

'Cheeky monkey,' Bella says, then to Ellie, 'On ye go, hen.'

Ellie at first does not know they mean her until Rose says, 'Come oan, hen, we huvnae goat aw day, ye ken.'

Ellie moves to climb the stairs when Bella shouts, 'Ye dinnae want tae be draggin the wee bairn up the stairs in amongst aw they smokers, come away inside wi us, hen.'

Ellie looks to Rose who shrugs, 'Oan ye go in then, hen. Ah'll git ye in a minute.'

When the bus moves off Rose humphs and wheezes up the stairs to collect the fares.

When she comes back down she is panting heavily. 'Where dae ye want tae get aff? Woolies again?'

Ellie kisses the top of Nat's head and touches the prayer book in her pocket; the book she took on impulse before she left the house. She looks up at Rose.

'Can you tell me how to get to Perth?'

Book Group Questions

1. The main character Ellie is West African and
    was brought up in a mission. How effective
    is her distinctive narrative voice and how
    does it help to define her character?

2. Within the book there are many voices/
    dialects used: Mr & Mrs Winski, Mary,
    Carol, Mrs Watson, The Pairty Line.
    How did the differences between each of
    the voices help your perception of their
    characters?

3. The character of Ellie's husband, James,
    moves from strong romantic in Africa to
    avoiding, almost passive aggressive when
    he moves back to Scotland. Discuss the
    reasons for this shift and do you feel it is
    necessary for the narrative?

4. How do you feel about James and Ellie's
    relationship?   On page 42 Ellie asks James
    why he married her. How honest were
    they about their (individual) motives for
    marrying?

5. How significant was the chapter with Ellie's
    trip into 'The Toon'? In what way did this
    episode effect what happened to Ellie after
    the event?

6. What is the purpose of the Pairty Line? How
    sympathetic were you to the two women
    on the call. The women are never directly
    named in the story, why did the author
    choose to do this?

7. Some of the conversations are not directly connected to Ellie. Why is this and did it make a difference to your enjoyment of the novel?

8. How important is Ellie's mother to the story? How important are the flashback scenes about her home country? Discuss.

9. Throughout the story many parallels are drawn between Scotland and Africa (e.g. old wives tales/witchcraft, tribalism/football supporters, celebration markings/religious symbols, tribal markings/tattoos, treatment of women). What does this show you about both countries in the sixties and today?

10. What do you make of the ending?

11. Mr Winski has a large presence in the first part of the book. What do you feel about his story and his outcome? In what way does his story impact Ellie's story?

12. Religion and the Catholic Church are shown in many different lights. What do you feel about the issues raised and Ellie's reaction to them?

13. The novel is set in 1966. How well is the period reflected? Why do you think the author chose this period over the present time?

14. How appropriate is the title?

15. What was your overall reaction to the book?

Acknowledgements and Thanks

My transition from business woman to writer would never have happened had it not been for the help and encouragement of others. I would like to thank in particular all those who read early drafts of the manuscript; my writing buddy David Allan who bullied me into finishing and spotted my many howlers; Frances Wright and Sarah Smith, my fellow Mitchell Sisters, for correcting my errors and making me laugh; Liz Small and Sara Hunt who gave me invaluable input in the later stages; Alan Bissett, Tawona Sithole and Gameli Tordzro for their generous quotes.

I would also like to thank Clare and Zander at Fledgling Press for their hard work in this production; my editor Anne Marie Hagen for her attention to detail; Thomas Crielly of TMC Graf'x for the stunning cover and George Lammie Photography for the wonderful portrait.

Some very patient tutors suffered my early offerings and I need to thank them all; Alistair Paterson started me writing in Borders Bookstore; Elizabeth Reeder opened the rusty cellar door and coaxed my creativity into the open; Laura Hird supported my early bids for publication; Frances Campbell fed my story with her theories on alienation and Ian MacPherson convinced me a Fife mining village was exotic. I am also grateful to all my Weegie Wednesday pals and The Hair Shop in Balfron for my regular, and necessary, doses of encouragement.

I had to research many aspects of the book and owe a huge debt to James Bauld, Fatoumata Brown, and the lovely people of The Gambia – thanks for allowing me into your worlds.

I also want to thank my family for keeping me grounded, with special hugs to my grandchildren, James and Caitlin, for helping out with the characteristics of Baby Nat.

And finally none of this would have been possible without the solid love and support of Colin, the quiet man who always finds the right words to soothe my doubts.